SNOWED

Bronzeville Books, LLC
269 S. Beverly Drive, #202
Beverly Hills, CA 90212
www.bronzevillebooks.com

Library of Congress Control Number: 2021949281

ISBN 978-1-952427-40-4 (hardcover)
ISBN 978-1-952427-41-1 (paperback)
ISBN 978-1-952427-42-8 (ebook)

First Edition

10 9 8 7 6 5 4 3 2 1

Cover Design: Reggie Pulliam
Book Design: Reggie Pulliam

SNOWED

TWIST PHELAN

BRONZEVILLE™
BOOKS

for erin mitchell and, of course, j

o, the families we make

Chapter 1

The tires skidded as her father sped through the turn. Phee Mahoney hoped they would crash. Not *crash* crash; she didn't want them to die or get hurt or anything. She'd be happy with sliding on a patch of ice and veering into the mounds of snow alongside the road. Just so they stayed stuck long enough for her to miss the field-trip bus.

The wind had come up. Snowflakes blew in every direction, like an explosion at a pillow factory. Phee wished she could vaporize them with her glare. Where was global warming when you needed it?

"Maybe the highway's closed," she said. There was only one road between Bristlecone and Silver Mountain Ski Resort.

"No, sweetie. I checked on the computer before we left," her dad said.

Phee felt her forehead. Was it a little warm? Maybe she was coming down with strep throat. She tried a cough.

"Gross! Germs," Brooklyn said.

"Germs," Scout echoed. The twins were five years old and so hyper, Phee sometimes had the impression they were triplets. Their dad was taking them to daycare after he dropped off Phee.

He pulled into the school's entrance. A bus was idling at the curb in front of the auditorium. With a resigned sigh, Phee got out of the car and slung her backpack over her shoulder.

Today her eighth-grade class was going to Silver Mountain, the local ski area. In a fit of optimism, or maybe temporary insanity, Phee had checked the INTERMEDIATE box on the permission slip. Which is what she'd be if she'd finished the Silver Scooters ski school her parents had enrolled her in when she was seven, instead of deciding she hated skiing the first day and refusing—okay, throwing a tantrum—when they tried to make her go back.

"Don't forget this," her dad said. He leaned over and handed her an orange piece of paper with the number 5 on it. Instead of being bussed back to the school, the students were going to be dropped off at central locations around town where their parents would pick them up. Phee would return on Bus 5. Assuming she survived.

"Have fun. Love you," her dad said. "Brooklyn, leave that seat belt alone."

"Love you, too," Phee said, shutting the door on Scout's wail as Brooklyn snatched her doll. Her dad pulled away from the curb and Phee watched him go, part of her wishing she was going to daycare with the twins. And she'd hated daycare.

She climbed up the bus's stairs and immediately saw her hat was wrong. Pom-poms might have been in two years ago. Now there wasn't a single pom in sight. She turned the red-and-purple hat inside out, put it back on, then slid into the empty seat beside Kimiko Watanabe.

"What's under your hat?" Kimiko said.

"My brain," Phee said.

Phee always felt ginormous beside her best friend. Everything about Kimiko was small and delicate—her pale oval fingernails, her earlobes with seed-sized pearl earrings, her size-five feet. Kimiko was nearly swallowed up by her pink-and-tan plaid boxy jacket, with lots of snap pockets, and tan baggy pants. Her helmet had stickers on it with names like Burton and Ride and DC.

Kimiko was sport-obsessed. Snowboarding, skateboarding, swimming were her current faves. She and Phee were on the school swim team together. Kimiko was good at backstroke. Phee wasn't; she always got water up her nose. If Kimiko wasn't doing sports, chances were she was watching them. Once, to Phee's horror, Kimiko sat next to Phee's older brother Zane and watched some of the Rockies game while she was waiting for Phee to get ready.

Kimiko leaned toward Phee and lowered her voice. "There's something I want to tell you. I'm—" She broke off and sat up again as the last student boarded, the doors whooshing shut behind him.

Chord Oakeson walked down the aisle. He was the only person who looked more rad than Kimiko. His jacket was camo-print and he'd tied a dark-green bandana below one knee. A turquoise backpack was slung over one shoulder. His boarder boots were unlaced, yet he managed to navigate the aisle without tripping. Phee knew she'd fall flat on her face if she went anywhere with untied shoes.

"Hi, Chord," Veronica Swingle said. She slid over to make room beside her on the seat. She and her friends sat a few rows ahead of Phee and Kimiko. Phee had an impression of pink. A lot of pink—Veronica's signature color, and thus her friends', too. Veronica headed up the Donner Party of cliques at Horace Tabor Middle School, cannibalizing her friends' personalities until each one dressed, talked, and liked the same TV shows as she did.

Phee had gone to Veronica's birthday party in sixth grade. The school rule was if you had a birthday party, you had to invite everyone in the class. Veronica's invitation arrived in a pink envelope addressed in dark pink ink. When Phee opened it, pink glitter sprinkled onto the carpet. At the party, there was even more pink. Veronica's room had pink curtains, a pink bedspread, and a fluffy pink throw rug. The furniture had pink Vs painted on it in cursive. The cake had pink coconut flakes on top, which Phee liked, and the goodie bag came with a tiny pink lipstick and mirror. Phee had gotten in trouble after she showed the twins how to use the mirror to start a fire with dried grass.

"Hey," Chord said to Veronica. Despite her obvious invitation, he passed by the Donner Partiers and took the seat across the aisle from Phee and Kimiko. Phee snatched off her hat, making her hair stand out straight from her head with static electricity.

"I'll take Causes of Bad Hair for one hundred," Joshua Grabenstein said. His voice had sounded like a chipmunk with allergies ever since a tetherball broke his nose in fourth grade. He sat in front of Phee and Kimiko. Phee kicked the back of his seat.

Joshua was obsessed with *Jeopardy*!. Failing the online test twice hadn't diminished his determination to become a contestant on the kids' version of the show. He turned answers into questions. If you asked him what the math homework was, he'd say, "What's the problem set on page 24?" Lately he'd taken to calling himself Alex after the long-time host of the show, Alex Trebek.

The bus pulled away from the school as Chord rummaged in his backpack. Phee noticed its blue color was almost the same shade as his eyes, then was annoyed at herself for noticing.

"What did you want to tell me?' Phee said to Kimiko.

Her friend waved a hand. "Forget it. It was stupid."

"Hey, Betty," Chord said to Kimiko. "You got a tool I can borrow? I wanna change my setup to centered."

"Gonna bust some insane air on a nine?" Kimiko said as she gave him what looked like a car remote. The initial K had been added with a Sharpie to the purple BETTY RIDES sticker on it.

Phee tried to arrange her face to look as though she understood what they were saying. Why did Chord call Kimiko Betty? Maybe they did like each other.

"I'll take Snowboarding for two hundred. The answer is backside one-eighty," Joshua-Alex said. Phee had started thinking of him as both names. She hoped it would switch to just Alex soon.

"A snowboarder with a big butt?" she said.

Joshua-Alex made the wrong-answer buzzer noise. "What is an aerial maneuver in which the rider makes a one hundred eighty-degree rotation off the jump, leading with the heel side?"

The bus groaned as it shifted gears. Phee realized they had started the final climb to the resort. She felt like doing some groaning herself.

Chord took an energy bar out of his pocket, unwrapped it, and bit off a generous chunk.

"Yuck! Plastic food," Kimiko said.

Chord grinned. "Gotta fuel the machine." He took a big bite, then glanced at Phee. "You riding or skiing?" he asked between chews.

"Skiing," Phee said. At least she'd have a better chance of knowing what people were talking about. Unless they'd invented a whole new lingo since Silver Scooters.

"You into poaching or gonna stay in the glades?" he said.

Apparently they had. "Glades," she said. The only poaching she knew about was what you did to eggs, and she didn't like them cooked that way. Too runny. At least Glade air fresheners were cute.

Chord settled back in his seat. "Remember—if you ain't fallin', you ain't haulin'."

Phee wondered if it was too late to fake the flu.

Chapter 2

Phee had thought more about the fake-sick ploy as she waited to get off the bus. Should she pretend to faint? Clutch her stomach and make retching noises? When the time came, though, she'd allowed herself to be swept up in the tide of people heading to the rental counter and now stood with Kimiko on the snow between the two main lifts.

"If I die, you can have my ladybug bracelet," Phee said. Her mom had brought it back from her last trip.

"You're not going to die. It's just skiing."

"That's like saying to Voldemort it's just a kid named Harry."

"I can hang with you if you want," Kimiko said.

One lift carried skiers to the blue runs. The other went to the green slopes. The sign in the lodge said blue meant intermediate and green was for beginners. Phee had committed this information to memory.

"It's okay. I've taken lesson," Phee said, careful to keep it singular. "It's something you remember how to do, like riding a bike." Of course, the first time Phee rode her bike without training wheels, she'd fallen and broken her arm, but that was beside the point.

A crumpled piece of orange paper lay on the snow. Phee picked it up. It read CHORD OAKESON BUS #4.

"Chord lost his bus ticket," she said.

Kimiko snatched the paper from her. "I'll give it to him."

Joshua-Alex penguin-walked toward them on his skis, his face red and sweaty. "I'll take Crushes for one hundred," he said. "The answer is Chord."

Kimiko glared at him. "Get a life." She stomped away. Her snowboard boots made for good stomping.

"Wait!" Phee called after her. Kimiko didn't turn around. Since when did Kimiko like Chord? Two days ago she'd told Phee that Moses Nguyen was cute.

The whole boy-crazy thing hadn't yet hit Phee. Boys were too messy and loud and, well, annoying. Although lately she got a funny feeling in her stomach whenever she looked at Peter Allerd. He wore nerd glasses that made him look cute and didn't use any of the goop Zane liked to trowel onto his hair. She and Peter had French together. She liked how he made the words sound like music. Her pronunciation was horrible; she could barely order a *pain au chocolat* at the bakery in town.

Sometimes Phee wished there were a shot she could take to delay the whole I've-got-a-crush thing until she was out of her training bra and wasn't the third-tallest person in class.

Phee shuffled toward the beginners' lift, stabbing the snow with her poles. Her feet felt like they were encased in cement. Her rental helmet was too big, so she had to keep tipping her head back to see where she was going.

"Told you she was a spore," said a voice behind her. Phee didn't have to turn around to know it was Veronica. Or one of her clones. Why was Veronica calling her a plant part?

"You know, the lift to the blue runs is the other way." Definitely Veronica.

With difficulty, Phee twisted around to face her adversary. Dressed in pink ski pants, pink and white parka, and pink-rimmed goggles, flanked by two girlfriends also wearing the same color, Veronica looked like Strawberry Shortcake come to life. If Strawberry Shortcake skied, that is.

"I'm waiting for somebody," Phee said.

"Look, there's Chord," said one of the Donner Partiers. All three girls turned to look at Chord standing in line for the lift to the advanced runs.

Forgetting about Phee, Veronica schussed toward him like she was on ice skates, accompanied by her friends. Their skis actually made that sound—*schuss, schuss, schuss.*

Phee continued toward the beginners' lift. She passed Joshua-Alex propped on his poles, panting. "I'll take Skiing for one hundred. The answer is *green*," he gasped.

"What runs are you going on?" Phee said hopefully.

"Correct! Wanna ride up together?"

Phee nodded. Her helmet dropped forward, like a mask on a suit of armor. Phee took it off and put on her pom-pom hat, inside out. She'd fix the helmet at the top.

She and Joshua-Alex waddled to the end of the lift line. Once there, they kept their skis parallel and pushed themselves along with their poles. The girl checking lift tickets pointed her scanner gun at Joshua-Alex.

"Argh!" He jerked and writhed like he'd been Tasered. The girl ignored him.

In Silver Scooters, Phee had taken the Magic Carpet—a moving walkway like at the airport—to the top of the bunny slope. She'd never ridden a chair lift before. Not that she'd ever wanted to; she was afraid of heights. Climbing to the top step of the ladder to help her dad with the Christmas lights made her dizzy.

It was her and Joshua-Alex's turn to get on the lift. Phee shuffled toward the red line in the snow marked LOAD HERE. The chair arced around the corner toward them. The edge of its seat thwacked against the back of her thighs.

"Oof!" She sat down heavily.

They started up the hill. Phee's stomach lurched as the ground fell away beneath them. Joshua-Alex pulled down the restraining bar. It looked very unsubstantial. Phee gripped it, the helmet balanced on her lap. Her ski boots felt even heavier. Could they pull her off the chair? She gripped the bar harder and squeezed her eyes shut.

"What's that lump under your hat?" Joshua-Alex said.

"My hair," Phee said through gritted teeth.

"Hey, check out that boarder!" Joshua-Alex said.

Phee cracked one eye. The terrain park was to the right of the lift. Coming toward them was a snowboarder in a jester's hat. He skimmed his board along a rail then launched himself off a ramp. The bells on the hat jangled as he sailed through the air. He landed with a *whump* and sped down the hill.

Watching the snowboarder made her queasy. She shut both eyes again. "How much longer?"

"Ten minutes," Joshua-Alex said. She sensed him turn to look at her. "What's wrong?"

"I'm afraid of heights."

"I'll take Head Cases for one hundred. The answer is *your problem*." When Phee didn't respond, he said, "What is acrophobia?"

Phee opened her eyes. Their chair passed over tall pines. The ground seemed miles below. "Are there wolves up here?"

"Only at night. I think."

Great. At least now she had something to take her mind off the landscape rushing by. "What's a spore?"

Joshua-Alex looked pained. "I ask the questions. I have to practice."

"I'll take Ski Slang for one hundred. The answer is spore."

"What is Stupid Person On Rental Equipment?"

The trees disappeared as they passed over a small canyon. Phee's stomach did flip-flops. This was stupid, all right.

Chapter 3

"See you at the bottom," Joshua-Alex said.

"Wait!" Phee said, brushing snow from her track pants. They weren't very warm but were the only thing she had that looked like ski clothes. "You said you'd show me what to do."

"It's easy." That was what he'd said when it was time to get off the lift, right before he crashed into Phee and they both fell. The liftie had to pull them out of the way so the skiers coming behind them didn't run over them.

"Make french fries when you want to go faster, make a pizza slice when you want to slow down or stop." He demonstrated, bringing his ski tips into a wedge, and then pulling them apart until they were parallel. His skis started to slip downhill.

"B-y-e-e-e-e-e-e-e!" Joshua-Alex headed down the mountain, his skis locked in a wedge as he picked up speed. He sideswiped a tree then dropped out of sight.

Phee shuffled forward a few steps. Her skis began sliding on their own. Not trusting her pizza-making ability, she plopped down on the snow. Her helmet fell forward, banging the bridge of her nose. She took it off and put on her hat. The cold seeped through her track pants.

Phee assessed the situation. She could ask to ride the lift down. Why not put those empty chairs to use? She hadn't seen anyone do it, though.

And what if Veronica or someone else saw her? Probability of success: low. Probability of humiliation: high.

She could follow Joshua-Alex. Probability of success: low. Probability of humiliation: high. Probability of death or serious injury: very high.

Thinking about injury brought her back to her original plan. If she was injured, wouldn't the ski patrol have to take her down the mountain? Probability of success: high. Probability of humiliation: medium.

Her butt had gone numb. If she didn't move, she'd have a real reason to call the ski patrol—frostbite. Phee rolled onto her side and tried to push herself up. Her skis slipped out from under her and she fell onto the snow. She tried again. This time she not only fell, her hat came off. She pulled it back on her head, pom-pom side out.

"Need a hand?"

Phee looked up. A teenaged boy sat on what looked like a chair seat attached to a single ski. He used short poles with mini-skis on their ends to push himself toward her. When he was close enough, he held out a hand. Phee grabbed it, and he pulled her to her feet.

"Thanks," she said. The boy wore a tight-fitting top with PARALYMPICS TRAINING CENTER lettered across the front in red, white, and blue. His face was a buttery tan and there was a smear of zinc oxide on his nose.

"You're Johnny Mercer," Phee said. Everyone in Bristlecone knew who Johnny Mercer was. A champion junior skier, he'd been on the fast track to the Olympics. That was before a hit-and-run left him a paraplegic three years ago

He lifted his goggles and put them on top of his helmet. "That's me." He grinned, his teeth bright against his tanned face.

"I'm Phee."

"What are you doing up here by yourself?"

"Trying to learn how to ski."

"The bunny slope might be a better place to start."

Phee sighed. "It's a long story."

"Want a ride? It's bumpy but fast."

"What? Oh, I don't think so. But thanks."

"How else are you gonna get down?"

Catching a ride from Johnny would be kinda cool. "Okay," she said.

"Take off your skis and give them to me. Cool hat, by the way. But you'd better wear your helmet."

He adjusted the helmet so it stayed put on her head. Following his directions, Phee sat on Johnny's lap and leaned back into his chest.

"What's this thing called?" she said.

"A sit-ski."

Phee laughed. "Makes sense. Are you sure I'm not hurting you?"

"The last time anything hurt my legs—at least that I felt—was when a car nailed me."

Phee glanced back and saw a look flit across his face. It was the same expression she'd seen on her dad when he talked about playing baseball in college, especially the game when he hurt his shoulder while a scout who'd come to see him was watching—happy and sad at the same time. *Regret.* She wondered if that was one of the little heartbreaks waiting for her in high school.

"I'm sorry," Phee said. "About the accident, I mean."

"It wasn't an accident," Johnny said. "Whoever was driving steered onto the shoulder and plowed right into me. Cops didn't find any skid marks; the person didn't brake or swerve. They were either drunk or gunning for me. Neither one's an accident, as far as I'm concerned."

"Did they catch who was driving?"

"Nope."

"That sucks."

"Yep." Johnny pushed the sit-ski forward with his poles. "Hang on!"

Thirty seconds later they were flying down the mountain. Johnny hugged Phee with his forearms while maneuvering the poles to steer. They swooped and cornered and went so fast that the trees and other skiers blurred. Tears streamed from Phee's eyes and her cheeks were numb with cold. Occasionally they'd hit a bump that sent them airborne. The landings jarred her tailbone and made her say *oof*! Phee felt as though she were flying on a magic carpet.

After what seemed only a minute or two, they reached the bottom of the hill. Phee was sorry to feel the ski slow down. As the lift loading area loomed ahead, Johnny abruptly turned the sit-ski ninety degrees, sending a rooster's tail of snow arcing through the air. He dug in his poles to bring them to a complete stop.

Phee climbed off as gracefully as she could. "That was SO awesome. Thank you."

Johnny unfastened her skis and poles from the sit-ski. "Anytime."

Phee bent down to pick up her skis. The sun glinted off a metallic disk on Johnny's jacket. She squinted at it. WEST REGION STATE LITTLE LEAGUE CHAMPIONS was lettered around the edge. Zane had one like it on his key chain.

"Do you know my brother Zane?" Her brother was a sophomore but had been good enough to play on the varsity team.

"Mahoney No Baloney's your brother? He played third base the year we went to regionals."

"He doesn't play baseball anymore." Mahoney No Baloney? Wait until she saw Zane again.

"Me, neither," Johnny said.

Could she be more of a dummy? "I'm sorry."

"Don't be. It's all good."

"Well, thanks again."

"See ya." Johnny poled the sit-ski around and headed for the lift line.

"Phee!" Kimiko slid to a stop beside her, sending an arc of snow against Phee's legs. "Was that Johnny Mercer?"

"Uh-huh. We went skiing together."

Kimiko cracked a grin. "Not bad for a spore."

Chapter 4

After hearing about her descent, Ms. Vlachos had excused Phee from skiing for the rest of the day. Phee was glad Ms. Vlachos was one of the chaperones. Introduction to Business was Phee's favorite class and Ms. Vlachos was her favorite teacher. She made the class fun and interesting so most everybody participated. Phee loved her polished leather boots, the strawberry Yoplait Lite yogurt she ate between classes, the cranberry-and-grape Koosh ball on her desk.

Phee returned the rental skis and helmet, bought a hot chocolate, found a quiet corner of the lodge, and took out her book. She always carried one in her backpack for situations like this. Curled up in the chair, she started reading. She had three chapters to go before she finished the latest Artemis Fowl. Spirits had possessed his little brother, making him more annoying than usual. Phee could sympathize.

"That thing on your hat reminds me of Ms. Vlachos's Koosh ball," said a boy's voice.

"Zip it," Phee said, her eyes still on the book.

"I like it."

This got her attention. Phee looked up to see Chord lounging in a battered leather armchair in another corner. He'd taken off his snowboarding boots and propped them on his backpack. Phee saw his socks had little reindeer on them.

"Why aren't you in the half-pipe"—she paused, remembering—"busting some insane air?"

"I got grounded. Slopes only for me."

"What'd you do?"

"Learned to play the violin."

Phee never heard of anyone getting into trouble for playing an instrument. It was not playing that was bad.

"I've been riding half-pipe awesome this winter. Got a sick trick to wow the Vans people at nationals this weekend." Chord flipped something purple and black into the air like it was a coin. Phee realized it was Kimiko's snowboard tool.

"I'll pretend I know what that means. So?"

"So my parents grounded me. My mom's afraid I'm gonna break my wrist." Flip.

"Haven't you been riding for a long time?"

"Since I was six. But since my dad got laid off, she's all worried we can't afford Bellermine if I don't get a music scholarship. So she told Ms. Vlachos I couldn't ride." *Flip. Flip.*

Bellermine was a private school south of Denver. Parents sent their kids there so they'd get good SAT scores and into Ivy League colleges, two things Phee didn't want to think about yet. Zane had told her eighth grade was the last time she wouldn't have to worry about her permanent record—something else Phee didn't want to think about—and she intended to make the most of it.

"Maybe after you get into Bellermine, she'll let you go snowboarding again."

"It'll be too late. I gotta show the Vans people the trick this year. Otherwise there goes my shot at the junior team." *Flip. Flip. Flip.* Chord missed the spinning tool on the last toss. It fell on the floor. He picked it up and stuck it in his pocket.

"Bummer," Phee said. It was what she usually said when the topic was parental actions. What else could you do?

"How soon until we're outta here?"

Phee looked at her wrist. Her watch was gone.

"I lost my watch!" She stood and looked all around the chair. Chord helped her. She found a quarter, a dime, and a gum wrapper, but no watch. She searched through her backpack, without luck.

It must have come off when she was riding the lift or falling down at the summit or zooming down the hill in Johnny's lap. Whatever, it was gone. Phee's heart sank. No way she'd find it in the snow.

She really liked that watch. Her mom had given it to her for Christmas. It had digital read-outs for dual time zones. "So you can synchronize it to where I am," her mom had said. Before her mom left on her latest trip, Phee had looked up the time difference for Australia and set the lower clock sixteen hours ahead.

Ms. Vlachos stuck her head into the lodge. "Three thirty," she called to Phee and Chord. "Time to find your bus." She left.

"Do you know where the bathroom is?" Chord said.

Phee pointed. "Down that hall."

"Sorry about your watch."

"Yeah." Phee headed for the door.

The lodge was uphill from the parking lot where the buses sat belching diesel into the frosty air. Phee took baby steps down the steep path, trying not to slip.

A door slammed. Phee looked right to see a man standing in front of a long metal shed, wearing a navy windbreaker and a black baseball hat with a lime-green logo. He carried two snowboards, one under each arm. One was red, the other blue, and each had a large sunflower decal on its deck. After a quick glance left and right, the man turned and disappeared around the far corner of the shed.

There must be a shorter way down the hill. Phee changed course to follow the man. It was snowing again, and the sodden flakes made the going difficult. She made it to the building and leaned against it while she caught her breath. She could see the man's footprints being rapidly filled by fresh snow. She tracked them to the edge of the building and beyond into an open field dotted with trees. Some of the resort's groomers were parked there, large machines used to smooth the snow for skiers.

Phee scanned the area. There weren't any paths leading downhill, at least none she could see. The snow was coming down with more enthusiasm now so it was hard to tell. She was about to retrace her steps when she noticed two people at the far end of the field standing beside a van with a red A on the door.

As she watched, one person got into the van and drove away. The other started back toward the shed. It was the guy who'd been carrying the snowboards, only he didn't have them anymore.

The wind began to blow sideways, spattering Phee with wet snow. She ducked behind the nearest groomer for shelter. When the man walked by, she'd ask him for directions to the buses.

She huddled beside the large machine's tread, shivering. Her hands prickled with cold. She took her gloves from her backpack and put them on. They made it hard to pull the zipper on the pack closed again.

The man should have passed her by now. Phee stepped out from behind the groomer. The man—and the shed—had vanished in a flurry of white.

She cupped her hands around her eyes and stared at the place where she thought the building should be. Was that its outline? The air was filled with swirling snow, tilting Phee's sense of space and making her dizzy. She walked forward a dozen steps, her legs like leaden weights, and stopped. The wind pulled at her clothes, nearly knocking her over. Was she going the wrong way? Blinking rapidly, shielding her face with her arm, she backtracked, leaning into the storm. After the third step, something jabbed her in the back. She screamed and jumped to one side. The ground disappeared and Phee was falling.

Chapter 5

Phee pushed herself to her feet. She was in a hole, a little shorter than head height and about three feet in diameter. The sides were packed snow, except for one corner where a tree stood. She'd scraped her jacket against its rough bark on her way down. The nylon had torn on her sleeve and down stuffing leaked out, quickly becoming lost among the snowflakes.

She pawed at the wall of snow in front of her, starting a small avalanche that quickly buried her boots. Okay, no climbing out that way. Maybe she could use the tree's branches as a ladder. The first one she stepped on broke. So did the second and third. The ones that could hold her weight were too close together; she'd never be able to climb through them.

Phee brushed strands of hair out of her eyes. Her gloves were sticky with tree resin and some of it stuck to her hair.

"Help!" Would the bus leave without her? What if she had to spend the night? "HELP!"

"Help yourself."

Phee looked up, squinting against the falling flakes. Chord's face loomed above her.

"Here, hold on to this." He extended the handle of a short shovel into the hole. Phee grabbed it.

"I'm going to pull you up. Don't let go."

Phee tightened her grip. "Okay."

"One…two…three!"

The handle was jerked upward. Phee held on and went with it, bellyflopping onto the snow, her butt and legs dangling in the hole.

"Thank—"

"Don't let go!" Chord said at the same time Phee felt the snow beneath her start to crumble. Chord dug in his heels and scrabbled backward, pulling Phee away from the widening hole. It was like being dragged from the mouth of a monster that was trying to swallow you.

When her toes were on solid ground, Chord dropped the shovel and sat heavily. Beside him was a red pack with a triangle patch on the front. The storm had eased; only a few late flakes floated through the air.

Phee rolled off her stomach and sat up.

"What happened?" she said.

"You fell into a tree well. The branches stop the snow from filling in around its base. They make a hole right next to the tree. You can't climb out by yourself. If you try, the snow can collapse and suffocate you."

"Well, um, thanks." Phee clapped her hands to loosen the snow stuck to her gloves. "How did you know I was there anyway?"

"I saw that thing on the top of your hat."

Phee reached up and touched the pom-pom.

"Plus you scream pretty loud."

"I scream the same way whether a wolf is chasing me or a tree branch touches my back." Phee got to her feet and brushed snow off her legs. "Think we missed the bus?"

"Maybe. Better hurry."

The shed was visible again—in the exact opposite direction she'd been heading. Phee started toward it. After a half dozen paces, she stopped and turned.

"You coming?"

"In a minute. I need to put my shovel away."

A shiver rippled through her, making Phee aware how cold she was. She resumed plowing through the drifts. When she was halfway to the shed, she turned to see if Chord was following. He was walking up the hill.

"Hey!" she shouted. "The busses are this way!"

He waved without stopping. Phee stood, undecided. Another shiver shot through her, making her teeth chatter. She began bounding down the hill like an awkward deer, if a deer could walk on its two hind legs.

Five busses were nose to tail in the parking area, engines idling. Phee ran toward them. Bus 5's doors whooshed open and she climbed up.

Kimiko sat in the fourth row. Phee plopped down beside her.

"You're all wet and your mascara is smeared under your eyes," Kimiko said, scooting to the far edge of the seat. She was doing something on her phone. Phee leaned over to see while licking her finger then rubbing under her eyes. She'd begun wearing makeup this year—mascara, blush, lip gloss, all bought at Walgreens. The mascara in the pink tube with the green top never stayed very well, even though it was supposed to be waterproof.

Kimiko was posting photos on Instagram. Some of the parents let their kids on social media, but Phee's didn't. Her dad did parenting in lunges of impetuous dad-ness, usually by forbidding her from doing things. Facebook and Twitter and Instagram were on the list, along with drugs, sexting—she still winced at the thought of him saying the word—getting a ride from someone who'd been drinking, and joining the Denver Junior Debutantes. Trouble was, her dad issued his edict only against activities she'd never dream of doing—sending photos of herself wearing just underwear? Seriously?—or after the thing had become so passé it was featured on Dateline.

Not being on social media was okay with her. She'd found out Zane's Instagram password—ZANEisAWESOME—and logged onto his account if she wanted to look at something. Otherwise, she happily did without the tweets on what Veronica was wearing that day. Pink was pink.

"I got caught in the storm," Phee said.

Kimiko frowned. "How? It just started fifteen minutes ago. That's why the buses are still here. They're waiting for the road to the highway to be plowed."

"I fell into—" Phee stopped talking. Two rows up Veronica was turned in her seat, listening, the beginning of a smirk tugging at the corners of her mouth.

"I was talking to Chord and forgot about the time," Phee said. Veronica's smile evaporated.

"Chord? Why were you talking with him?" Kimiko said. Her brown eyes were hard and shiny, like a bird's.

"Phee and Chord sittin' in a tree," sang Joshua-Alex from the row behind them.

"It's not like that," Phee said. "We were just talking."

"Whatever," Kimiko said with a sour expression. The bus lumbered forward with a growl of its engine. "You know, that hat is really dorky."

Phee pulled it from her head. She held it in her lap and untangled some of the pom-pom's strands. If she hadn't been wearing it, would Chord have seen her? She put the hat back on.

"It's my favorite," she said.

Chapter 6

The next morning, the snow crackled and squeaked under her boots as Phee headed to the bus stop. The Mahoneys lived at 54 Fir Lane. Whoever named things in Colorado was obsessed with trees. She wondered how you got the job of naming streets and towns. Probably you had to know the governor.

Her family had moved to Bristlecone from Denver when Phee was four. She didn't really remember living in Denver. Sometimes when they went to a museum or the mall, her mom would drive down a certain street and point at a gray brick house. "There—that's where we used to live." Phee would stare at the house, scrutinizing the ivy growing up the chimney, the brass number plate on the mailbox, the swing on the porch. She didn't recognize any of it.

When she was in third grade, Phee thought their current house looked like a face, with its red front-door mouth and window eyes fringed with black shutter eyelashes. Now she thought it just looked like the other houses on the street—nice, but not so fancy that you felt you'd get in trouble for running across the lawn or walking on the living room carpet. It was two stories, big enough for all of them to have their own room—Phee, Zane, and the twins. The only people who shared a room were Mom and Dad.

As Phee walked down the street, the front door to number fifty-two opened. She looked over, expecting to see Mrs. Heckler. When the older woman broke her hip last year, Phee had taken to rolling her trash bins to the curb on Tuesdays. She still did it, even though Mrs. Heckler could walk okay now. Phee also bought her bags of yellow Citrons at the Sweet Factory. Mrs. Heckler was addicted to the sour lemon candy. Phee felt the same way about gummi bears, the ones from Germany in the gold bag. She liked that Mrs. Heckler didn't smell like other old people and that she called her Phee instead of Ophelia, unlike most adults.

But instead of Mrs. Heckler, a boy about Phee's age appeared. He had red hair with a spiky cowlick and wore a ratty gray hoodie.

"Rusty?" Phee said.

Until three years ago, Rusty Risborough and his mom, Mrs. Risborough, lived with Mrs. Heckler. Mrs. Risborough was Mrs. Heckler's daughter and divorced. Phee and Rusty had been sort-of friends when they were in elementary school. They talked while they waited for the school bus every day, and sometimes Phee went to Mrs. Heckler's house on Saturday mornings to watch cartoons with him. He'd helped her build a huge snowman the winter of the really big blizzard, and then came to the funeral she held when the snowman melted. Once they got to fourth grade, Rusty started hanging with the emo kids so he and Phee didn't do much together anymore.

Rusty jumped off the top step and slogged across the lawn, making fresh footprints in the snow.

"Hey, Phee." He stood in front of her, his big hands dangling at his sides like ping-pong paddles. There was a grungy Band-Aid wrapped around one of his fingers.

She punched him in the arm, but not too hard. "Where have you been? Why did you leave without saying good-bye?"

Rusty jammed his hands into the pockets of his hoodie. That made his hands look even bigger. One finger poked through a hole at the seam. He looked over her head at something in the distance. Phee resisted the urge to turn to see what it was.

"I didn't know we were leaving until my mom told me right before we had to go." He hunched his shoulders. "I'm sorry," he said to his shoes.

Ah, the divorce. Mr. and Mrs. Risborough had lived apart awhile, but Phee knew kids could be moved around like checkers. Last year her friend Natalie had to move to California to live with her dad, even though her parents had been divorced for three years. She didn't even get to finish seventh grade at Horace Tabor.

"So are you moving back?" Phee said.

Rusty shook his head. "Mom says Grammy can't be by herself anymore. She's going to come live with us."

"Where?" Phee said, feeling a little sad. She liked Mrs. Heckler. Maybe Phee could mail her some Citrons.

Rusty addressed his shoes again. "I'm not supposed to tell."

Not tell? Phee's mind shifted into imagination mode; it spent a good amount of time there. Maybe Rusty and Mrs. Risborough and Mrs. Heckler were going to become secret agents somewhere. Before she could ask, the door to number fifty-two opened again.

"Rusty! Come here right now!"

Mrs. Risborough still sounded like the old parrot at the pet store—squawk, squawk, squawk.

Rusty's face went pale. "Gotta go," he mumbled.

Phee watched him hurry across the lawn, legs churning. When he got to the top of the steps, Mrs. Risborough grabbed his arm and yanked him through the open door, all the time whispering fiercely into his ear. Rusty kept his eyes on his shoes.

"Hi, Mrs. Risborough!" Phee yelled.

The door to number fifty-two slammed shut.

Chapter 7

Phee was feeling sleepy by the time Intro to Business began. All that skiing the day before must have tired her out. She wished she liked coffee. It always perked up her dad, and had turned Brooklyn into a human SuperBall the time he'd drunk half their mom's iced mocha at Starbucks without her noticing.

"Ophelia?" Ms. Vlachos's voice roused her.

"Here," Phee said automatically.

The snicker from the class ascended in volume as it surged toward Phee's seat in the back row like an avalanche cascading down a mountain. She turned away from the window in time to catch Veronica's eye roll.

"Here, here, here," Joshua-Alex said.

Phee kicked the back of his chair. If she hadn't gone on the stupid field trip, Ms. Vlachos and the rest of the class wouldn't be looking at her like she'd just started babbling in Swahili.

"Congratulations," Ms. Vlachos said.

Phee's mind raced, looking for a clue. What would Ms. Vlachos be congratulating her for?

"Joshua," Ms. Vlachos said.

"I'll take Winners for one hundred," Joshua said. "The answer is Alex."

"Veronica," Ms. Vlachos said. "And Chord, who's out today. Congratulations to all four of you."

Phee was really confused now. What could she have done that put her in the same boat as three people she couldn't have less in common with? She raised her eyebrows at Joshua-Alex.

"The answer is the Junior Entrepreneur winners," he whispered.

Ah. The essay competition. Everyone in class had written up a marketing idea for Trent Snowboards. The top four got to spend a day at the company. Phee hadn't thought her idea—that the company give away miniature snowboard key chains—was that great. It wasn't exactly up there with the Energizer Bunny.

But she was glad she'd won. Maybe one day she'd start her own company. First, though, she'd have to invent something. Her dad had told her, "Necessity is the mother of invention." What did she need? She thought about babysitting her brother and sister. A diaper alarm would've been handy when the twins were little.

The bell rang while Phee was imagining a flashing red light attached to a pair of Pampers. A siren would be nice, too.

Ms. Vlachos raised her voice to be heard over shuffling feet, books being slammed shut, students' chatter.

"We leave Thursday morning. I'll pick you all up in front of the bus circle. Don't forget to pick up a permission slip before you leave."

Kimiko nudged Phee with an elbow as they walked into the hallway.

"Trent Snowboards—how cool is that?"

Phee thought of the man in the Trent jacket she'd seen yesterday during the blizzard. She couldn't see the appeal of snowboarding. It seemed that even if you were good, you still fell down a lot. Maybe she should let Kimiko take her place. She and Chord could talk about backsides and Betties and all that other boarder stuff.

"Where's Chord?" she said.

Kimiko scowled. "Why do you think I'd know?"

"Um, I don't. I was just asking."

"Well, I don't know." Kimiko quickened her pace. "I gotta go."

Phee watched her friend push through the crowd of students. *I'll take Crushes for one hundred.*

Chapter 8

Phee went around to the side door of her house, left her boots in the mudroom, and walked into the kitchen. She dropped her backpack on the floor.

"Hello?"

The only answer was Homicide's half growl, half purr. Homicide was their one-eyed tabby cat. He had to take what Phee's dad called kitty Prozac. You shouldn't pet him if he was off his meds.

Phee glanced through the window at the house next door as she opened the fridge and took out a container of hummus and a handful of carrot sticks. What was up with Mrs. Risborough? Phee didn't know much about Rusty's mom, other than she was a nurse who gave out stale candy from the dollar store at Halloween. When Phee and Rusty were friends, they spent most of their time at Phee's. Mrs. Risborough worked nights at the hospital and slept in the afternoons.

As Phee spooned hummus into a bowl, she thought about the kid in the movie she'd watched at Kimiko's the previous week. He had a weird disease that made his skin fall off. He escaped from the hospital and went around touching everyone who'd ever been mean to him so they'd get it, too. Maybe Rusty had a contagious disease and was trying to get away. She was glad she'd always been nice to him.

Phee fanned the carrot sticks around the edge of the bowl, creating an orange daisy. She took paprika from the spice cupboard and sprinkled some on the hummus. It didn't look red enough, so she added some cinnamon, too. The magazine she'd flipped through at the dentist's one time said it was important to make an effort with "presentation" at meals. She wasn't exactly sure what that meant, but the photo showed a table with flowers and candles and cloth napkins folded to look like birds.

She was putting the hummus away in the fridge when her brother cruised into the kitchen and grabbed several of the carrot sticks. He bit off the ends, then stuck them into the bowl and scooped up some hummus. Her flower looked like it had been attacked by aphids.

"Zane, you double-dipped!" Phee pushed the bowl toward him. "Yuck."

"I'm starving," Zane said around a mouthful of carrot. "Are there any pizza bites left?"

"Dad ate them for breakfast. Mom's coming back day after tomorrow."

Before she left on a business trip, Phee's mom had stocked the fridge with healthy stuff from Whole Foods. She said if she didn't, Dad would feed them nothing but junk. As far as Phee was concerned, last night's dinner of popcorn cooked in bacon fat, with bacon bits and spicy peanuts sprinkled on top, and mango gelato for dessert covered all the major food groups.

Phee's mom was a geologist who looked for oil for petroleum companies. She'd been in Australia for three weeks and two days. She'd sent Phee a postcard with a kangaroo on it. HOPPY BIRTHDAY. WE'LL CELEBRATE WHEN I'M HOME. XXOO MOM. Phee's gaze went to the window over the sink. Did it snow in Australia? She imagined kangaroos hopping around with snow in their pouches. Her mom had said something about winter being summer there, so Phee wasn't sure.

Zane flopped onto the couch, picked up the TV remote, and turned on the Weather Channel. He was a sophomore at Bristlecone High and less than a month away from getting his driver's license. He'd started leaving brochures for Fords—mostly the Mustang and F-150 pickup truck—on the kitchen table.

Brooklyn and Scout clattered down the stairs, followed by her dad.

Although she'd never asked, Phee was pretty sure she knew how her parents had come up with all their names. It had to do with their love of reading. Zane was in honor of the author of the Westerns her dad collected. Ophelia came from her mom's Shakespeare craze. Homicide arrived when her dad was hooked on crime fiction. As for Brooklyn and Scout, her mom always read the cover of *People* magazine when she was in the checkout line. At least she hadn't named them Beckham and Willis.

"I won the Junior Entrepreneur contest," Phee said. "I get to go to Trent Snowboards. You have to sign the permission slip."

"You won a snowboard? That's nice, honey," her dad said as he scrawled his signature. "Zane, I'm not telling you this again. Please put away the things you left in the garage."

Phee's brother made money by cleaning up houses after people moved out. He'd started doing it last summer. A real estate agent friend of their mom's got a listing to sell a rental house the tenants had trashed. She'd hired Zane to clean it up so she could show it to potential buyers. When he asked what to do with the tenants' stuff, the agent had said, "Throw it away, keep it, sell it on eBay." Zane sold it and made thirty-four dollars. The real estate agent hired Zane for more jobs, and also gave his name to her agent friends. Zane got so busy, he made one of his baseball teammates, Austin, a partner in the business. Soon the Mahoneys' garage was full of tenants' abandoned items, awaiting listing on eBay.

"Okay," Zane said. He didn't move from the couch.

"Brooklyn, take that carrot stick out of your nose." Phee's dad had turned his attention to the twins.

Brooklyn chased Scout around the dining table with the carrot stick, which now had a big booger on the end. Brooklyn's hair went past his shoulders like his sister's, and streamed behind him.

Phee's dad slid his laptop into a case. "I'm leaving early for class because of the snow."

Phee's dad worked in a bank, something to do with giving money to people to buy houses. Once a week he taught a computer class at the senior center. Phee helped him assemble his handouts. The previous lesson had been how to copy and paste text into a Word document. How sad was that? All those people were going to die soon and they were only on copy and paste.

"Pizza for dinner fine with everyone?" her dad said.

The twins stopped running.

"I want pepperoni!" Brooklyn shouted.

"I want pineapple!" Scout said.

"I want mushrooms!" Brooklyn said.

"Mushrooms are fungus, you know," Zane said.

"Ewww," said Scout.

"Double ewww," said Brooklyn, and started chasing his sister again.

"Phee, do you mind watching the twins tonight?" her dad said. Phee's parents paid her ten dollars an hour to babysit the twins.

"That's so cool," Kimiko once said. "You can make money whenever you want to." So Phee let her watch the twins that day for two hours and keep the twenty dollars. Kimiko never asked if she could do it again.

"I have to finish my history paper," Phee said. She and her dad both knew the twins required undivided attention.

"I'll be home by six thirty." He opened his wallet and handed Phee three twenties and a ten. "That's to cover the pizza, too." Her dad pulled on a baseball cap, the brim facing backward. It was as wild as he ever got in public. Still, Phee liked how it made him look younger than most of the other dads in Bristlecone. Not like Rusty's mom. She had gray hair. Did she know how to copy and paste?

"Mrs. Risborough came back," she said.

Her dad slung his laptop case over his shoulder. "Didn't you used to play with her son, Rusty?"

Phee scowled at the use of the word play. "I saw him, too. He wouldn't tell me where they'd moved. He says they're taking Mrs. Heckler to live with them."

Zane turned up the TV volume. The weather girl said, "An earthquake in the South Pacific—" Zane changed the channel.

"Go back to the Weather Channel," Phee's dad said.

"Can't you just look on the Internet? The game's gonna start," Zane said. There was a no-fly zone between the TV and Zane when Colorado's teams were on. Tonight was Nuggets basketball.

"Zane, turn to the Weather Channel *now*."

Phee looked at her dad in surprise. Mom usually wore the bossy pants; he was the easygoing one.

On TV was a map of an ocean with a red dot off to the right. Wavy lines shot out from the dot, running into a yellow section marked Australia.

Chapter 9

Phee yawned and stretched, clearing the last of the being-caught-in-a-tsunami dreams from her brain, then kicked off the covers. It didn't take long for the cold air on her feet to drive her from the bed.

Her dad had skipped the senior center last night—the old people would have to wait another week to find out what Google was—and stayed home to phone the place where Phee's mom was staying. None of the calls went through. He sent a bunch of emails, but they either weren't answered or came back as undeliverable.

Phee pulled on her favorite purple leggings and a cream sweater and wondered why her dad hadn't wakened her. Every morning he knocked on her door ten minutes after her alarm went off to make sure she was *on track*. Phee brushed her hair and imagined a train like the miniature one in the park, running from her bed to the bathroom to the kitchen to the bus stop.

Downstairs, she saw her dad sitting at the kitchen table, red-eyed and unshaven. He wore red plaid pajama bottoms and a T-shirt that said Mom Likes Me Best that Zach gave him last Father's Day. The twins were eating cereal. At least Scout was. Brooklyn was building a stack of Cheerios on his spoon.

"Did you talk to Mom?" Phee said.

"Not yet. But I talked to the people at the embassy. They're trying to get in touch with her, too." Her dad gave her what was supposed to be a reassuring smile. Instead, he looked like he just ate something bitter. "Don't worry, honey."

"I won't," Phee said, meaning it. Her mom had been in scary situations before. She'd been in Peru when the earthquake hit, Italy when the volcano erupted, and on that ferry in India when it sank. Each time she'd come home perfectly fine and with amazing stories to tell. Phee's dad wanted her mom to take a safer job, and they had argued about it. "I have more lives than Hercules does," her mom had said.

Brooklyn flipped his spoon. The little Os scattered across the table and dropped onto the floor.

"I want Lucky Charms!" he declared.

Scout had taken the Lucky Charms box out of the cupboard (only Zane was supposed to eat them because Mom said sugar made the twins hyper). She rooted through the cereal, picking out the marshmallow bits.

"Scout, give me that," Phee said.

She wrested the box away and put it as high as she could reach in the pantry while her sister wailed. Her shoes crunched Cheerios. Time to ask for a raise. Last time she did, her mom had said the Thirteenth Amendment didn't apply to kids. Phee didn't get it but her dad had laughed.

She was getting the vacuum from the front hall closet when the doorbell rang.

"I'll get it." She opened the door. "Aunt Helen! What are you doing here?" Phee flushed. "I mean, I didn't know you were coming."

Aunt Helen smiled. "No worries, sweetie. It was a last-minute thing."

Aunt Helen was Dad's sister. She lived in Texas and had a pool and horses in her backyard. It was one of the best places to visit, and Aunt Helen was one of Phee's favorite people. Aunt Helen didn't have kids, so she treated Phee and even the twins like they were rational people with valid opinions and common sense. Which Phee was—something not always appreciated by her parents.

The twins had come to see who was at the door.

"Aunt Helen! Aunt Helen!" They converged for a group hug. Phee felt Aunt Helen's soft sweater and smelled the vanilla of her skin lotion.

"Is your dad here?" Helen said, disentangling herself.

"Dad!" Brooklyn yelled.

"Brooklyn, I've asked you not to—Helen! I didn't hear the door. Thank you so much for coming." Phee's dad appeared and gave his sister a kiss on the cheek.

He asked her to come? Phee thought. They never had guests when her mom was away. And her dad never came downstairs, much less to the door, in his pajamas.

"Any news?" Helen said quietly. Phee's dad shook his head, his eyes creased. For a second, Phee could see what he would look like when he was a lot older.

"Come into the kitchen," he said. "Everybody."

They all sat around the kitchen table, including a sleepy Zane, who had stayed up late with Austin picking up stuff from a house.

"Your mother's not coming home today," her dad said.

"Why not?" Zane said.

Phee's dad exchanged looks with Aunt Helen. "There was an earthquake in the ocean near Australia," he said. "That made a big wave, called a tsunami."

"Soon-na-me," said Scout.

"That isn't how you say it, dummy," Brooklyn said.

"Don't call me a dummy! You're the dummy!"

"That's enough!" Phee's dad used the same voice as when he'd told Zane to turn back to the Weather Channel the night before. Both twins stared at him, wide-eyed.

"The tsunami hit the part of Australia near where your mom is," he said. "It knocked out the phone and Internet and washed out the roads to the airport."

"So how is she going to get home?" Zane said.

"I don't know right now. Things are still pretty confused. That's why

Helen is here. She's going to help out until your mom gets home."

The twins began to cry.

"I want Mom," Brooklyn sobbed.

Aunt Helen scooped him into her arms. "It's only going to be for a few days. Now, do you want to see the presents I brought?"

Phee watched Brooklyn setting up his Stomp Rocket and Scout sorting through the beads of her bracelet-making kit. She wished she were five again, too little to know what the hard questions were, the ones the adults weren't answering or even asking. What if her mom wasn't coming home? What if she was dead? Phee always felt a weight settle around her heart whenever her mom left, lifting when she returned. The weight would crush her if she never saw her mom again.

Aunt Helen put her arm around Phee's waist. Her aunt wore her hair puffed out like a dandelion and some of it brushed Phee's cheek.

"I know you're worried, sweetie. Your mom is one of the smartest people I know. If anyone is going to make it through, I'm putting my money on her."

Phee nodded. She was afraid if she said anything, she'd start crying like the twins. Brooklyn jumped on the stomp pad. The plastic and foam rocket shot skyward. It hit the ceiling then fell back onto the carpet, followed by sprinkles of chipped paint. Brooklyn picked up the rocket and prepared to launch it again.

"Brooklyn, that's an outdoor toy," Aunt Helen said. She handed Phee a wrapped package. "This is for you."

Aunt Helen gave good presents—no scratchy sweaters or toys Phee was too old for. Last Christmas Aunt Helen had taken Phee to a pet store and they'd come home with a hamster. He was brown and white with bright brown eyes. Phee named him Marvin. About two weeks later, she came home from school to find the door to his cage open and Marvin gone. Brooklyn confessed to playing with the latch, even though it was on the list of Things Never To Do, along with taking knives out of the kitchen drawer and playing with superglue. Aunt Helen had offered to get Phee another hamster, but she didn't want any more pets.

Phee held the package now, savoring the knowledge something good was inside but not knowing exactly what it was. She pulled off the ribbon, slid a finger under one of the taped ends, then peeled the wrapping paper back to reveal a book. *The Master Spy Handbook: How to Secretly Sleuth, Crack Codes, and Snare Suspects*. She opened to the table of contents. *How to Tail Someone . . . Seeing Behind You . . . Secret Messages . . . How to Know If Someone Is Lying . . . .*

"It reminded me of our Bourne marathon," Aunt Helen said. She and Phee had shared a late-night-movie-and-popcorn session during her last visit. "I hope you like it."

Phee closed the book and held it to her chest. "It's perfect. Thank you." Maybe she'd become a secret agent, like Jason Bourne. How did you apply for that job? Wouldn't it be, well, secret?

Brooklyn had discovered that pressing the stomp pad without the rocket in place produced a startlingly realistic fart noise. He hit the pad over and over while Scout giggled.

A car horn sounded outside. Phee looked out the window. A white van was parked in their driveway with the driver's-side window down. Johnny Mercer sat behind the wheel.

Chapter 10

Johnny waved at her.

"I'll be right back," Phee said.

Aunt Helen had seen the van, too. "Who's that?"

"Someone I met on the ski trip."

"Would your mom care if you went out to talk to him?"

"No," Phee said.

Her mom wasn't like most adults. It seemed like her friends' moms wanted their daughters to be afraid of boys. Or more like wary. In person, online, texting—every encounter with a boy was potentially dangerous in their view. Phee's mom was more relaxed about it. They'd talked about staying safe with friends and strangers and using her common sense, and that bad things didn't happen as often as they seemed to on TV and the Internet. Her mom also said Phee couldn't date until she was sixteen, but at least she didn't freak out whenever Phee was with a friend who happened to be a boy.

"Okay," Aunt Helen said.

Phee put the spy handbook on top of the refrigerator where the twins couldn't get it, put on her outer gear, and opened the door.

It had snowed during the night. She stood still for a moment, enjoying the iciness on her face and the heat from the house on her back. This was how Phee liked snow—draped and mounded over the bushes and lawn, twinkly in the sunlight, with a warm house to retreat into.

She waded through the snow toward the van. Phee liked making first tracks—it was like you were starting over at the beginning, with no mistakes yet.

"Sorry about the honking," Johnny said when Phee stood beside his open window. "I usually call but I didn't have your number. And walking to your front door is a bit of a hassle."

"It's okay," Phee said. She peered into the van. The driver's seat had been removed, replaced by a wheelchair. "You can drive just using your hands?"

"Yep. Want to see how it works?"

"Okay." Phee slogged around to the other side of the van and got in. As soon as she shut the door, a dog appeared beside her seat. He swiped her face with his tongue and gave her a blast of dog breath.

"Kirby!" Johnny said. "Lie down."

The black and white dog complied, his bright eyes bouncing between Phee and Johnny.

"He's beautiful," Phee said. "Is it okay if I pet him?"

"Sure."

Phee stroked the soft coat. Kirby's tail thumped. "What kind is he?"

"Border collie. So if you have any sheep that need herding . . . "

Phee laughed.

"The only thing he goes after for real is Frisbees." Johnny scratched under the dog's chin, jangling the tags on his collar. "That's my good boy, yeah," he crooned. Kirby's eyes closed in bliss. Phee thought it was funny how guys babbled that way to dogs.

"Look what I found," Johnny said. He plucked a shiny gold object from the center console and held it up. "I think this is yours."

"My watch!" She pulled off her gloves and fastened it around her wrist. "Where'd you find it?"

"In the front pocket of my jacket. It must have fallen there when we went down the hill."

"Thanks." Seeing the oil well on the dial made Phee's heart feel funny.

She changed the subject. “So how does it work?” She nodded at the van’s steering wheel. Two chromed levers extended from the base of the steering column. One was topped by a red knob, the other, a green one. Yet another knob was welded onto the steering wheel.

“Green is the gas and red is the brake,” Johnny said. “I have to drive one-handed. That’s what the knob on the steering wheel is for.”

“How do you get your wheelchair into the car?”

“There’s a motorized lift on my side. I roll onto it, press the button, and up I go.”

“Like an elevator!”

“You got it. There’s also a ramp I can pull out from under the van.”

“This sort of reminds me of Mr. Bean’s car,” Phee said, then dipped her chin in embarrassment. Johnny probably had never watched the show.

Johnny laughed. “I remember that episode.” The comedian had tied an armchair to the roof of his Mini Cooper, operating the steering wheel with rope and the pedals with a broom handle. “Want to see it in action?”

Phee nodded. He pushed against the green lever and shifted at the same time, and the van backed out of the driveway. Phee grabbed onto the armrest.

“It’s okay,” Johnny said. He pulled on the red lever. “See? I can stop.” The van halted at the street’s edge.

Phee relaxed her grip. “Cool,” she said.

“I’ll go around the block.”

They started down Fir Lane. As they passed Mrs. Heckler’s, Rusty came out the front door with his mom.

The van’s windows were tinted dark. Phee lowered hers and said, “Can you honk the horn?” Johnny obliged. The Risboroughs looked up and Phee waved. Rusty raised his hand and waggled it back and forth, a sad expression on his face, while Mrs. Risborough stared at them, her mouth half open. Did she think it that surprising an eighth grader would be going for a ride with a guy in high school?

Phee flipped her hair over her shoulder like Veronica did. Mrs.

Risborough clamped on to Rusty's arm and pulled him inside the house. She wore a flowery dress that was wide through the hips and looked like a rolling meadow when she walked.

"Who're they?" Johnny said.

"Our neighbors. I mean, they used to be our neighbors."

"Not very friendly."

"Rusty's okay," Phee said. "But his mom is kinda antisocial."

They made it back to Phee's without incident. "Thanks for the ride," Phee said as she opened the door. "And for bringing my watch."

"Sure. Tell Mahoney No Baloney I said hi."

I sure will, Phee thought, already making up a rhyme in her head. *Mahoney No Baloney as big as a pony 'cause he eats too much macaroni . . . .*

Chapter 11

Phee dropped her purple plaid backpack under her desk and slid into her seat in health class. She looked down at her leggings. She hadn't had time to change before the bus came. They were wrinkled where they'd gotten wet and her legs looked like elephant skin. Wrinkled purple elephant skin. Phee wondered if she should rethink her favorite color. Maybe red?

Kimiko half turned in the seat in front of her. She wore an orange fedora, Ashlee Simpson T-shirt under a man-style vest, and skinny jeans. On Kimiko the clothes looked fashionable. On Phee, they'd look like she shopped in the '90s section of Goodwill.

"I am so screwed," Kimiko whispered.

"What happened?"

"I have to get braces!"

Phee's mom had started talking about Phee getting braces. "I don't want that overbite to cause you jaw problems later," she'd said.

"Bummer," Phee whispered to Kimiko, thinking, what if Kimiko had to get the metal kind? Would her lips freeze to them when she went snowboarding?

"Do you want a boy or a girl?" Kimiko said.

"Huh?" Phee had trouble imagining a boyfriend, let alone a husband and kids. She looked out the window. Was her husband-to-be looking out the window at his school, too?

"Boy or girl?" Kimiko repeated.

"Both," she said.

"You can't have—"

"Kimiko, Ophelia," said Mrs. Moss. "Do you have something you'd like to share with the class?" Mrs. Moss had red hair and wore a lot of green, which Phee thought funny because of her name.

Kimiko slid down in her seat. "No," she said into the collar of her shirt.

"No," said Phee. Two rows over Veronica smirked.

"School for one hundred. The answer is kids headed for detention," Joshua-Alex whispered. "Who are Kimiko and Phee?" Kimiko gave him a dirty look.

Mrs. Moss opened a large carton beside her desk and took out a fake baby. Now Kimiko's question made sense.

Last year an eighth-grader had gotten pregnant. She stayed in school until her stomach got too big to fit behind the desks. It looked like she had a basketball—no, a beach ball—under her shirt. All the parents were afraid more girls would have babies, as if you got pregnant the same way you got chicken pox. So this year every eighth-grader had to take care of a robot baby for a day. The idea was that it'd be such a pain, you wouldn't want a real one, at least not while you were in middle school.

Phee liked babies. She'd been happy when the twins were born. She liked their milky smell and soft skin and how they opened their mouths like baby birds when she fed them spoonfuls of mashed peas. But she didn't want to have a baby when she was in middle school. She didn't need to carry around a robot to know this. The fake babies were for the parents, not the students. Kids had to do a lot of things just to make grown-ups less anxious. It could be annoying.

"Each of you will be responsible for an infant for three days. They require constant attention, including feeding, burping, rocking, and diaper changes."

Joshua-Alex raised his hand. "Do they make fake poop?" he said.

"No, they don't." Mrs. Moss turned the robot around and held up its shirt. “The baby will cry until you figure out the correct action key.” She held up a ring of colored keys. “There are keys for food, changing diapers, and so on, to insert into a slot in the baby’s back.” She pulled the baby’s shirt down and set it on the desk. “Software inside the baby records how well you do as a parent. It also allows me to set the level of difficulty—easy, medium, or hard.”

“Like a crack baby,” Veronica said, looking at Phee.

Evan Ackerman leaned toward Kimiko. “Can I be your baby daddy?”

Kimiko made a face. “If you were, I’d give the kid up for adoption.”

“There aren’t enough babies for everyone so you’ll be taking turns,” Mrs. Moss said. She began to call names and hand out babies. “Joshua Grabenstein…”

Joshua-Alex picked up his baby by one arm. It started to cry. Joshua-Alex fumbled through the collection of keys. The baby cried louder. Mrs. Moss found the right key. When the baby was quiet again, she said, “They also cry if you don’t hold them properly.”

“I guess that means no bungee jumping.” Joshua-Alex looked into the bland plastic eyes. “Right, Miley?”

“Miley?” Phee said.

“I’ll take Baby-Faced Singers for one hundred,” Joshua-Alex said.

“Ophelia Mahoney.”

Phee retrieved her baby. She looked at the little plastic face and couldn’t help but think about Chucky, the serial killer doll in the movie she’d made the mistake of watching once when babysitting the twins. “But I’m going on the business-class field trip tomorrow.”

“Then I hope you know a good babysitter,” Mrs. Moss said.

Chapter 12

The bell rang. Phee slung her backpack over her shoulder and picked up Tron, the name she'd given her robot baby. When she walked into the hallway, Ms. Vlachos was standing there. "Phee, could you come with me to Mr. Sandoval's office?"

When a teacher, even a favorite one, asked a student to come to the principal's office, nothing good ever happened. You weren't going to find out you were so smart you got to skip the rest of eighth grade, or they'd made a mistake counting the votes and the homecoming queen was you instead of Veronica. No, it was always bad news.

Phee racked her brain for what she might have done wrong. There was the paper on the Civil War due in two days that she hadn't started, but Ms. Vlachos wouldn't know that. Her mom was the parent who kept up with homework assignments, making sure Phee "budgeted her time." But since she'd been gone—

Phee came to a dead stop in the middle of the hallway. A student bumped into her from behind.

"Watch it, idi—" The student saw Ms. Vlachos and kept walking.

"What is it, Phee?" Ms. Vlachos said.

It's my mom, Phee wanted to say. You're taking me to Mr. Sandoval's office to tell me something terrible happened to my mom. But the words were stuck in her throat.

"Are you okay?" Ms. Vlachos said.

Phee's grip tightened on Tron. He started to cry. The mechanical wail broke through her paralysis. "I'm fine," she said, sorting through the keys. It took three tries until she found the right one and inserted it. "I'm fine."

Phee walked into the principal's office with heavy feet. She expected her dad to be there, and maybe Aunt Helen. Instead, there were a man and woman she'd never seen before. They sat in the chairs across from Mr. Sandoval's desk.

"Hello, Ophelia. Thank you for coming,"

Like I had a choice, Phee thought as Mr. Sandoval stood. He wore a light blue short-sleeved shirt and fingerprint-smeared glasses. He extended a hand. At first Phee thought he wanted her to shake it, then realized he was gesturing for her to sit down on the bench under the window. Ms. Vlachos stayed by the door, one hand kneading the other like it was a Koosh ball.

"This is Mr. and Mrs. Oakeson," Mr. Sandoval said.

"Hello, Ophelia," Mr. Oakeson said. Mrs. Oakeson just stared at Phee with clear blue eyes fringed with dark lashes. Chord's eyes. The last name clicked.

"I told them you were the last person to see—" Ms. Vlachos began.

"Ophelia, I understand you spent some time with Chord on Monday," Mr. Sandoval said.

Phee nodded cautiously. This felt like one of those courtroom shows, where the lawyer acted all friendly and asked the witness a bunch of easy questions. Then *bam!* came the zinger. Phee clutched Tron and waited for the zinger.

"What did you talk about?"

Phee glanced at Mrs. Oakeson. Her skin gleamed the same yellow-white as the fluorescent lights overhead.

"Um, snowboarding." Tron cried again. Mrs. Oakeson flinched. Phee dug in her backpack for the keys.

"Let me take your baby," Ms. Vlachos said.

Phee handed Tron over. "You put a key in—" But the robot baby had quieted as soon as Ms. Vlachos started rocking him.

"Anything else?" Mr. Sandoval said.

"Violin and—" Phee glanced at Mrs. Oakeson. *How you wouldn't let him snowboard because he might get hurt and screw up his chance for a scholarship to Bellermine.*

"That's about it," she said.

"Did he say anything about where he was going after the field trip?"

"No."

"Where did you last see him?"

Phee hesitated. She didn't really want to say *beside a tree well that he pulled me out of.* "On the way to the bus to go home."

"Did you actually see him get on the bus?"

"No, just before. He was assigned to a different bus than I was."

Phee heard a low moan. She thought it was Tron, but Mrs. Oakeson began to rock back and forth in her chair, hugging herself like she was cold. "I thought he was spending the night at a friend's," she whispered. "But yesterday when he didn't come home after school and then missed dinner, too . . ."

Mr. Sandoval said, "Chord wasn't on the bus home from the field trip and no one has seen him since Monday."

Chapter 13

When Phee got home from school, the house was empty. Empty of kids, that is.

"The twins are at a playdate and I don't know where Zane is," Aunt Helen said. "I was about to go grocery shopping." She covered a yawn. "Excuse me! I guess Scout and Brooklyn wore me out."

"Tell me about it," Phee said.

"I'll go, Helen," her dad called from the den. Phee was surprised. Her dad was usually still at the office when she came home.

"Take Phee with you. Anyone who ate peanut-butter-and-pickle sandwiches on cinnamon toast should not be in charge of grocery shopping." To Phee, she said, "Make sure he brings home some fruit and vegetables. Ones listed in the ingredients on a label don't count."

Her dad joined them in the kitchen.

"Did Mom call?" Phee said.

"No, honey. I'm still trying to get in touch with her." He ran a hand through his hair. Phee noticed it was starting to gray by his ears.

"I can't reach anyone at the oil company who knows what's going on," he said to Aunt Helen. "They say it isn't their responsibility to account for her because she's an independent contractor. They can't even tell me what job site she was at!" He ran his hand through his hair again, making it stick up like Homicide's did when he was mad.

Phee knew her mom was pretty independent, but the contractor part didn't make sense. Trina Elliot's dad was a contractor, and he'd built houses until the economy got bad and he had to get a job at Home Depot. Phee's mom didn't build houses.

While her dad got ready to go to the store, Phee watched some YouTube videos of the tsunami coming ashore. Water roared through the streets, turning cars into bobbing boats and knocking over houses. She hadn't seen any people drown, but the news said thousands were dead and just as many were missing. Phee still wasn't worried. Her mom was a geologist. She knew where to go to be safe. Not like those people who got in their cars or ran into one-story buildings. Phee imagined her mom climbing to the top of a tree, waiting for the water to go down.

Usually her dad listened to music in the car, but tonight they drove in silence. Phee had Tron on her lap. Would Mrs. Moss be able to tell he wasn't in a car seat? She slipped her seat belt over his chest.

"Did you really eat peanut-butter-and-pickle sandwiches?" she said.

"Every day."

"Until when?" Phee said.

"Hmm?" her dad said. He was staring at the road, both hands on the wheel, but Phee got the feeling his mind was somewhere else.

"When did you stop eating them?"

"Oh, I don't know. One morning I woke up and didn't like them anymore."

Phee thought of things she used to like a lot and then didn't like at all. My Pretty Pony. Justin Bieber singing "Baby." Strawberry gelato. But no people. Everyone she liked she'd always liked—Kimiko, Ms. Vlachos, even Joshua-Alex. He was weird, but nice-weird, not creepy-weird.

Snow had begun falling again, the flakes startlingly white in the beam of their headlights. Her dad switched on the wipers. They sank back into silence. Her dad wasn't one of those people who thought talking about anything was better than just being quiet.

The car dinged. Her dad frowned at the gauges on the dashboard.

"What is it?" Phee said.

"I'm low on gas again. Something must be wrong with the injectors."

No, Phee wanted to say. The car was low on gas because Zane had been using it. Three weeks ago she'd caught him driving their dad's car back from a house cleanup. He'd told her it was an emergency—"Austin had a doctor's appointment and his car isn't working." Apparently Austin had a lot of doctor appointments.

They pulled into the parking lot and went into the store. Her dad pushed the cart while Phee pulled things from the shelves. She and Aunt Helen had made a list. She'd read the section in *The Master Spy Handbook* on how to make invisible ink, so she added erasable gel pens to their purchases. According to the book, the pen's heat-sensitive ink turns clear when it reaches a certain temperature; rubbing it with the eraser generates the necessary heat. The ink reappears when it gets cold. To read an erased message, you just had to pop the page in the freezer. Phee wasn't sure who she was going to send secret messages to, but she wanted to be prepared.

What if her mom was actually a spy? Phee thought as she followed her dad to the next aisle. Maybe instead of looking for rocks that had oil, she was really looking for terrorists. Maybe she hadn't been anywhere near the tsunami but had been taken prisoner by—Phee put the brakes on her brain. Sometimes her imagination took her to crazy places before she realized it. Her mom was a geologist. *And she's going to come home.*

While her dad figured out which paper towels to buy (her mom always did the math and chose the "best value"), Phee wandered to the end of the aisle with Tron in her arms. He was too little for the baby seat in the shopping cart. The pharmacy section ran along the rear wall of the store. Several customers stood in line waiting to pick up prescriptions.

Phee did a double take. Standing at the register was Mrs. Risborough. She wore a red plaid coat over white nylon pants and white Crocs. Phee did not like Crocs. Even her practical mom drew the line at the ugly rubber shoes.

"I'll be right back," Phee called to her dad. He didn't look her way, focused on tapping numbers into his phone calculator. "Mom likes the ones with the lumberjack on them," Phee said in a louder voice. Her dad didn't act like he'd heard her.

She headed toward the pharmacy area. Mrs. Risborough was walking away from the register, carrying a white bag. Phee trotted toward her.

"Mrs. Risborough? Mrs. Risborough!"

Rusty's mom stopped and turned. Her eyes went wide.

"It's me, Ophelia," Phee said. She didn't want Mrs. Risborough to think she was a mugger, although she was pretty sure no one had ever been mugged *inside* a supermarket. "Aunt Helen told me that you came by—"

Mrs. Risborough's eyes widened and she backed away from Phee. Sweat shone on her face. Phee whirled around to see what was scaring her. But nothing was there, unless you counted the cardboard Jolly Green Giant.

Phee turned back in time to see the red plaid coat squeeze past someone pushing a cart through the exit doors and disappear into the darkness of the parking lot. She frowned. What was going on? *Adults are so weird sometimes.*

A red glove was on the ground. Phee picked it up. Mrs. Risborough had been holding a pair of red gloves. She wondered if she should take the glove and drop it off at Mrs. Heckler's. What if Mrs. Risborough ran away from her again?

Phee walked over to the pharmacy register. No one was in line.

"Mrs. Risborough dropped this," Phee said to the young woman behind the counter. Her blond hair was pulled into a ponytail and she wore a crisp blue jacket. She tapped on the keyboard of the computer in front of her.

"There's no Mrs. Risborough in the database."

"But she just picked up a prescription." Phee described Mrs. Risborough, down to the red plaid coat and red gloves.

The woman read the information on the computer screen. "I know the customer you're talking about, but Risborough isn't her last name."

Phee frowned. "Oh. Okay. I'll just take the glove to her house. Thanks."

A customer walked up to the drop-off window and hit the little bell on the counter. As the pharmacist walked away to take the new order, Phee leaned across the counter until the edge dug into her stomach. She squinted at the computer screen.

PATIENT NAME: MARY ROSENBERG. INSURANCE: NONE. OXYC—

Phee couldn't read the rest of the word; the printing was too small. The next section said DOSAGE: 60 MG TWICE DAILY.

Phee slid off the counter. Maybe Rosenberg was Mrs. Risborough's last name before she got married. Tron began to wail. Phee found the right key and turned him off. People were staring at her. Did they think she still played with dolls?

"It's a fake baby," she announced to no one in particular.

"There you are!" It was her dad. His cart was half full. All Phee saw in the way of a fruit or vegetable was a jar of salsa and some grapes. No one liked grapes except the twins. Brooklyn threw them and Scout squished them. Phee thought about asking if they should get apples or broccoli, but a glance at her dad changed her mind. He didn't look like he was in a produce mood.

As they started for the checkout stand, Phee noticed her dad had picked out the wrong paper towels. When they passed the display, she grabbed the right brand and switched it for the one in the cart.

Phee put their items on the conveyor belt. She added a bag of Citrons from the display for Mrs. Heckler, and after a moment's hesitation, a Hershey's dark chocolate bar, the only candy her mom liked.

"Are these for your dolly?" the checker asked as she scanned the candy.

"He's not a—"

"Hey, Phee."

Phee turned to see Peter Allerd standing behind her—tall, dorky, and moderately handsome. She immediately regretted wearing her Hello Kitty T-shirt. She hadn't even liked Hello Kitty since sixth grade. But when her mom was gone, laundry tended to not get done.

She pulled Tron close to block the white cat from view.

"Hi," she said.

Peter nodded at Tron. "I had to carry one of those around last month."

He looked at her—his eyes were lake-clear blue—and smiled. Phee's heart thumped against her ribs.

"Mmm," Phee said. Even though she'd come in third in last year's spelling bee—she'd gotten *lemur* right but screwed up *toucan*—and had finished more books than anyone else on the extra-credit reading list, her proficiency in the English language suddenly deserted her.

"Hello, Ophelia." Peter's dad set a carry basket filled with packages of cheese and crackers and beef jerky on the belt. He wore a tan uniform with a shiny badge pinned on his belt. He was Bristlecone's sheriff. Seeing the badge made Phee feel slightly guilty, even though she hadn't done anything illegal, at least not that she could think of.

"I understand you're looking for a lost boy," Phee's dad said. Phee had told him about Chord. "Any news?"

"No."

"How long has he been gone?"

"Forty-eight hours," Sheriff Allerd said.

Phee caught the look that passed between the two men. She knew what they were thinking. *After a couple of nights outside in this cold, Chord is probably dead, but because our kids are here, we can't say that.*

"I saw one of your billboards," Phee's dad said.

Sheriff Allerd made a face. "Not my style. But then I've never had one of my deputies run against me before."

The checker gave Phee's dad his receipt. "Have a nice day."

"Thank you."

"See ya," Peter said to Phee. He stepped forward and their elbows bumped.

"See ya," Phee managed to echo before hurrying after her dad.

Phee's dad loaded the groceries into the car and they started for home. Phee could still feel the spot where she and Peter touched and had to resist the urge to rub it.

When they'd gone about a mile, her dad said, "How's school?"

The answer to that question was a list of not-so-great things. *Veronica and the Donner Partiers are being mean to me, Chord might be dead, and I think I like Peter Allerd but no way does he like me back.* "Um, fine."

"That's good."

A bunch of orange lilies, her mom's favorite flower, stuck out of one of the bags. Her mom thought it was better to buy them before they bloomed. *I like seeing them unfold, plus they last a lot longer.* Her dad preferred them in full flower, each petal curled like a panting dog's tongue. *I want you to enjoy them now*, he'd say to her mom. *If they wilt after a few days, I'll get you more.* You could tell a lot about her parents by the way they chose flowers.

Her dad noticed her looking at the lilies. "They're for your mother." Each bud was closed up tight. Because it was how her mom liked them? Or because her dad thought it would be a while before she came back?

She and her dad were quiet the rest of the way home.

Chapter 14

Phee helped carry the groceries into the kitchen. Zane and the twins were there with Aunt Helen. The twins were frosting cupcakes and Zane was eating them. Scout and Aunt Helen wore beaded bracelets. Scout's was crusted with white frosting. Homicide sat on the window seat and watched the goings-on through slitted eyes.

"Hi," Phee said.

"What's that?" Brooklyn pointed at Tron.

"My baby," Phee said.

Zane snickered. "So immaculate conception can happen."

"A baby?" Scout said.

"What's immaculate concentration?" Phee said.

Zane guffawed. "That isn't how you say it!" Aunt Helen was trying not to smile. Phee went hot with embarrassment.

"We're not the littlest anymore!" Brooklyn said. He banged his spoon against the counter in celebration.

"It's a fake baby," Phee said.

"Let me see that." Zane grabbed Tron, who whimpered. Homicide hissed and stalked out of the room.

Tron's whimper grew louder. Zane turned the robot baby upside down and shook it. "How do you turn it off?" Tron screamed.

Scout clapped her hands over her ears, smearing frosting in her hair. "Be quiet!" Brooklyn continued banging his spoon.

Zane thrust Tron at Phee. "Make it shut up!"

Phee stuck keys into the slot until the speaker switched off. "I have to keep him for three days."

"How do you know it's a him? Did you look?" Zane said, snickering again. Phee hated it when he did that.

"It has a pee-pee?" Brooklyn said. "Can I see?"

"No," Phee said. "It doesn't."

"We made bracelets at Sarah's," Scout said. "I made one for you." She slid off the stool and walked to the kitchen table, where she picked up a string of beads. "It's your favorite color."

Phee took the purple bracelet. "It is," she said, glad she hadn't changed it to red. Scout helped her tie the bracelet on her wrist.

"I'll make one for the baby," Scout said.

"That would be nice," Aunt Helen said. "Let's finish the cupcakes first."

Phee set Tron on a chair. She noticed Zane's black Carhart pants and beige button-up shirt with the arm patch.

"Did you get paged?" she said.

Her brother belonged to the Bristlecone Rescue Patrol, volunteers who backed up law enforcement. He'd joined last year, Phee thought mainly because the group was on call day and night, which meant there was a good chance he'd be paged out of class once or twice a month. But Zane took it seriously, passing written and practical tests in search and rescue, emergency care, water and avalanche rescue, winter survival, and communications. He and Austin directed traffic at special events, helped firemen roll up hoses and refill oxygen tanks, and performed grid searches for evidence for the sheriff's department. Last summer when a guy held up a gas station and then ran away on foot, shooting as he went, the volunteers were sent out to find the casings. They also looked for and helped rescue people, usually "grandpas with Alzheimer's or dumb hikers," according to Zane.

"Yep," he said now through a mouthful of cupcake. "Sheriff's department wants to do a grid search for that kid from your class who got lost on the field trip." He put on his black baseball hat with SEARCH & RESCUE printed across the front. "I heard the teacher didn't even notice he was gone until the parents called. What a dummy."

"Ms. Vlachos isn't a dummy. She's a great teacher."

"Don't you mean *used* to be a great teacher? If I were the principal, she'd be so fired."

"It wasn't her fault!" Phee's voice trembled. "There was a snowstorm and—"

"Zane, do you need a ride?" Aunt Helen interjected.

"No, thanks. Austin's picking me up."

"I want to go, too," Phee said. What if Chord had fallen into a tree well? His hat didn't have a pom-pom so it'd be harder to find him.

"Me, too!" Brooklyn announced. He waved a spatula in the air.

"You, wandering around in the woods at night?" Zane said to Phee. "I don't think so. You'd end up getting lost and then we'd have to look for you, too."

"I would not!"

School had been buzzing with rumors after news of Chord's disappearance leaked—he had run away, was lost, kidnapped, dead. Phee didn't pass on any of the rumors but she may have had something to do with the leaking. She couldn't avoid telling Kimiko about her visit to the principal's office, which led to Kimiko breaking into tears, which led to Mr. Fordiani, their algebra teacher, asking what was wrong, which led to Kimiko blurting out the news, which led to Veronica and the rest of her clique lapsing into mild hysteria, and that was that for solving linear inequalities, which was okay by Phee. She'd stayed up late reading *The Master Spy Handbook* instead of graphing $A + B > C$ and the other homework problems.

The first chapter in the handbook was titled "Do You Have What It Takes to Be a Spy?" Phee had gone through the checklist. *Razor-sharp wits*—check. *Amazing powers of perception*—sort of check. (She'd noticed Mrs. Risborough wore red gloves. Not seeing the tree well hadn't been her fault.) *Perseverance*—check. *Curiosity*—check. *Patience*—well, four out of five wasn't bad. She'd work on patience.

"I want to go," Phee repeated.

"I think it's best if you stay here. If they find him, I'm sure your brother will call." Aunt Helen threw a look at Zane, who frowned, then said, "Oh, yeah, right."

"Bath time for you two," Aunt Helen said to the twins, who looked like they were wearing more frosting than the cupcakes were.

"Me first," Scout said.

"No, me!" Brooklyn said. They ran from the room.

"The lady next door came by," Aunt Helen said to Phee as she put the cupcakes in a container.

"Mrs. Risborough?"

"She didn't leave her name. When I said you weren't here, she got a little upset. I asked her if there was something I could do, but she said she'd come back later and left."

"Are you sure she lives next door?"

Aunt Helen suppressed a smile. "Well, I watched her walk across our yard and go into the yellow house." Check off *amazing power of perception* for Aunt Helen.

Phee tried to work out why Mrs. Risborough would have stopped by. She couldn't know Phee had her glove. Unless she'd seen Phee pick it up? Then why not ask her for it at the store? Maybe she'd come to apologize. But why had she been so rude in the first place? Phee gave up. *Patience.*

Someone rang the doorbell.

That didn't take long. Phee picked up Tron and the glove and went to open the door.

Joshua-Alex stood there, wearing a brown watch cap, navy down jacket, and ski pants. "Is Zane ready?" he said.

"I'll see." Phee cupped her hands around her mouth and called into the house. "Zane? Josh—uh, Alex is here."

"Just a minute," came Zane's shouted reply.

Phee turned back to Joshua-Alex. "You're in rescue patrol, too?"

"Not officially. You have to be in ninth grade to sign up. But Brian's going with his brother, and he said I could come, too." Over his shoulder Phee saw Austin's idling pickup truck. It was the kind with the bitty backseat, black with flames painted on the doors.

"Where's Miley?"

"I'm paying my sister to watch her."

Phee thought again about Chord rescuing her from the tree well. What if he'd gotten lost in the snow afterward? It'd be her fault. "I'm coming, too."

"I told you, no," Zane said behind her. "Question Boy shouldn't, either." He opened the foyer closet, pulled his heaviest parka from a hanger, then took out his rescue patrol backpack, red with a black and white triangle patch sewn on the front pocket. From snooping in it when her brother wasn't home, Phee knew each volunteer carried food, a flashlight, a headlamp, first-aid kit, matches, lighter, knife/multi-tool, rope, water and water purification tablets, survival blanket, and compass.

"Okay," Phee said. "I'll stay home and talk to Dad about why his car is getting such bad gas mileage."

Zane paused with his arm halfway through a sleeve. "You'll do what?"

"He mentioned it on the way home. I was thinking he might want to check the odometer as well as the gas tank."

"You'd tell him I've been driving?" Zane's whisper was sharp with outrage.

Phee shrugged. "Of course, if I go with you, I can't talk to him . . ."

"That's extortion!"

"Pretty much."

"The doll stays here," Zach said.

"Nope. I have to take him with me."

Zane pushed past her with a resigned look. "You're all riding in the backseat. Now hurry up."

"I have to tell Dad," Phee said. She found him in the kitchen with Aunt Helen. He was nibbling on a cupcake while Aunt Helen loaded the dishwasher.

"I want to go with the rescue patrol to look for Chord," Phee said.

"I don't think so, honey," her dad said. "It's late and you've got school tomorrow. And I don't want you up on the mountain after dark."

"It'll be okay. Zane'll be there, and Sheriff Allerd." She wasn't sure about Peter's dad, but figured it was a safe bet. "Dad, Chord is a friend. I *have* to look for him."

Her dad exchanged looks with Aunt Helen. Phee noticed the deep creases in his cheeks and how bloodshot his eyes were. She'd almost changed her mind about going when he said, "Okay, but you have to stay with your brother every minute."

"I promise," Phee called as she ran to get her coat.

Chapter 15

Phee and Alex stood in front of the lodge, now shuttered tight against the winter night. Tractor growls and backup beeps from unseen snowcats grooming the runs split the quiet. The snow had stopped, leaving the air dry and icy. Phee zipped Tron into her jacket and tugged her pom-pom hat down around her ears. She tried to take shallow breaths; the cold air seared her lungs.

Parked where the buses had picked them up was what Zane called the mobile command center, a former ambulance converted to rescue patrol use. Radio antennae bristled from its roof. One of the rescue patrol officers had used the vehicle's bullhorn to divide the volunteers into teams of five people. Most of the patrol were men, but Phee saw a few women in the mix. Maps were distributed, with each team assigned approximately one square mile to search.

The officer had turned the bullhorn over to Sheriff Allerd. He thanked the volunteers for coming and explained the sheriff department's working theory: instead of getting on the bus to go home, Chord had caught the lift for one last run just as the storm hit. He'd become disoriented and gotten lost.

Each team formed a line at one edge of its designated search area. Keeping about twenty feet of space between members, the teams advanced slowly and in unison, scanning the ground and trees for Chord or evidence that he'd been there. Their headlamps and flashlights traced scraggly constellations on the dark hill.

Phee and Joshua-Alex wanted to join Zane and Austin's team, but Sheriff Allerd wouldn't let them. "Untrained civilians can't be part of the squad. While I appreciate your concern for your friend, it would be safest for everyone if you two went home or waited in one of the cars."

"I want to look," Phee said. Joshua-Alex nodded his agreement.

The sheriff's radio spit static. "Fine," he said as he keyed the device. "You two were on the field trip, right? Search between here and where the buses were parked. Maybe there's something we missed."

Phee watched Zane vanish into the darkness with the rest of his team, his red pack bobbing among the others. She felt a little guilty about breaking her promise to her dad, even though the sheriff had said she couldn't go with her brother.

"If they missed something, we'll find it," Joshua-Alex said after the sheriff had left to join the others on the hill. Phee wasn't so sure. Sheriff Allerd said searchers had combed the area the day before. Since then, fresh snow had fallen.

Joshua-Alex went to Austin's truck, popped the back hatch, and took out something that looked like the tube from a small canister, with a round flat showerhead on the end. He carried it over to Phee.

"What's that?" she said.

"I'll take Modern-Day Treasure Hunting Tools for a hundred," Joshua-Alex said. "The answer is beachcomber's favorite."

Phee studied the doughnut-shaped head, the wires running up the metal shaft, the dial and gauges on the small black box attached to the top. "I give up."

Alex made the buzzer sound. "What's a metal detector?" He flicked a switch on the handle and pointed it at her. She heard *click click click* when it got close to the zipper on her jacket.

"Where did you get it?"

"My uncle Bernie in Florida got a fancier model, so he sent me his old one. He says you wouldn't believe what people lose in the sand—watches, cell phones, coins. Once he even found a war medal."

"It works in the snow?"

"Yep. Down to almost a foot, according to the manual."

"How will it help find Chord?"

"If he can't hear us, like if he's unconscious or in a snow cave asleep, it'll beep when it detects the metal on his clothes." They'd learned to build snow caves at Outdoor Scouts camp. If you got lost, you could use tree branches and packed snow to make an igloo that would keep you warm, or at least warmer than if you were just outside.

"Let's start here," Phee said. She started down the road she'd taken the day before to the bus, stepping carefully so she wouldn't fall where the ground was iced over. She carried her dad's camping flashlight, and the beam skittered off the frozen ruts.

Joshua-Alex followed, the detector giving off a faint click now and then. When Phee came to the metal shed where she'd seen the man with the snowboards, she veered to the right.

"Hey, the road goes this way," Joshua-Alex said, pointing down the hill.

"I know. But let's try over here." Phee slogged across the field. Sweat dampened her inner layer of clothes and her head felt hot under her hat.

Joshua-Alex struggled after her, sweeping the metal detector right and left. Phee stopped a few feet from the tree and the hole she'd fallen into. "Let's look in this area."

Joshua-Alex tramped around the tree, widening the circle with each circuit. When he was about fifteen feet away on the uphill side, the metal detector began clicking rapidly. The light on the handle flashed.

"I got something! Start digging!"

Phee dropped to her knees, stuck the flashlight in the snow like a candle, and scooped the snow away from where the detector had registered the strongest reading.

Even though she had on her heavy gloves, her fingers quickly went numb. Her legs were chilled all the way through where they pressed against the snow. Tron hadn't uttered a sound since they got out of the car. Maybe the cold had knocked out his electronics.

"I can't feel my fingers," Joshua-Alex complained.

"I've got an extra glove." Phee handed him Mrs. Risborough's, which was still in her pocket.

"Only one?"

"If it was good enough for Michael Jackson . . ." Phee said. He put it on.

Phee got a branch that had fallen off the tree and used it to poke through the white crust.

"Forget it," Joshua-Alex said. "Let's go back before we freeze to death."

Phee shot him a look.

"I didn't mean to say that," Joshua-Alex said quickly. "I mean—"

"Hold the flashlight." Phee resumed digging with new energy. Less than a minute later, her stick hit something hard. Like metal.

"I got it!" She burrowed her hand into the loosened snow. Her fingers found something smooth and round. She pulled it free. "Shine the light on it."

A moment later, Joshua-Alex blew out an exasperated breath. "It's just somebody's snowboard tool."

Phee stared at the purple Betty Rides sticker with the K marked on it. "Not somebody's. It's Kimiko's."

Chapter 16

Their discovery of the snowboard tool created a hubbub among the rescue patrol and sheriff's personnel. Phee stood encased in a volunteers' spare parka and listened.

"The girl says he was in this vicinity late Monday afternoon," one said.

Another measured the snow depth where the tool was found. "It was buried under four inches," he said. "That means he was here this morning."

"Are you sure?" asked Sheriff Allerd.

The man nodded. "It would have been buried much deeper if he'd lost it Monday afternoon."

If Chord was here this morning, Phee thought, where did he spend the last two nights? Only after the chief and several of the volunteers turned to look at her did she realize she'd spoken the question.

"You've been really helpful, Phee," the sheriff said. Phee could tell from his tone what was coming next—he was sending her home. "Austin and Zane are still up on the mountain. I'll have one of my men take you and Joshua home."

"My name's Alex," Joshua-Alex said. But the sheriff had resumed talking with the patrol.

Phee and Alex walked down to where they'd caught the bus on Monday. A squad car pulled up. Phee didn't realize it was their ride until the deputy got out and opened the door to the backseat for them.

Joshua-Alex gestured at Phee to go first. As she climbed in, she felt his hand on top of her head, pressing down on her hat's pom-pom. She shook it off and scooted across the seat.

"What were you doing?" she said as he sat beside her.

"Making sure you didn't hit your head while your hands are cuffed behind you. They do it all the time on TV."

"Do you see handcuffs on me?" Phee pulled off her hat.

"I'll take Modern Police Gear for one hundred. The answer is flex-cuffs."

Phee sighed. "I give up."

"The question is, what replaced handcuffs? Flex-cuffs are like giant zip ties."

"Well, I'm not wearing those, either," Phee said crossly. She hoped Joshua-Alex got on kids *Jeopardy!* soon, or else she'd be seriously tempted to strangle him.

The deputy shut the door. There was no door handle on the inside and the doors automatically locked. The interior smelled faintly of vomit. Phee didn't want to think about who'd last been sitting where she was.

They started down the mountain.

"Are the windows bulletproof?' Joshua-Alex said to the deputy.

Phee thought about the tool she'd found and realized what else was missing. "What about his snowboard?"

Joshua-Alex looked at her. "Huh?"

"Chord's snowboard. Where is it?"

Joshua-Alex shrugged. "Probably at the lodge."

The deputy turned onto Joshua-Alex's street. "It's the white house," Joshua-Alex said. "Do you think you could turn on the siren?"

"It's almost eleven o'clock," the deputy said.

"It's okay. My mom will still be watching TV and I don't care about the neighbors. Benny Cosgrove let his dog pee on my bike so I hope *he's* asleep."

"You live next door to Ashley Cosgrove?" Phee said.

"She just moved there," Joshua-Alex said.

Phee and Ashley had become friends through Girl Scouts. Starting in second grade when they were Brownies, they had sold cookies together every year, and every year they made themselves sick eating a whole box of Thin Mints. They sat next to each other in class, had sleepovers at each other's house, and shared secrets.

Then last summer Ashley went away to dance camp for two weeks and came back wearing pink like it had always been her favorite color. It wasn't. Ashley dropped Girl Scouts and went out for cheerleading instead. She also sat at the Donner Partiers table at lunch, even though under all that pink Phee knew she was the same Ashley she always was. Phee didn't know if that made it harder or easier to lose Ashley as a friend. Phee had sold cookies by herself last month, and she didn't eat one Thin Mint.

Joshua-Alex pressed his hands against the metal grill that separated the front and back seats. "Ple-e-e-e-ease?" He sounded like Brooklyn when he wanted something. Annoying in a five-year-old, *really* annoying in an almost-teenager.

"Okay," the deputy said. He let loose a squawk as they pulled up to the curb. The porch light flicked on and Mrs. Grabenstein ran out the front door to see what was going on. She wore a baby blue Juicy Couture tracksuit and flip-flops with crystals on them. Diamond studs sparkled in her ears. Some of the kids called her tacky, but Phee thought she looked elegant, or at least more than her mom did in the cargo pants and old button-up shirts she wore around the house.

The deputy opened the door to the backseat. "I was framed, Ma!" Joshua-Alex said as he leaped onto the sidewalk, brandishing his metal detector like it was a lightsaber. As he embraced his puzzled mother, a light came on next door. A moment later, Ashley Cosgrove and her sleepover guest emerged from the house. Ashley wore a pink bathrobe with a fancy A embroidered on the chest. It matched the one worn by her sleepover guest, except the guest's robe had a V stitched on it.

V for Veronica, Phee realized as the two girls walked to the edge of the brick portico. She slumped low in her seat, wishing the deputy would get into the car so they could leave, or at least shut the rear door. Instead, he stood with Mrs. Grabenstein and Joshua-Alex while Joshua-Alex showed him how the metal detector worked.

Ashley stepped off the portico onto the grass. Phee scrunched down further. "Phee? Is that you?" she said, peering through the darkness.

"Oh…my…god," Veronica said, spacing out the words for emphasis. "Did she get arrested?" It was hard to miss the glee in her voice.

Phee sighed. She was going to be a dweeb forever. Her mom had told her when you're in middle school, *forever* lasted only until the end of eighth grade, but that was long enough.

Ashley's front door opened wider. Mrs. Cosgrove appeared. She wore a plaid bathrobe that was way too large for her. Probably Mr. Cosgrove's. If they didn't get out of there soon, Phee would know what everyone on Joshua-Alex's street wore to bed.

"Ashley! Veronica! Come back inside!" Mrs. Cosgrove said.

"But Mom, it's Phee," Ashley said.

"Phee?" Mrs. Cosgrove said. She peered at the police cruiser, then frowned as her mom instinct took over. "Go inside. Now."

The two girls scampered into the house just as the deputy said good night to the Grabensteins, closed the back door of the cruiser, and slid behind the wheel.

As they pulled away from the curb, Phee thought, *A minute and a half.* That's how long it would take Veronica to post PHEE IS A FELON on her Facebook page. And Ashley would let her use her computer to do it.

"Want me to turn on the siren when we get to your house?" the deputy asked.

"No, thanks," Phee said. "By the time we get there, everyone will already know I'm a criminal."

Chapter 17

"I need to get another baby from Mrs. Moss," Joshua-Alex said. "My dad ripped the battery pack out of Miley."

Phee regarded the eviscerated robot. "She looks like an organ donor."

Joshua-Alex stuffed Miley into his backpack. She didn't quite fit; one arm stuck out of the top as though she were signaling for help. "It's not my fault my little brother hid those dumb keys."

They sat on the bench in front of the school, waiting for the bus that would take them to Trent Snowboards. Phee unzipped her backpack and looked for her scarf. Only the pom-pom hat was there. The snow was coming down fast so Phee pulled it on.

Her dad had waited up for her last night. Over the milk and cookies he'd slipped into the grocery cart when she wasn't looking, Phee told him about finding the snowboard tool.

"But it didn't do any good," she said. "We still didn't find Chord."

"Then he might not be on the mountain."

"What do you mean?"

"He might have gone to a friend's house or somewhere else he doesn't want his parents to know about." Her dad waved a cookie for emphasis. "Not that I want you to ever do something like that. But it's a possibility."

On the table was a notepad with a list of names and phone numbers.

"Nothing from Mom?" Phee said.

"No."

"So it's like you said about Chord. She might not have been where the storm hit. And there might be a reason she doesn't want to call home from wherever she is."

"You're right, honey." When her dad got up to put the milk away, Phee noticed he still had on the clothes he'd worn the day before.

Kimiko sat beside Phee on the bench, jarring her back to the present. Ms. Vlachos had picked her to fill Chord's slot. "The hat again?"

"I'm starting a trend," Phee said, swallowing a yawn. Tron had woken her twice during the night.

White crystals floated onto Kimiko's dark hair, sparkling like sequins. "Are you seriously taking the doll with you?"

"That's the point," Phee said. She had found one of the twins' baby carriers in the garage. Now Tron was strapped to her chest like a tandem skydiver in the air show. "You're supposed to see what a pain it is to have a baby."

"I don't need to drag around a fake one to know that," Kimiko said. "Anyway, when I have a baby, I'm going to get a nanny to carry it."

A white Mercedes stopped at the entrance to the circular drive in front of the school. The passenger door opened and Veronica got out. A pink plaid scarf was wound around her neck, the same shade as her backpack.

"I'll take Spoiled Things for a hundred," Joshua-Alex muttered. "The answer is Veronica."

"Who is the most spoiled kid at Horace Tabor Middle School?" Kimiko said.

"Cor-r-r-rect!"

"Don't encourage him," Phee said.

"You know, she never takes the bus anymore," Kimiko said. "Her mom drives her every day."

Veronica slammed the car door and stalked away without looking back. As she walked toward where the others waited, she adjusted the scarf so that it protected her from the snow. Phee admired how it draped over her head, like the hood of a cape in *Game of Thrones*. Maybe she'd ditch the pom-pom hat for a scarf. Trouble was, every time she'd tried to tie a scarf over her head, she ended up looking like a mummy or someone with a serious head wound.

"Hey," Joshua-Alex said as Veronica joined them. Phee moved over to make room on the bench but Veronica didn't sit. Instead she took out her cell phone and started texting. Phee yawned again.

"Did you hear if they found anything else last night?" Joshua-Alex asked Phee.

"I didn't talk to Zane." She'd been asleep by the time her brother came home. She'd planned to talk to him at breakfast, but when she came downstairs Aunt Helen said he'd left early. "Something about a pickup for his eBay store, sweetie."

"Wait a minute, you guys went looking for Chord?" Kimiko said.

Joshua-Alex flexed his biceps. "We were out with rescue patrol. Phee found the crucial piece of evidence."

"What did you find?" Kimiko said, her tone sharp.

"That thingy you used to adjust your snowboard, um, foot thingies," Phee said.

"My Zip?" Kimiko said. Phee thought about Chord flipping the tool like a coin in the lodge and she felt a funny ache in her chest.

"I guess so," Phee said.

Kimiko crossed her arms. "Why did you think it was mine? Every boarder has one."

Not with a BETTY RIDES sticker marked with a K. "I thought it looked like yours, that's all," Phee said.

"Well, it's not, 'cause I still have it." Kimiko chewed on her lower lip. "Have they stopped looking for him?" She really does like Chord, Phee thought.

"My dad says no one can survive overnight in the mountains, not without the right gear," Veronica said without looking up from her phone. Phee stared at her. Veronica had been in hysterics at the thought of Chord being lost in the snow. Today she acted like all he'd done was miss the bus.

"That isn't true," Phee said. Her dad had said the same thing that morning, but she didn't want Kimiko to get more upset. Phee felt bad about Chord. She couldn't get the sound of Mrs. Oakeson's moan out of her head. It was worse than any noise Tron made. She wondered if a rescue patrol in Australia was looking for her mom.

Veronica gave her a condescending look. "What would a spore know about the mountains? And aren't you supposed to be in jail?" She took out a lip gloss from her purse and swiped the wand across her already shiny lips. Last month, Phee had bought the same kind. But every time she wore it, her hair got stuck to her mouth so she'd given it to Scout.

"Why are you supposed to be—" Joshua-Alex began.

"I'm not." Phee's tone made it clear he should drop it. She thought of telling Veronica she'd gone for a ride with Johnny Mercer, but decided not to. It wasn't like it had been a date or anything. Her parents wouldn't let her go on one. Her mom didn't even let her go to school dances until this year, which was useless because everyone knew only seventh graders went.

"Veronica's right," Kimiko said. She stared at the ground. Her hair fell forward, hiding her face.

"His parents don't think so," Joshua-Alex said. "They have a mountain man looking for him."

Kimiko looked up. "What are you talking about?"

"They hired some Joe-pro guide who can track animals. He was there last night."

"But it snowed all night," Kimiko said. "There wouldn't be any tracks to follow." Her voice cracked on the last word. Phee reached out to hug her, forgetting about Tron. When she squished the robot baby against Kimiko, it wailed.

"Shut that thing up!" Kimiko said, pushing her away. Phee was still looking for the right key when a small school bus—the one used for special-needs kids—pulled up in front of them. Its doors whooshed open. Ms. Vlachos stood on the top step. She wore skinny black pants and the boots Phee loved. Some of the teachers wore mom jeans and ten-year-old

Gap sweaters. Not Ms. Vlachos.

Phee was happy to see her. She was afraid the school wouldn't let her be chaperone again.

Ms. Vlachos smiled at them. Phee thought she held it a fraction of a second too long, her mouth stretching a fraction of an inch too wide.

"Are my award winners ready for their tour?"

Chapter 18

Ms. Vlachos said Trent Snowboards was located on the edge of town, less than a half hour away from school. As the bus rumbled along the pavement, Phee leaned her head against the glass and looked out at the dirty snow edging the road. Kimiko had walked past her to sit by herself in the back of the bus. Veronica and Joshua-Alex were a few rows ahead, talking with Ms. Vlachos.

The bus stopped for a red light. A van came up beside them in the next lane and honked its horn. The driver's window lowered. Johnny Mercer waved. "Hey, Phee!"

Phee unlatched and pushed down her window. Snow went down the front of her shirt. "Hey! How'd you know it was me?"

"Can't miss that hat!" The light changed and Johnny pulled away. Phee closed the window.

"How can he drive if his legs are paralyzed?' Joshua-Alex said.

"The van's got extra levers on the steering wheel for the gas and brake. He took me for a ride. It's pretty cool."

"You and Johnny are hanging out?" Kimiko said. "Way to go, girl."

Veronica gave Phee a sour look, then went back to texting. Phee figured rumors about her and Johnny would be all over school before the day was over. She patted Tron's head. "If they say he's your father, don't listen to them."

Ms. Vlachos walked toward them. "I want to talk to you about Chord." Her mouth twisted and Phee thought she might cry. "If the sheriff's department and the rescue patrol . . . if he doesn't . . ." The bus went around a corner and Ms. Vlachos grabbed the seatback to steady herself. "If there's a need, the school has made arrangements for extra counselors . . ."

Whenever something bad happened, that's what the school did—bring in counselors. If Phee's mom didn't come back, would she have to see a counselor? She wasn't sure about telling a stranger how she felt if her mom . . . like Ms. Vlachos, her brain wouldn't say the word. But if she talked about it with her dad, it would make him sad, too. Like the time he'd found her crying after she got a second-place ribbon in the sixth-grade science fair. By the time they finished talking, she felt better but he was a mess. Maybe the counselor was a good idea.

Phee had a new thought. What if her dad married someone else? Jenny Feingold's mother had died of breast cancer four years ago. Her dad had gotten a new girlfriend right away, named Kristen. Jenny called her Kristen, or when she wasn't around, Crummy Kristen. Jenny kept it up even after her dad married Kristen. But when Phee was at Jenny's house for Girl Scouts last month, she'd heard Jenny call her Mom.

Phee huffed on the glass, fogging it. She wrote her mom's and dad's initials in the condensation, then drew a heart around them. She'd never call anyone else Mom. Maybe Aunt Helen would live with them. Then her dad wouldn't have to get married again. Phee wiped away her drawing. Her eyes felt hot and she pressed her fingers against them.

"You feeling okay, Phee?" Ms. Vlachos said.

Phee lowered her hands and looked through the clear patch of glass where the heart had been.

"Allergies," she said.

"If you ever want to talk, I'm here," Ms. Vlachos said.

Emo moment. "I think it's the pollen," Phee said.

"Here we are," the bus driver said.

The building had no windows, only a brown metal door. Barbed wire wrapped around the top of the chain-link fence that enclosed an asphalt area next to the building on the right. As everyone got off the bus, Phee noticed the two security cameras in the building's eaves. The whole place reminded her of a prison. People must really love to steal snowboards. The snow was coming down harder, so Phee and the others dashed into the building.

The lobby was plain—four white walls and a concrete floor. A hallway lined with closed doors was at the far end, behind the receptionist desk. In between the doors were vertically mounted snowboards. Chairs made out of old skis and snowboards were lined up along two of the walls, a table with snowboarding magazines in the corner between them.

While they stood on the rubber mat just inside the door and stomped the snow off their boots, Ms. Vlachos approached the receptionist.

"We're here to see Trent Barton," she said.

"He's in a meeting but should be finishing up soon. I'll let him know you're here." The receptionist waved at the chairs. "Take a seat."

Phee chose the chair closest to the door. The deep seat sloped backward and her butt slid down until it was stopped by the chair back. Her legs stuck out straight in front of her. She jiggled Tron and patted her pocket, making sure the keys were handy.

A door in the hallway opened and a man emerged. He had on a navy windbreaker, dirty jeans, and a black baseball hat with a neon lime-green logo on the front.

It was the man Phee had tailed the day of the ski trip, hoping to find a shortcut to the bus.

Chapter 19

The man's gaze swept the group in the lobby, then came back to Phee. Did he remember her? How could he? It had been snowing—

Phee pulled her hat off her head. Pretty hard to miss it, even in a blizzard. It was as distinctive as the splotch of neon on his baseball hat.

"Jungen, the chemicals delivery should be here in an hour," the receptionist said.

"Thanks. I'll go clear the snow off the loading dock," he said in a thickly accented voice. German, maybe. After another look at Phee, he left through the front door.

While Phee was still thinking about Jungen, the door in the hallway opened again. Two men emerged. One was in his late thirties, dressed in a thermal shirt and jeans. The other wore a khaki uniform. As they walked into the lobby, Phee tried to sink lower into her seat and pulled the front of her jacket over Tron. The man in uniform was Peter's dad.

The men walked to the door, stopping beside where Phee sat.

"Thanks for coming," the man in jeans said. "I appreciate the top guy coming out on a burglary call."

"We'll let you know if we turn up anything," Sheriff Allerd said.

"I'm not hopeful. That's the trouble with intellectual property. It's probably halfway to Vermont or Canada by now." The man made a face. "Our stuff could even be up the freeway in Breckenridge. It doesn't take very long to reverse engineer a snowboard."

They shook hands. As Sheriff Allerd reached for the door handle, his gaze dropped. "Is that you, Phee?"

"Hi," she replied from the depths of her jacket, her chin resting on top of Tron's head. Out of the corner of her eye, she saw Veronica smirking at her. After last night she was probably hoping the sheriff would arrest Phee.

"Any word on your mom?" Sheriff Allerd said.

"No. But my dad said we'd probably find out something today." He hadn't, but all Phee wanted to do was get Peter's dad out of the building before he saw Tron or, worse, the fake baby had a crying attack.

"That's good to hear. You take care." He opened the door and stepped into the swirling snow.

Ms. Vlachos was introducing the other man to the group of students.

"And this is Phee," she said. "Phee, meet Mr. Barton."

"Hi," Phee said as she struggled to get out of the chair. The upward slant of the seat made it difficult.

"Call me Trent. Everyone does." He smiled, revealing super-white teeth and dimples, then winked at Ms. Vlachos. As a general rule, Phee thought grown-up men who winked were creepy, but Ms. Vlachos didn't seem to mind. She gave him a smile back, the first one Phee had seen from her since they got on the bus that morning.

Trent cleared his throat. "I'm sorry Chord Oakeson couldn't join us today. I . . . I was part of the sheriff's search party." He looked genuinely sad, Phee thought. Trent went on. "I hope he comes home safe and sound. He was doing some steezy stomping last time I saw him on the hill. He was"—Trent corrected himself—"is a promising rider. No one practices harder than he does—always first down and last through the pipe. That's what it takes if you want to be a champion."

They all stood awkwardly for a few seconds until Tron started to whimper. Phee knew by now it would become a scream in about fifteen seconds. Deftly she took the keys from her jacket pocket and silenced the fake baby. Trent looked at her with a quizzical expression.

"I'm a product tester," Phee said. "This week is dolls."

Joshua-Alex frowned. "You are not—ouch!" Phee had stepped on his foot.

"We have product testers, too," Trent said. "The best boarders out there—Olympians, world champions, top pros. They all want to ride Trent boards."

Phee heard the pride in his voice. She imagined making something all the people who were best in the world would want. She imagined an Olympian on the podium, holding up his medal. "I couldn't have done it without my Ophelia snowboard." Imagining the name of her snowboard company made her think of the BETTY RIDES sticker on Kimiko's tool. Was Betty a real person? Did everyone have her sticker on their snowboard tool? Or just Kimiko?

"Phee?" Ms. Vlachos said.

"Here—I mean, coming." Phee followed the others down the hallway past the snowboards on the wall. Underneath each one was a placard with a different year written on it—2009, 2010, up to the present. "What's *steezy stomping* mean?" Phee asked Kimiko.

"Rad tricks with an afterbang."

"That isn't helpful," Phee said.

"I heard Ms. Vlachos is going to get fired," Joshua-Alex whispered.

Phee stopped. "What?"

"I'll take Why I Was Let Go for five hundred," Joshua-Alex said, still whispering. "The answer is losing a kid on a field trip."

Phee started walking again, more slowly this time. Poor Ms. Vlachos. And poor her. Eighth grade was so much harder than seventh, and not just the stuff they were learning. When her mom was on one of her trips and had been gone a long time, sometimes Ms. Vlachos's class was the only reason Phee went to school.

Chapter 20

Trent opened the door at the end of the hallway and ushered them into a large concrete building. There were work boots and work gloves and rubber smocks hung on hooks in a corner beside racks of snowboards and shelves of bindings and boots. Men worked at various complicated-looking machines on snowboards in various stages of completion. Pipes snaked among the large industrial lights on the ceiling. Even though fans roared, the chemical smell was strong enough to make Phee wrinkle her nose.

"Some of the companies farm out their board production. We make all our decks on site," Trent said. "It's still largely done by hand." He pointed at one of the machines. "Our construction method is called a sandwich process. The first thing we lay down is the bottom sheet, a thin piece of steel. Then the edge is wrapped around the base's circumference." He gestured at one of the workers, who was using a tool with a whirling disk at one end to bend and polish the strip of metal around the rim of the bottom layer of the board.

Kimiko was listening intently, as was Joshua-Alex. Phee wondered if snowboard construction had ever been a category on *Jeopardy!*

"What's that?" Kimiko said, pointing to a strip of yellow tape that one of the workers had started to lay around the just-polished edge.

"That's gummy," Trent said. "It moves with the board so when it's being flexed, all the materials inside it can shear just a little bit on each other and that holds the board together." He put his palms together horizontally and rubbed them against each other. Phee's mom had done the same thing when explaining tectonic plates to Phee. Thinking about her mom brought a jab of pain to her chest. She hugged Tron.

Phee was certain she would know if her mom was dead or really hurt. She closed her eyes. This wasn't that kind of pain. This was the I'm-really-missing-you ache she sometimes felt when her mom was gone on one of her longer trips. The feeling had never been this intense before. Other people had been hurt, even killed, in the tsunami, but not her mom. Feeling reassured, Phee opened her eyes.

"Next comes the core," Trent said. "It's a combination of foam and composite engineered wood to make the boards really snappy. On top of the core we put carbon fiberglass." He pointed to another machine. "It's goopy when it goes on, but after it hardens in the mold, it becomes really springy, like a diving board."

"This is so boring," Veronica muttered. "I mean, how is this going to help us run a business?"

"I guess it shows you have to know how the stuff you're selling is made," Phee said. "You can't just sit in the boss's office."

Veronica's eyes became angry slits. "What's that supposed to mean?" she hissed.

"Um, just that you have to know everything about your company."

"Well, sometimes you can't. Sometimes people hide things from you and then when you find out there's a problem, it's too late," Veronica said. Before Phee could answer, she turned on her heel and walked away. Phee watched her go.

"What'd I say?" she whispered into Tron's ear.

Trent was showing Kimiko and Joshua-Alex how plastic was added on top of the fiberglass.

"Once the top sheet goes on, then the sandwich is complete," he said. "Then the deck is polished and painted." He indicated the area where workers in safety glasses and canvas-looking jumpsuits were trimming, polishing, and applying decals and paint to various snowboards. Phee was having a hard time concentrating. The loud machines hurt her ears and the chemical smell made her head swim.

"How do you know what's the best thing to make boards out of?" Kimiko said. "I mean, all this seems like following a recipe. How do you know what ingredients to put in?"

"Our secret weapon tells us," Trent said. He led them to what looked like a large pizza oven in the corner of the building. "This is the TMX 2010. It heats whatever we put in it to a hundred and thirty degrees, and then a laser melts the plastic onto itself. It's like building a loaf of bread one slice at a time."

Joshua-Alex frowned. "I don't get it."

"This machine lets us build anything we come up with. If an engineer or a rider has an idea for a board or a binding or any piece of equipment, this machine can turn it into a prototype that can be tested. No one else in the business has one like it. It's what puts Trent Snowboards on the cutting edge of innovation. Come this way."

He led them through a metal door into what looked like a conference room. There was a tall table with stools and a regular-height table with chairs. The tall table had drawings on it. The regular-sized table had computers and printers. The chemical smell was gone and the machine noise had been reduced to muffled thumps and whines.

"This is where the magic happens," Trent said. "This is where we work on design innovations with our engineers and team riders to make the boards ride better and faster. Then we use the TMX 2010 to make the prototypes."

"I heard you were going to bring a new design to nationals," Kimiko said.

Trent smiled at her. "All I can say is, if you like great snowboarding, be at Gold Mountain this weekend."

Gold Mountain was the ski resort that backed up to Silver Mountain on the west. It was huge, four thousand acres. If Silver was family friendly, then Gold was the fancy resort. Ski "ambassadors" dispensed cups of hot chocolate in the lift lines. Valets picked up your skis at the end of the day so you didn't have to carry them. It had one of the best terrain parks in the country. The Snowboarding National Championships were being held there that upcoming Saturday and Sunday.

"Can we see the new design now?" Joshua-Alex said.

"Sorry. We sponsor certain riders. So do our competitors. If our team does well riding on our new board, it's good advertising for the company. We don't want anyone to know what the new board looks like beforehand."

"How do you keep the new boards secret?" Joshua-Alex asked. "Don't your riders have to practice on them before the competition?"

"Good question," Trent said. "We have a private half-pipe that we take the prototype boards to. Our team rides them there. After they're finished for the day, we take the boards back here and lock them up. We keep the design studio locked, too." His cheeriness dimmed for a moment.

Phee thought about what the sheriff and Trent had been talking about. She wasn't sure what *intellectual property* was, but it sounded like it had to do with things written down. "Have any drawings been stolen?"

Trent made a face and leaned away from her, like Palmer Hill did whenever anyone farted. "No, of course not." The skin around his eyes tightened as his gaze became hard. "We have a top-notch security system."

"Oh," Phee said. "I mean, that's good." Trent regarded her for a few more uncomfortable seconds, then looked at his watch.

"It's almost noon. Lunch is waiting for you in the cafeteria. I'll have my assistant take you there."

"Is there a bathroom there?" Joshua-Alex said.

"I hope you can join us," Ms. Vlachos said to Trent. "I know we'd all like to hear how you started your company."

"Sure. I have some e-mails to answer first. I'll meet you there."

As they followed a short, stocky girl through the loading dock area, Joshua-Alex said, "Ms. Vlachos likes Trent."

"You're crazy," Phee said.

"She's flirting with him." He turned to Veronica. "You're the expert. What do you think?"

Instead of delivering a barbed comeback, Veronica acted as though she hadn't heard him. She'd been more aloof than usual today, except for when she got mad at Phee. Which was fine with Phee—a quiet Veronica was easier to be around than a talking one.

Phee didn't get why Trent lied about the new boards being stolen. Usually you wanted people to know your stuff was gone in case they saw it. Maybe he'd been talking to Sheriff Allerd about something else that was missing.

"This isn't the way we usually take visitors," Trent's assistant said. "But it's the fastest way to the bathroom." She smiled sympathetically at Joshua-Alex.

They passed an open bay where a truck was being unloaded. Workers duck-walked sealed buckets of what were probably gummy and goopy chemicals. Several glanced their way, but only one stopped to stare. Jungen.

Phee let the others pass her. If Jungen saw her on Monday, he might have seen Chord, too. Did he know Chord was missing? What if he'd seen something that could help find Chord?

She walked toward the edge of the platform. "Excuse me," she said.

Jungen turned his back to her and began sweeping the loading dock, although all the snow had been pretty much cleared off.

"Um, Mr. Jungen?" Phee said. Even though some of her friends' parents said it was okay for her to call adults by their first name, she thought it was weird. "On Monday at Silver Mountain, did you see the guy help me out of the, um, tree well? Did you see where he went after that?"

Jungen kept sweeping. "I was not where you said." His accent turned *was* and *where* into *vas* and *vere*. He didn't understand me, Phee thought. She tried again.

"On Monday, at the ski resort—"

"You haf me mixed up with someone else."

Phee looked at his baseball hat with its neon logo. "Sorry. I thought—"

He stopped sweeping and turned to face her. His eyes were dark and hard. "You did not see me. I was not at the Silver Mountain on Monday."

Chapter 21

Kimiko slept with her head on Phee's shoulder. Phee had taken off her hat and was using it as a pillow against the glass. Across the aisle, Veronica paged through one of those magazines full of photos of ex-Disney stars and the latest boy bands. She couldn't have looked any more bored and still be conscious, Phee thought. Joshua-Alex alternated between reading *Jeopardy! for Dummies* and blowing straw wrappers off the bundle of straws he'd pinched from the Trent cafeteria. Ms. Vlachos sat several rows ahead of them, staring out the window.

Trent had told them during lunch how he'd gotten into snowboarding, made his own board in shop class, then started his company in college. After hearing him talk for fifteen minutes about the differences among *directional freeride* and *twin tip freestyle* and *shovel-nosed carving* boards—a topic only Kimiko appeared interested in—Phee decided against starting her own company. According to Trent, he "ate, drank, breathed, and dreamed about snowboards twenty-four/seven the first five years." Phee couldn't imagine anything she'd want to think about all the time, not even Peter Allerd or Jason Bourne movies. Her brain wasn't wired that way. Every time she went to the salad bar, she chose a different type of dressing.

A small car zipped past the bus, then darted in front of it. The bus driver hit the brakes hard. Kimiko and Phee's upper bodies whiplashed against their seats. Kimiko's backpack slid off her lap onto the floor.

Kimiko stirred. "Are we there?" she asked groggily.

"Not yet," Phee said.

Kimiko's forehead scrunched into squiggly lines. "Do you think Ms. Vlachos will get fired because of Chord?"

"Hope not. It wasn't her fault, not really."

"If they do fire her, do you think they'll do it right away? I mean, aren't they going to wait a little to see if Chord shows up?"

Phee looked out the window. The failing afternoon light made the trees look spooky. She thought about how cold the nights were. Would it be Chord or only his body they'd find? "I don't know."

Kimiko went back to sleep. Joshua-Alex looked up from his book. "Nine-letter words for four hundred," he said to Phee. "A marker on a grave or an Old West Arizona town."

"My middle name isn't Google," Phee said.

"Tombstone," Veronica said.

Joshua-Alex looked at her in surprise.

"What, you don't think I know the answers to your dumb questions?" Veronica snapped. "My parents took me horseback riding there when I was six."

"Actually, you have to know the questions that go with the answers," Joshua-Alex said. He consulted his book. "How about All About Art for eight hundred: He had a blue period in 1901 and a rose period in 1905."

Veronica rolled her eyes. "Who is Picasso? I thought these were supposed to be hard. Like, everyone's been to the *museu* in Barcelona."

Phee wasn't sure where Barcelona was. The way Veronica said *museu* made it sound Spanish. Mexico, maybe?

Joshua-Alex flipped to the back of his book. "Okay, you asked for it. Foods That Are Good for You: Chinook or Atlantic."

Veronica flipped her hair over her shoulder. "What is salmon?"

Joshua-Alex raised his hands, fists clenched. "Correct!"

"Our chef made it all the time. Poached is best."

Poached salmon? Phee imagined a fish crammed into a little cup that sat in boiling water, its eye looking up at her. *No, thank you.*

"You should totally try out with me," Joshua-Alex said excitedly.

Veronica made a face like she'd bitten into something rotten. "As if."

"Did you know that even if you lose on the new kids *Jeopardy!*, you still get a thousand dollars? Second place gets two thousand, and the winner gets to keep what they made during the game or fifteen grand, whichever is more. Some kid won almost fifty thousand dollars!"

"Wow," Phee said.

"The winner gets fifteen thousand dollars?" Veronica said. Phee was tempted to ask, *What do you care?* The Swingles were rich. No one else in Bristlecone took their kids horseback riding in Arizona or to *museus* in Mexico. She thought about what she'd do if she had that much money. First she'd buy a car. She'd let Zane drive it until she got her license, as long as he took her places, too. And a babysitter for Scout and Brooklyn, one that lived with them. Then she had another idea. She'd give it to her parents so they'd have enough money and her mom wouldn't need to go on so many business trips.

"It's for real. You can check on the website," Joshua-Alex said.

"So that's why you want to get on the show?" Veronica said. "For the money?"

Joshua-Alex's enthusiasm went out of him like air from a beach ball with the plug pulled. "No," he said curtly. He resumed reading his book, shoulders hunched. "I don't care about the money," he said into his collar.

Veronica gave him a baffled look. "Whatever."

Something rolled against Phee's foot. She leaned down. Kimiko's backpack was unzipped. Lip gloss, a pen, gum, an iPod touch, sunglasses, Purell, some coins, a *Hannah Montana* CD, and a mini hairbrush had spilled out. The *Hannah Montana* was unexpected. She always thought Kimiko was too cool for early Miley.

Being careful not to wake Kimiko, Phee started putting everything back into the pack. There wasn't a lot of room. Kimiko had a box of energy bars wedged in beside her books, along with packets of peanut butter and a can of Muscle Milk. Phee had been ravenous after the trip down the mountain with Johnny. She figured you'd need to eat a lot if you were, well, actually skiing. Or in Kimiko's case, riding.

She groped around the floor to make sure she'd gotten it all. Her fingers touched a piece of paper. Even though she knew she shouldn't snoop, she unfolded it. There was a single line of text: CHORD OAKESON BUS #4.

Phee stared at the orange piece of paper. Kimiko hadn't given Chord his bus ticket. Had she forgotten?

Kimiko shifted beside her and mumbled something. Phee quickly refolded the bus ticket. She was leaning down to slide it into her friend's backpack when Kimiko opened her eyes.

"What are you doing?" she said.

"Stretching," Phee said. She wadded up the bus ticket and, using a huge fake yawn as a decoy, stuck it into her own jacket pocket.

Chapter 22

They arrived at school ten minutes before classes were over and the buses that took students home were pulling up to the curb. Parents weren't supposed to drive into the bus circle; they had their own drop-off and pickup spot. Everyone obeyed the rule except for Veronica's mom. Her white Mercedes always idled at the front of the line of buses. Like it was today.

The field-trip bus parked behind the others. Veronica was the first off. Her phone pressed to her ear, she cut across the bus circle—another rule disregarded—toward her mom's car.

Joshua-Alex paused at the top of the steps. "I'll take Olympics for a hundred. The answer is the Olympic long jumper who landed outside the pit." He crouched down and pendulumed his arms back and forth a few times. "Who is Bob Be-e-e-e-eamon?" he said as he jumped down. He cleared the four steps and landed on the concrete. His fists shot into the air. "A new Olympic and world record!" He took a step. "Ouch!" He hobbled toward the busses.

"I'll take Idiots for five hundred," Kimiko said to Phee as they followed Ms. Vlachos off the bus. "The answer is Joshua Grabenstein."

"Who just broke his ankle?" Phee said.

"How did you like today, Kimiko?" Ms. Vlachos said. They stood by themselves, except for one of the dads waiting to pick up his kid. He stood about thirty feet away, leaning against a light pole, dressed in a navy down jacket, jeans, and hiking boots. He wore sunglasses, too, even though it wasn't really that bright out.

"It was pretty cool," Kimiko said. "I liked seeing how the boards were made."

Ms. Vlachos turned to Phee. "How about you, Phee? What did you think was most interesting?"

That guy lying about not being at Silver Mountain on Monday. "I, uh, thought it was an interesting glimpse into the entrepreneurial experience."

Kimiko rolled her eyes and Ms. Vlachos pursed her lips so as not to smile. The phrase was one she'd used when announcing the Trent contest to their class. Phee felt her cheeks get hot with embarrassment.

"I mean, that is—" The school bell rang. Several pairs of double doors crashed open and students flowed outside. Instead of looking for a face in the crowd, the man in the navy parka walked over to them.

"Kimiko Watanabe?"

Kimiko's eyes narrowed. "Who wants to know?"

The man took off his sunglasses. "My name is Gus Krueger. The Oakesons hired me to look for their son, Chord. I was told you and he were friends. I'd like to ask you some questions."

"We're not," Kimiko said. She snapped her rubber-band bracelets against the inside of her wrist. "Friends, I mean." *Snap. Snap.* "I just see him sometimes on the mountain when I'm snowboarding." She backed away. Snap. Snap. Snap. "I gotta go. I don't want to miss my bus." She turned and dashed toward the lines of students waiting to board the busses. *Which don't leave for another ten minutes*, Phee thought.

Mr. Krueger didn't look bothered by Kimiko ditching him. He said, "You're Mrs. Vlachos, aren't you? The teacher who was in charge of the ski trip?"

Tell him it's Ms., Phee thought. But Ms. Vlachos was retreating like Kimiko had. She shook her head. "Sorry, I can't talk to you."

"Why not?" Mr. Krueger said. "I'm just trying to find a lost boy for his parents." More head shaking by Ms. Vlachos. "Don't you want to help?"

A shake became a tentative nod. "Yes, but my lawyer—" The head shaking resumed. "I told the police everything I know. See you tomorrow in class, Phee." Ms. Vlachos pulled her sweater around her and walked away, ducking into the closest set of school doors.

Mr. Krueger took a tablet out of his jacket pocket and checked the screen. "Phee? Are you Ophelia Mahoney?"

"Yes," Phee said.

Chapter 23

When Phee got home, the house was uncharacteristically quiet.

"Hello? Anybody here?"

No answer. She knew her dad was at work. Zane was probably doing a house cleanout. Where were the twins and Aunt Helen?

The interview with Mr. Krueger had been brief. Phee told him pretty much the same thing she'd told Mr. Sandoval and the Oakesons about what she knew—and didn't know—about Chord's disappearance.

She called the house voice mail to see if there were any messages. When the recorded voice came on, she almost dropped the phone. It was her mom, instructing the caller to leave a message. Phee let it run through twice before keying in the voice-mail retrieval code. After the initial shock, it wasn't upsetting to hear her mom's voice. Just the opposite, in fact. She seemed more real, more in the world than a minute ago.

No messages, said the voice-mail lady. Phee hit the disconnect key and wandered into the kitchen for a Snapple. A note from Aunt Helen was on the counter. TWINS WITH ME. DINNER AT SIX THIRTY.

Six thirty seemed like a long two hours away. Phee got an apple out of the bin. When she swung the fridge door shut, she saw the photo. She hadn't really looked at it before. Stuck under a ladybug magnet was a picture of her and her mother taken during a family trip to San Francisco. They stood on the Marina Green with the Golden Gate Bridge in the background. The wind had blown their hair across their faces right when the photo was snapped. Phee could see one of her mom's eyes peeking out, a bit of her nose, half of her smile.

Phee closed her eyes and touched the watch her mom had given her. She could imagine her mom completely—the set of her shoulders, the color of her hair, the scar on her knee. She could smell her, too; the peppermint oil she dabbed on her wrists "for good energy." And her voice was clear in Phee's head. Whenever her mom left for a trip, she never said good-bye. Instead, she said *hasta luego*. Phee had looked it up. It was Spanish for *see you later*.

Phee's eyes snapped open. What if she wasn't going to see her mom later? She looked at the photo again. Would her memory dim, so that she only remembered bits and pieces of her, until all that was left was a general feeling and nothing more? She rubbed the face of her watch. Touching it made her feel a little better, but it didn't help her remember.

A car pulled into the driveway. Happiness swelled in Phee's chest when she saw it was her mom's blue Volvo, then deflated just as quickly when Aunt Helen opened the driver's door. Phee's brain had known it wasn't her mom, but her heart had been sidetracked by hope. Mrs. Moss said hope and jealousy were wasted emotions. Maybe so, but that didn't make Phee stop feeling them. A tear went splat on Tron's face. She watched it trickle down his plastic cheek before wiping it away.

The twins barreled into the kitchen.

"We went to the Sweet Factory," Scout announced through red-stained lips. "I got cherry bombs!"

"I got gummy worms!" Brooklyn shouted. He pulled a blue one from his pocket and thrust it at his sister, who obligingly shrieked and ran into the living room. Brooklyn gave chase.

Aunt Helen sank into the kitchen chair beside Phee. "I know the last thing they need is more sugar and your mom doesn't like them to have candy, but I thought it would be okay while she's . . ."

Missing? Dead?

"Away," Aunt Helen said.

If you were an orphan when both your parents died, what were you if only one did? Was there even a word that meant half-orphan? Phee didn't think so, and this made her more annoyed. If one of your parents died, it was a big deal. There should at least be a special word for it.

Aunt Helen put a white paper sack on the table. "Scout told me that you like these."

Phee pulled the sack over and looked into it. Inside was a cellophane baggie of hard yellow candies. "Citrons," Phee said. She closed the sack. "I actually buy them for my neighbor. But thanks." She heard the snippiness in her voice and was sorry. It wasn't that she didn't like Aunt Helen being there. It was what her being there meant.

Aunt Helen put her hand on top of Phee's. "I wish I weren't here, either. At least not under these circumstances."

Phee forced a smile. "If you weren't, Dad would be giving us a bag of sugar and a spoon for dinner."

In truth, Phee thought her dad was as good a parent as her mom was. Together they had the nice-to-strict parent spectrum covered. And each had different specialties. Her mom helped with math homework. Her dad taught the kids to ride a bike. She made sure they ate healthy and kept the car radio tuned to NPR. He brought hot dogs and marshmallows on camping trips and let them watch Adam Sandler movies.

Phee picked up the white sack and stood. "I'm going to deliver these."

"Why don't you feed Homicide first," Aunt Helen said.

Phee hurriedly mashed up one of the cat's pills, mixed it into a can of food, and dumped everything into the bowl Scout had painted with Homicide's name at the do-it-yourself pottery place. Actually, she'd written HOMCID but Phee didn't think the cat cared. It wasn't like he could read. While Homicide gobbled down his meal, Phee groomed his coat with the special brush. As far as she could tell, dogs had owners, but cats had employees.

With Homicide taken care of, she grabbed the sack of candy and cut through the sparse hedge that separated the Mahoneys' property from Mrs. Heckler's. Phee headed for the front door, then thought better of it. The way Rusty's mom was acting, who knew if she'd let Phee in. Instead she tramped around to the rear of the house. Mrs. Heckler used the den on the first floor as her bedroom because she couldn't climb upstairs any longer.

A lamp was on in the room. The rest of the house was dark. Mrs. Risborough and Rusty must be out.

Phee rapped on the glass. "Mrs. Heckler?"

Moments later a pale face with a corona of white curls appeared at the window. Phee made an unlatching motion and pointed at the window lock. After some difficulty, Mrs. Heckler opened the window. There was no screen.

"Ramona! What are you doing here?" Mrs. Heckler said.

"Um, that's my mother, Mrs. Heckler. I'm Phee."

"Of course you are! I knew that. How are you, dear? Why don't you come in out of the cold?"

"Thanks, but I can't." She thrust the bag through the opening. "I brought you something."

Mrs. Heckler took the sack. "You are so thoughtful." She looked inside. "Citrons!" Mrs. Heckler always acted surprised to see the little yellow candies, even though Phee never brought her anything else. Now Phee wondered if she was acting or if she didn't really remember.

Mrs. Heckler offered the sack to Phee. "Would you like one?"

"No, thanks."

Mrs. Heckler popped a hard candy into her mouth. "The Citron was always my favorite. Especially yellow."

"I thought that's the only color they come in," Phee said.

"Oh, no. I've seen blue, too, and red. But yellow's the best."

"Of course," Phee said. She didn't see the harm in letting Mrs. Heckler think the candy came in different colors.

A car approached, its tires swishing through the slush. Mrs. Heckler's eyes widened in fright. She rolled the bag of candy closed. "I have to put this away," she whispered.

Mrs. Heckler shuffled across the room to her bed. The car rolled by. She stuffed the bag between her top and bottom mattresses then returned to the window, her tan slippers scuffing against the wood floor.

"She takes things without asking, then blames her brother," Mrs. Heckler whispered. "But I know she did it." She pulled her sweater closer around her and bent her shoulders against the cold.

When Phee first told her mom Mrs. Heckler was forgetting things and not always making sense, her mom had explained about Alzheimer's. Phee hadn't thought her mom was afraid of anything—she was good with snakes, driving in New York, heights.

But when Phee's mom explained what was happening to Mrs. Heckler, she'd seemed nervous. After hearing other adults talk about Alzheimer's, Phee figured it out. They were all thinking, *I don't want it to happen to me.* Phee wondered what it would be like to not remember people in your family, or to walk into a room and then forget why you were there.

"Be careful or she'll take your car, too," Mrs. Heckler said.

Phee was lost. "Do you mean Scout? My sister?"

"Yes!" Mrs. Heckler said.

Should she go along with Mrs. Heckler's version of reality or tell her the truth? Phee decided if she were the one mixed up, she'd want to know. "But Mrs. Heckler, I don't have a car. Zane's the one who's getting one. At least he thinks he is."

Mrs. Heckler shivered. "I'm sorry, dear, but I'm feeling a little tired. I think I'll lie down for a bit."

"Okay. Be sure to lock the window." She helped Mrs. Heckler slide the glass shut before she cut back across the yard.

As she headed for her house, her mind was still on Mrs. Heckler. She was glad it would be a long time before she was old.

Chapter 24

Zane had opened the garage door. He and Austin were unloading boxes from the back of the black pickup. Phee walked over to see what they'd found. Moths flitted around the outside lights and her breath hung in wisps in the chilled air.

"Did you get anything good?" Two months ago Zane had brought home a Wii system he'd found in a closet. It had the tennis game and Phee liked playing it when Zane wasn't home to tell her not to.

Zane dropped the cardboard box he'd been carrying onto the garage's cement floor.

"Don't know yet," he said. "We found these boxes in one of the closets. Haven't looked in them."

The tape that held together the box he'd dropped had split on impact. One of the top flaps had flopped open, exposing a tangle of clothes.

Zane pulled out a light pink sweater and held it up for Austin to see. "Girl stuff," he said and made a face.

"Where's it from?" Austin said.

Zane checked the tag in the sweater's neck. "J. Crew."

Austin nodded approvingly. "We'll get more on eBay than Craigslist for those kinds of labels. And that's a good color."

Zane tossed the sweater back into the box. "You're in charge of that listing, GQ-boy."

While the boys unloaded more boxes, Phee picked up the sweater. It had ribbon trim around the collar and little flower buttons and looked like it just came off the store shelf. Phee wondered why someone would leave it behind. She rummaged through the rest of the clothes. They all looked pretty new and were pricey brands—Brandy Melville, Anthropologie, Abercrombie. Austin would be pleased.

At the bottom of the box she found a knitted watch cap. It was pale pink with a cream stripe around the bottom. She fingered the material, softer than any wool she'd ever worn—cashmere, according to the label. Phee pulled it on. She liked how she could barely tell it was on her head, and it didn't feel scratchy like her pom-pom hat did.

"Hey, look at this!" Zane said. "It's an RC helo!"

"An RC what?" Phee said.

"A radio-controlled helicopter," Austin said as Zane lifted the miniature machine out of a carton. It was electric blue, about eighteen inches long, and looked just like the real thing.

"Will it fly?" Phee asked.

"Its tail rotor is broken but I can fix it," Zane said.

"Here's the remote," Austin said.

"Does it have batteries?" Zane said.

"Yup." Zane set the helicopter on the concrete. Austin pressed some buttons on the remote. The helicopter's blades began to spin, lifting the whirlybird off the ground. But instead of hovering, it tipped forward and went spinning into the ground. Austin shut the engine off.

"That's because it doesn't have a tail," Zane said. He rooted through the carton. "Here are the pieces. All I have to do it superglue them together and it'll be good to go."

"We could turn it into a drone," Austin said.

"Yeah!" Zane said. "We could spy on people."

"Like Missy Fairheitz when she's tanning in her backyard," Austin said.

"You mean when she doesn't have her top on?" Phee said.

Phee and Rachel Fairheitz were in the same grade, and had been book-report partners the previous summer. They had to choose five books from a list to read and write a report together on their favorite. The Fairheitzes had a large deck where the girls would lie out and work, most of the time, on their report. Missy, Rachel's older sister, had been home for the summer after spending her junior year at college in France. She'd returned scornful of "American puritanical values"—at least that's what she'd said when she flopped down on a chaise longue and took off her bikini top. The deck was visible from the top of a neighboring hill, and the hiking trail to the summit enjoyed a surge in popularity among teenaged boys until Missy went back to school in the fall.

Both boys' faces reddened. "What are you still doing here?" Zane said.

Phee ignored him. "What's a drone?" she said.

"None of your business," Zane said.

Phee folded her arms. "I can go inside and google it. But then I'd probably have to tell Aunt Helen why I wanted to look it up. And what you wanted to use it for."

"A drone is a UAS," Austin said. "Unmanned aircraft system." Seeing Phee's look of puzzlement, he added, "It's anything that can fly without a pilot."

"The government has ones that can blow up missiles after they've been launched," Zane said. "Or go into houses and caves to blow up terrorists."

"Or they put cameras on them and use 'em to spy on criminals," Austin said.

"Ooh, Missy Fairheitz is such a criminal," Phee said.

Zane scowled. "Don't you have homework or something?"

"I'll leave if you let me have this," Phee said. She was becoming quite the accomplished blackmailer. Granted, Zane gave her a lot of material to work with.

"Have what?" Zane said. He'd moved on to another carton and was flipping through a stack of CDs. "Jonas Brothers, One Direction, Justin Bieber," he read off the jewel cases. "How lame was the person who used to own these?'

"Maybe that's why they didn't take 'em," Austin said.

Phee pointed at her head. "This. The hat."

"Five dollars," Zane said, barely glancing up from the CDs.

"But you got it for free!" Phee said.

Her brother shrugged. "That's capitalism."

"I'll feed Homicide for three days," Phee said.

"Even his pills?"

Phee sighed. "Even his pills."

"Deal," Zane said.

Leaving the boys bent over the helicopter, Phee pulled her new hat over her ears and went inside to stand in front of the mirror in the foyer.

She looked like one of the stoner kids. She pushed the hat to one side and fluffed it up a little to make it look like a beret.

"*Bon jour*," she said to her reflection. It was one of the few French phrases Missy had taught her. But Phee didn't sound French. And she didn't look *chic*, another Missy word. Phee wasn't exactly sure what made someone or something *chic*, but Missy said all French women looked that way all the time.

Phee straightened the hat. "Hello," she said to the mirror before heading for the kitchen.

Chapter 25

The next morning there still hadn't been any word from her mom, although Phee's dad had tracked down the island where she and the other geologists had been working.

"It's part of Vanuatu," he said.

"That's in Australia?' Phee asked as she scooped cat food into a bowl for Homicide.

"No, it's a separate country," her dad said. "A group of islands off the east coast of Australia. The storm took out all their communications and swept most of their boats away. The Australian Navy is overwhelmed right now, but they said they're hoping to get a craft out there in the next day or so. And Japan is sending in some ships to help, too."

"A *day* or so?" Phee said. "Why don't they get an airplane and fly there?"

Her dad ran a hand through his hair. "That's all they could tell me." There was a half-full glass of wine beside him on the counter. Phee couldn't tell if it was leftover from the night before or had been poured that morning.

"Shouldn't you, like, be going there to look for Mom?" Zane said.

"I tried, but the flights are for emergency personnel only right now. After that, the waiting list is a mile long. Best thing is to sit tight and wait for your mom to call."

Which she can't do if she's dead, Phee thought.

Their dad got his wallet from the kitchen counter. He gave both Phee and Zane a ten-dollar bill. "I didn't have time to make your lunches. Afraid you're going to have to eat cafeteria food today."

"Earth to Dad—the last time I brought lunch from home was, like, freshman year," Zane said as he stuffed the money into his pocket.

"Thanks," Phee said, wondering if she should tell him ten dollars would buy lunch for three days. Her mom didn't like her to eat cafeteria food. "It has too much fat and isn't organic." She didn't know Phee and Kimiko, who always bought lunch, traded on Tuesdays. Tuesday was mac and cheese day. Kimiko hated mac and cheese. Phee loved it, especially the brown crust on top. None of the Donner Partiers ate mac and cheese. They always chose the limp green salad with two pale cherry tomatoes and a slice of cucumber on top. Ashley did this, too, even though Phee knew she loved mac and cheese as much as Phee did.

Brooklyn dashed into the kitchen with Scout in pursuit. He was bare-chested and barefooted and wore pajama bottoms with cowboys on them. His sister had on a nightgown over a pair of cords and sneakers. Brooklyn held a sheet of paper over his head as he ran.

"He took my drawing!" Scout said. "The one we're supposed to do for school!"

"Did not! It's mine!"

Scout chased her brother in a circle around the table. Aunt Helen appeared in the doorway that led to the rest of the house. When Brooklyn ran by her, she grabbed him. He squirmed and flailed but Aunt Helen held firm. She plucked the piece of paper from his grasp.

"Whose drawing is this?" she said.

"Mine!" the twins said simultaneously.

Aunt Helen scanned the sheet. "Brooklyn, unless you've started drawing pink ponies and changed your name to Scout, this belongs to your sister." She handed the drawing to Scout. "Go upstairs and finish getting ready for school." She kneeled so she could look Brooklyn in the eye.

"Where's your drawing?"

He averted his gaze. "Dunno," he muttered.

"Did you make one?"

This was answered with a nearly imperceptible shake of his head.

"Why not? Did you lose your crayons again?"

Another head shake. Phee, Zane, and their dad stayed quiet, caught up in Aunt Helen's gentle interrogation.

"Then why didn't you—"

"I tried! But I couldn't do it." Tears wobbled down his cheeks. "I kept thinking about Mom!"

"Oh, honey." Aunt Helen enfolded him in her arms. "We should have more news today."

As awful as it was, Phee was glad Aunt Helen hadn't said their mom would call or come home soon. She hated it when adults lied to kids, even when it was supposedly for their own good. What did that mean anyway? How could hearing anything but the truth be good? It'd come out eventually.

"Let's go upstairs and finish getting you dressed," Aunt Helen said. "Then you and I are going to work on a drawing. Don't worry about catching the bus. I'm driving you and your sister to school today."

Brooklyn sniffed loudly and allowed himself to be steered out of the room. Phee's dad stared after them, his mouth twisted like Phee's whenever she was upset.

Phee stroked the face of her watch. Her mom had better come home soon. Otherwise her family was going to fall apart.

A horn sounded outside.

"That's Austin," Zane said. He grabbed one of the toaster waffles their dad had set out and went out the kitchen door, letting it slam behind him. But not before Phee heard the shout from outside.

"Mahoney No Baloney!"

She went to the window over the sink. At the end of the driveway, in a fluoro green jacket and bike helmet, was Johnny Mercer. With him was his dog Kirby, sporting neon orange snow booties. Kirby was wriggling in ecstasy as Zane knuckled his back and talked to Johnny. Who was on the strangest-looking bicycle Phee had ever seen.

Chapter 26

"I've got a part for that helo. I'll put it in your locker," Johnny was saying to Zane as Phee walked up. She'd picked up her lunch, backpack, and Tron, put on her new pink hat, kissed her dad good-bye, and walked down the driveway to where the boys stood. Johnny didn't bring on the fluttery feeling in her stomach that Peter Allerd did, but she was happy to see him.

"Thanks, man," Zane said. He checked his phone. "We gotta jet. If I get one more tardy to first period, I'm pulling lunch detention." He and Johnny went through the latest handshaking/-slapping/-bumping ritual. Johnny saluted Austin, who'd stayed in his truck, as Zane hopped into the passenger side. The pickup roared away, sending up a spray of slush.

Phee looked over Johnny's vehicle. It had three wheels, one in the front and two in the rear. A hammock was suspended along the top of the white-painted metal frame that connected the axle between the two rear wheels to the front wheel. Long handles extended back from the front wheel. Attached to them were brake levers and what looked like gears and a chain from a regular bicycle. The whole thing was only a few inches off the ground.

Johnny lay in the hammock with his feet propped up on footrests. His legs were sheathed in bright blue tights that were mottled with roadside slush. Attached beside the left wheel was what looked like a long aerial with a bright orange triangle-shaped flag on top. On it were printed the Olympic rings.

"Like my hand bike?' Johnny said, then added with mock severity, "Don't even think about calling it a tricycle."

"I've never seen one. Isn't it hard to make it go just using your arms?"

"They're geared to make it as easy as possible. The two rear wheels coast, so I'm only pushing and steering the front one."

"You can go uphill?"

"Yup. Downhill, too." He grinned. "That's the best part." He thumbed one of the brake levers. "I try not to touch these."

"The roads are a mess. Wouldn't it be better to wait until the snow is gone?"

"I've got studs on." Phee looked at the knobby tire that was between his feet. Needle-thin metal spikes protruded from the raised part of the tread.

"They give me pretty good traction on plowed roads," Johnny said. "Of course I can't go as fast as on my summer tubulars, but it's a decent workout. I'm training for the Paralympics."

"Wow," Phee said. Could she have said something more lame?

"I have to make the team first. I'm shooting for the road race. I can try out as soon as I turn eighteen."

A school bus turned onto the far end of the street and lumbered toward them. Kirby pulled on his leash and barked.

"I'd better go," Johnny said. "Kirby hates getting splashed by those big tires." He cranked the handles and the front tire bit into the snow-splotched pavement. He gained speed after several revolutions, forcing Kirby to break into a trot. The orange pennant whipped back and forth above his head in time with his pedal strokes.

Phee walked to the corner, beating the bus by a few seconds. Its doors wheezed open and she climbed in. Kimiko had claimed two seats toward the rear.

"Was that Johnny Mercer?" she said after Phee sat beside her.

"Yeah. He wants to try out for the Paralympics."

Joshua-Alex popped up behind their seat like the twins' jack-in-a-box. "Phee and Johnny sittin' in a tree—"

"Get a life," Kimiko snapped. She lowered her voice so only Phee could hear her. "Did you find out anything about your mom?"

"Turns out she's on some island, not even Australia," Phee whispered back. "My dad said they gotta send a boat there."

"That's good, right?"

"I guess."

"Your mom's cool. I wish my mom were like her."

"Yours is okay." Mrs. Watanabe didn't work. Whenever Phee went to Kimiko's after school, Mrs. Watanabe had a snack set out for them. She reviewed Kimiko's homework every night.

"Not like yours. Remember when she helped us build a rocket?"

"I remember Rusty setting it off too soon and the rocket going through the carport roof," Phee said. Her mom had bought a rocket kit and was helping Phee and Kimiko put it together in the Mahoneys' carport. Rusty wandered over to watch. When the rocket was finished, Kimiko and Phee and Phee's mom went to set up the launch pad in the driveway. Rusty had apparently missed all the don't-play-with-matches lectures. Phee heard a *whump* and a rush of air and had turned to see Rusty staring up at a hole in the carport overhang and the rocket arcing over their fence.

"Your mom didn't get even a little mad. Mine would have been yelling her head off. Assuming she'd helped us build it, which is a big *not*." Kimiko sighed. "Your mom treats you like you're a grown-up. Mine acts like I'm still a baby."

Phee's fingers found the smooth face of her watch. She thought it might be nice to be treated like a baby now and then. She changed the subject.

"You know how we were supposed to go to my house to do the science project today? Well, I was wondering if we could go to yours instead. I mean, my mom won't be there to help us and . . ." Phee's voice trailed off. *And there's a good chance my dad is gonna find out my mom's dead so I don't want to be there.*

Kimiko clapped a hand to her head. "I meant to ask you! Is it okay if we do it tomorrow? I'm supposed to go to the dentist today."

"Okay," Phee said.

"Thank you, thank you, thank you," Kimiko said. She turned to the boy sitting across the aisle. "Hey, Wyatt, did you do the math homework? I really don't get factoring."

As the two talked, Phee gazed out the window. She didn't know where Kimiko was going after school, but it wasn't to the dentist. Everyone Phee knew went to Dr. Bell. His palms didn't smell like hand sanitizer like Dr. Jansen's did. Phee had briefly considered being a dentist, until she thought about what it would be like to look into open mouths all day. Yuck and boring.

The Bells lived down the street from the Mahoneys. Dr. Bell loved to play golf. As soon as the snow melted and the local course opened, he was there on Saturdays and Sundays as well as after work on weekdays. During the winter, he and Mrs. Bell went to their condo in Arizona for a week every month so he could play. When they were gone, they paid Zane to take in their mail. Like he was doing this week.

Phee pressed her forehead against the window, cold seeping through the pink cashmere to her skin. This hat wasn't as warm as the pom-pom one. If you were a girl, you could have lots of friends, but you had to have one special person be your bestie, your home girl, your BFF. Ashley used to be Phee's. Then Kimiko was. But now Kimiko was acting like she wanted to dump Phee. If Kimiko started wearing pink, Phee was going to barf.

Tron whimpered.

"Tell me about it," she muttered as she rummaged in her backpack for the keys.

Chapter 27

Phee had gym fifth period. The teacher, Ms. Sobel, wore navy blue shorts every day, even in the winter, along with a whistle on a cord around her neck. Her legs were sturdy and tan and her hair was shorter than most of the boys'.

The girls' locker room was a modular building on the edge of the playground. *Athletic field*, Phee mentally corrected as she joined the rest of her gym class in the narrow room. The faint funk of sweaty bodies hung in the air. Metal locker doors banged over the hubbub of voices as thirty girls changed into their gym suits. The one-piece jersey outfits were blue and white striped tops attached to blue shorts. When they were babies, Brooklyn and Scout had similar onesies.

Ms. Sobel clapped her hands to get their attention. She was big on clapping when she wasn't blowing her whistle.

"Listen up, everybody," she said. "It's strength and agility day."

The girls responded with a collective groan, Phee among them. Undeterred, Ms. Sobel continued. "Everyone meet in the gym in five minutes." She left.

Phee was lacing up her gym shoes when a voice behind her said, "You stole Veronica's hat."

Phee twisted around to see Ashley glaring down at her. Her eyes were rimmed with black liner and her eyelashes were thick with mascara, which made her look like Johnny Depp in *Pirates of the Caribbean*. Her pink hair ties, signifying her status as a Donner Partier, were the same shade as the rubber bands around her braces. It looked like bubble gum was caught in her teeth. Had Phee been wrong about Ashley? Maybe she *had* changed.

Ashley pointed at Phee's head. "That's Veronica's."

The pink hat was so lightweight and soft, Phee had forgotten she had it on. "No, it isn't," she said.

Ashley crossed her arms and flared her nostrils. "So where'd you get it?"

Phee didn't want to say she'd found it in a box of junk picked up from an empty house. "My brother gave it to me."

"You're lying!" Ashley said with all the drama of a cop or lawyer on TV. Had Ashley's parents watched a lot of *Law & Order* right before she was born? Right now, Phee wished she'd exercise her right to remain silent.

"I am not," Phee said, hearing less conviction in her voice than she would have liked.

Ashley snatched the hat off Phee's head. Static electricity crackled and Phee felt strands of her hair stand up. Ashley turned the hat inside out. She held it up in front of Phee and stabbed a polished fingernail at the label. "It's from this year's Bartholomew & Holmes collection. They only made like fifty of 'em and Veronica bought the only one Nordie's had. You stole it!" Ashley's voice rose on the last three words. The locker room din lessened as some of the other girls turned to look at them.

"I didn't," Phee said. Now almost everyone in the locker room was listening. Phee's cheeks felt so hot she half expected her eyelashes to char.

Girls your age are fickle, her mom had told her when Phee explained why she and Ashley weren't selling cookies together anymore. *You two will probably be friends again in high school.*

Phee had to look up what *fickle* meant: suddenly changing. She hadn't been fickle to Ashley. And high school was further away than Christmas, her birthday even. Knowing Ashley might be her friend then did nothing to make her feel better now.

"Let's ask Veronica if it's hers," Ashley said. She glanced down the long room. "Hey, Ronni?" There was no answer. Phee didn't see Veronica's buttery blond head among the girls. Ashley flipped her hair over her shoulder. "Whatever. I'll ask her in class."

"Give me my hat back," Phee said.

Ashley bared her teeth like Homicide did right before he was going to pounce on a bug and eat it. "Come get it."

Phee stood and reached for the hat. Instead of handing it to her, Ashley tossed it over her head. Lindsay, another Donner Partier, caught it. Phee stepped over the bench, her hand outstretched.

"C'mon, Lindsay," she said.

Lindsay tried to throw the hat back to Ashley. Her effort fell short, and the hat landed on the ground. Ashley and Phee both scrambled for it, Phee getting there first. She was about to grab the hat when Ashley elbowed her hard in the stomach.

"Oof!" Phee said as she landed hard on a bench. About a third of the class had gathered around to watch the drama like it was the UFC. Phee heard *way to go, girl* and *get her, Ashley* but only one *cheap shot*. Her knee throbbed where it'd hit the wood. Tomorrow she'd have a huge bruise.

Ashley triumphantly dangled the hat in front of Phee, "Nyah, nyah—"

Almost without thinking, Phee stiffened her hand and did a perfect karate chop on Ashley's wrist.

"Ow!" Ashley cried. She dropped the hat and clutched her wrist.

Phee picked up the hat. *Where did that come from?* She'd never hit anyone before. And all over a hat someone had thrown away? She wished she could talk to her mom, who was good at explaining why Phee did something even when Phee didn't know why.

Lindsay was at Ashley's side, her arm wrapped around Ashley's waist as though Ashley was about to fall down, although to Phee it looked like Ashley was standing just fine by herself. She wasn't even holding her wrist anymore. She was glowering at Phee.

"You hit like a boy!" Ashley said.

Phee stood. Her knee throbbed. "You throw like a girl."

"Well, duh," Lindsay said.

"It wasn't a compliment," Phee said. Trying not to limp, she started for her locker. The other girls moved out of her way. Some looked a bit scared.

Great. Now everyone thought she was a mean girl.

Chapter 28

The door to the locker room opened. Ms. Sobel stuck her head in. "Why are you so slow today? Let's get going!" she said.

Led by Ashley and Lindsay, the class filed out of the locker room. Phee stayed behind to put the pink hat in her locker. She snapped the combo lock shut and hurried to catch up. Sometimes Ms. Sobel made the last person in the gym run laps.

She cut down one of the aisles and nearly ran into Hui Zhong and Veronica. Hui jumped back, startled. A paper floated to the ground. Phee picked it up. She recognized the previous night's algebra homework. It had taken her an hour to multiply and divide all those integers without her mom's help.

Hui's face was bright red. "That's, that's mine," she said. Hui was a genius, one of the don't-be-surprised-if-she-cures-cancer kind.

Phee handed her the paper. "Number thirteen took me forever."

Hui nodded. "If you multiply negative two—"

"This is a private conversation," Veronica said, glaring at Phee.

"Sorry," Phee said. As she left the locker room and jogged down the tunnel that led to the gym, she wondered why Veronica was cheating. Phee had heard she got mostly Bs, sometimes a C, and didn't seem to care about doing better. Phee understood why Hui would help her. With favors like a seat at the Donner Partiers lunch table at her disposal, Veronica would be tough for someone like Hui—always on the outside but desperately wanting in—to refuse.

The gym smelled like sweaty socks and floor wax. Light from the high windows gleamed off the polished wooden floors. The room was filled with an array of equipment. There was a bar for pull-ups, a mat for sit-ups, areas for jumping jacks and lunges. In the corner was a portable climbing wall.

"Okay, girls," Ms. Sobel said. "Divide yourselves into groups of three then go to a station." Phee quickly crossed the gym and stood by Vinushu and Hayden, the only two girls who were possibly less athletic than Phee. They stood by the sit-up mat. Two stations away were Ashley and Lindsay.

Phee hated strength and agility day. It was worse than dodgeball, which Phee considered the American version of stoning. She especially hated the climbing wall. Her fear of heights made it an exercise in misery. She stared glumly at it, the last station of the day, waiting to humiliate her. Probability of success: low. Probability of humiliation: high.

"Do each exercise for one minute," Ms. Sobel said. "The first time will be for practice. During the second go-round I'll record the results."

And do what with them? Phee thought. Were the number of push-ups she could do in a minute something that needed to go on her permanent record?

The door to the gym opened and Veronica ran across the shiny floor.

"Sorry," she said to Ms. Sobel as she joined Ashley and Lindsay. The three girls bent their heads toward each other and Ashley whispered animatedly. After about twenty seconds, three pairs of eyes looked over at Phee.

"Get ready," Ms. Sobel said. Phee lay down on the mat with her knees bent. She tugged on the cuff of her shorts. Her mom had accidentally washed her gym suit in hot water and now the shrunken shorts tended to ride up.

Ms. Sobel blew the whistle. The gym filled with slapping sounds as feet and torsos hit the mats and floor. Phee clasped her hands behind her head and pulled her elbows toward her knees. *One.* She lowered herself down to the mat and did it again. *Two.* Beside her Hayden went up and down like a metronome, while Vinushu simply lay on the mat, arms and legs outstretched like a gingerbread man, staring at the ceiling. She might have been doing yoga. Or sleeping.

After a long minute Ms. Sobel blew the whistle again. “Rotate!”

Phee got to her feet and hustled to the jumping-jacks area. Once more came the whistle. As she jumped up and down, Phee’s gaze went to the Donner Partiers on the far side of the gym, where Veronica, Ashley, and Lindsay did push-ups. Or at least they tried to—Ashley’s back was so bowed her stomach almost touched the mat. Lindsay’s braid had lost its pink hair tie and her arms trembled as she pushed herself up. To Phee’s surprise, Veronica was doing boy style and not too badly. Before she could slide her gaze away, Veronica looked up and their eyes met.

Phee braced herself for a frown, a sneer, a dirty look. Instead, Veronica gave her a little nod then resumed her push-ups. Phee was surprised enough to stop jumping. *What was that about?*

“Phee, time isn’t up yet,” Ms. Sobel called. Phee resumed flapping her arms, trying to catch Veronica’s eye, but the other girl never looked her way again. Ms. Sobel blew the whistle. “Next station.”

Phee’s group stood in front of the climbing wall. “I’ll go first,” Hayden said. She stepped into the harness and cinched it around her waist. She clipped the rope dangling from the top of the wall to a D-ring on the harness and grabbed two handholds designed to look like rocks. At the sound of the whistle she climbed upward, reminding Phee of a spider crawling across its web. Before she knew it, Hayden had made it to the top, slapped the top beam, and begun her descent. Her feet touched the ground before the second whistle.

“Way to go,” Phee said.

“I have to go to the bathroom,” Vinushu said. She trotted out of the gym.

Phee wished she’d thought of that. Some of the girls used the I-got-my-period excuse to get out of PE, but Phee’s hadn’t started yet. Besides, it was kind of embarrassing to say, even to Ms. Sobel. She sighed and trudged toward the base of the climbing wall.

Chapter 29

In reality it was less than twelve feet tall, but from Phee's perspective, the climbing wall looked like a cliff face on Everest. She strapped herself into the harness and attached the safety rope, then wiped her palms on her shorts, gave her gym suit's hem a final tug, and latched on to a pair of handholds. The fake rocks were just big enough for her fingertips to crimp down on. The whistle blew.

Her feet scraped against the base of the wall as she tried to pull herself up.

"Step onto the footholds," Hayden said. "It's easier to climb with your legs instead of your arms." That didn't make sense to Phee, but she felt her way to a fake rock with her toe. She tried to step on it, but her foot kept slipping off.

"That's a handhold," Hayden said. "The footholds are the ones with the green tape. Yellow is for hands."

"Thanks," Phee said. She managed to get her feet balanced on a pair of green-marked bumps. Maybe she should have paid closer attention at the beginning of the term when Ms. Sobel had explained how to climb.

"Step up onto a foothold with your right foot and then reach for a handhold with your right hand," Hayden said. Phee did as she was told.

"Now do the same thing on the left side."

Phee felt for a fake rock with her left foot. Was it green or yellow? Phee couldn't tell. No way was she looking down.

"Good!" Hayden said. Taking that to mean she'd gotten lucky and found a foothold, Phee balanced on the bump and reached for a handhold. Her knee scraped against the rough stucco, and she felt blood trickle down her leg.

"Keep going!" Hayden said. "You've got the rhythm."

"You got this," Phee whispered to herself as she climbed, hand over hand, step by step. She kept her eyes on the fake rock in front of her.

The whistle blew.

Time to climb down. She tipped her head back and saw she was nearly at the top of the wall. How far off the ground was she? Her muscles locked up. She couldn't move.

"Didn't you hear the whistle? Come down," said Hayden's voice below her.

"Working on it," Phee muttered. Her brain wanted to go, but the message wasn't reaching her arms and legs. Her fingers were getting sore from holding on so tightly.

Let go of your right hand, then step down with your right leg. Phee mentally repeated the instructions twice, three times. But she stayed where she was. It was like there was a dead zone in the middle of her body, where all calls from her brain got dropped before they could reach her limbs.

"Phee, are you okay?" Ms. Sobel said.

"Um, sort of."

"Want me to talk you down or do you want me to lower you on the safety rope?"

She wanted to say *talk me down*, but "the rope would be good" was what came out of her mouth. Probability of safe descent: high. Probability of humiliation: off the chart.

Two minutes later, accompanied by Ms. Sobel's encouraging words and the stares of the class, Phee was lowered to the gym floor. When her shoes hit wood, she closed her eyes and sighed in relief. From now on, she planned to limit her climbing to stairs.

"Let's fix up that cut on your leg," Ms. Sobel said. Phee looked down. A thin line of blood stretched from the scrape to her sock.

"It's okay," Phee said. But Ms. Sobel insisted on getting the first-aid kit from her desk in the office next to the gym. The first swab of alcohol made Phee suck in her breath with a hiss. After that, it wasn't too bad, except for the stares and whispers of the other girls, who had resumed rotating through the stations. Ashley and Lindsay smirked at her whenever they passed. Veronica, on the other hand, never looked her way.

Ms. Sobel closed the first-aid kit. "That should do it. Be sure to tell your mom what happened so she can be on the lookout for fever or infection."

"I-I will. Okay if I go change?"

"Sure. Monday is lap day. You and I can work on climbing when everyone else is running."

"Can hardly wait." Phee headed for the locker room. Maybe she could get out of there before the Donner Partiers and the rest of the class arrived.

Phee slammed her locker shut just as the door burst open and her class trooped in. She hurriedly stuffed the pink hat into the outer pocket of her backpack.

"There she is," Ashley said, striding toward Phee.

Phee considered making a run for it before the ridiculousness of the idea kicked in.

"She took your hat, Ronni," Ashley said. "No wonder she got arrested the other night."

A girl one row over gasped. The murmur—*Phee was arrested*—swept across the locker room like an incoming wave over sand.

"I wasn't—" Phee shut up. It was pointless to argue against the Donner Partiers. It would only make her look guiltier.

"Let's see the hat," Ashley demanded. Lindsay stood behind her, trying to look fierce.

Anger rushed through Phee. If Veronica wanted the stupid hat, she could have it. She grabbed it out of her pack and thrust it at Veronica.

"Here. Take it."

Veronica did, holding it with two fingers as though it had cooties. She rotated the hat so she could see the label, then regarded it for a few seconds. "This isn't mine," she said.

"But it's Bartholomew & Holmes," Ashley said. "Last winter's collection."

"Nope. It's a knockoff." Veronica pitched the hat at Phee. It landed on the floor. "All yours." She sauntered to the end of the room, a catwalk worthy of *America's Top Model*, with her entourage hurrying to catch up.

Phee picked up the hat. "I could swear it was—" she heard Ashley say as she slipped out the locker room door. Once outside, Phee pulled her pink trophy onto Tron's head.

"Don't tell anyone it's fake," she said.

Chapter 30

Phee turned in Tron to Mrs. Moss after gym. She felt curiously light and free without the robot baby. Although she'd never admit it, she kind of missed him. Keeping Tron happy was easy—feed him, let him sleep, cuddle him. If only everyone else were so simple.

Phee was one of the first to arrive for Ms. Vlachos's class. But Ms. Vlachos wasn't there. Instead a man with red hair wearing cargo pants sat at her desk.

"Who are you?" Phee said.

"Mr. Duffy. I'm subbing today." He picked up Ms. Vlachos's Koosh ball and squeezed it.

"What about Monday?" Phee said, her eyes on the ball.

"I never know until they call me in the morning," Mr. Duffy said. He tossed the ball into the air and caught it—one, two, three times. The third time he missed and it fell on the floor. Phee stepped on it, her snow boot covering the ball. Mr. Duffy squatted and peered under the desk.

"Did you see where that went?"

"Sorry, no. Is Ms. Vlachos sick?"

Mr. Duffy straightened up. "They never tell me the reasons why a teacher is out." The second bell rang. "Time to take your seat."

Mr. Duffy walked to the blackboard and began writing his name in chalk. While his back was turned, Phee scooped up the Koosh ball and slipped it into her backpack.

Mr. Duffy talked about inventions and patents and infringement. Phee wasn't really paying attention. She stared out the window. No snow today. There were patches of green where the sun had melted spots on the lawn.

Did Ms. Vlachos get fired?

After the final bell, Phee walked to the curb where the buses waited. She stood apart from the other kids, keeping an eye out for Kimiko. She didn't see her friend. Maybe she should make that ex-friend. She still didn't buy the dentist story.

Although it wasn't snowing, it was cold, and she put on the pink hat. Phee wondered where Zane had gotten it. If it was a knockoff, did that mean he'd found other fake stuff? What if he got in trouble for selling it on eBay?

"Hey."

What if the counterfeiters, or whoever they were, wanted their stuff back? What if they tracked Zane down and came to their house?

"I said, *Hey*."

Phee blinked. Peter Allerd stood in front of her. He wore a navy puffer jacket and his cheeks were red, probably from the cold. He wasn't wearing his glasses. His eyes were bluer than his dad's, with long lashes. She'd seen him a couple of times at school from a distance since they'd talked two nights ago. Every time she did, her stomach felt funny. Night-before-Christmas funny, not I-think-I'm-going-to-be-sick funny. Although now it was feeling more like the second one.

"You were a million miles away," he said and grinned.

Her mouth felt dry and she made herself swallow. "More like seven and a half. That's how far it is to my house."

His smile disappeared. "Did you find out something about your mom?"

"Oh, um, no. I was thinking about something else." They stood silently for a moment. Phee's mind raced, trying to think of something else to say. "Hey, does your dad know anything more about Chord?"

"Uh, no." Peter shifted his weight from one foot to the other.

"Bummer," Phee said. She kicked at a chip in the sidewalk. Could she have sounded more like an idiot? She wished she still had Tron.

"My dad still has deputies and the rescue patrol looking for him," Peter said. He folded his arms across his chest. "And it's not just because of the election."

"It's his job to look for people, isn't it?"

Peter ran a hand through his hair, making it stand up like hers did after she took off her hat. On him, it looked kinda cute. "Some people say he shouldn't be wasting taxpayer dollars looking for somebody who's"—he hesitated—"who's probably not going to be all right."

Phee was getting tired of all the euphemisms. "You mean somebody who's dead."

"Yeah."

"But what does an election have to do with it?"

"My dad's running for reelection. One of his deputies is running against him. He says my dad is making a big deal out of the search for Chord to cover up the fact he hasn't done a very good job. But he has! It's not his fault that people all of a sudden are stealing stuff."

"There's a crime wave in Bristlecone?"

"Not exactly a wave. But, yeah, stuff is being stolen. Like from the auto parts store. Probably the biggest thing is Trent Snowboards' prototypes got boosted."

"I heard about that when our Biz class went there yesterday." Phee twisted a strand of her hair, then realized what she was doing and snatched her hand away.

"My dad would probably win if he arrested somebody before the election. If you hear about a crime and know how to solve it, let me know, okay?" He grinned, but Phee could tell he wasn't totally joking.

"Sure. Although I bet your dad wins anyway."

Peter made a face like he was sucking on one of Mrs. Heckler's Citrons. "The deputy who's running against him is a real tool. The guy accidentally shot off part of his toe practicing at the range. He had it replaced with a rubber one."

Phee's stomach muscles quivered. She clamped her jaw shut, willing herself not to laugh. Someone shot himself and she found it funny? Peter would think she was creepy-weird. *Don't don't don't laugh.* Her shoulders shook with the effort.

The corner of Peter's mouth twitched. "His name's Robert. Now everyone calls him Roberto."

Phee lost it. Peter began laughing, too, so hard that he dropped his backpack onto the ground and propped his hands on his knees. He snorted every time he drew a breath. Each snort made Phee laugh harder until she was doubled over, arms wrapped around her ribs.

She was the first to get the hysteria under control. "I get these laugh attacks and I can't stop." She wiped her eyes. There went the mascara again. "You must think I'm crazy."

"I don't think it's crazy at all. Laughing is the best way to forget about bad stuff, at least for a little while."

That put the brakes on Phee's mirth. Had he heard about the fight with Ashley in the gym?

Peter glanced over his shoulder. "I gotta go. My bus is going to leave." He hoisted his backpack onto his shoulder, leaned toward her, hovered for a second, and then kissed her. After what seemed like both an hour and no time at all, he backed up a step.

"Um, see ya," he said.

"See ya," Phee managed to say. She knew her face was full-on tomato. Peter Allerd had kissed her! Right on the lips in front of school!

She stayed where she was, watching him run for his bus. At the last minute, right before he started up the steps, he turned and smiled at her. That made her feel almost as good as the kiss did. Almost.

A horn honked, then honked again. At the entrance to the bus circle, a pickup truck was idling—black with flames painted on the doors. Two snowboards jutted out of the bed. What was Austin doing here? She checked the line of kids waiting to board her bus. Did she have time to run over and ask him where the pink hat had come from? She didn't want to say anything to Zane about counterfeit stuff until she was sure the hat was fake.

She walked quickly toward Austin's truck. A girl dashed out of one of the school's side exits and headed for the pickup. Austin leaned over and pushed open the passenger door. The girl climbed in, giving Phee a clear view of her face.

The good feelings from the kiss with Peter dissolved. Phee turned on her heel and hurried for her bus.

She didn't want Kimiko to catch her staring.

Chapter 31

Mrs. Heckler was standing on her front porch when Phee walked up the street after being dropped off by the bus. The elderly woman wore two coats under a lab coat, with a windbreaker on top of everything. Lace-up snow boots made her feet look huge. On her head was a beret with a pink shower cap peeking out underneath.

"Hi, Mrs. Heckler," Phee called, waving.

"Hello, Phee. Would you like to come in? I have some Cheetos that Kathryn doesn't know about." Mrs. Heckler giggled. "With her back the way it is, she can't look under the furniture."

Phee assumed Kathryn was Rusty's mom. The way Mrs. Risborough had been acting, Phee didn't really want to run into her, but she didn't see Mrs. Risborough's rental car anywhere.

"Okay. Thanks." Phee walked up the path to where Mrs. Heckler stood. She dragged her wheeled backpack over the steps behind her.

Up close, she could see Mrs. Heckler wore thick striped socks and galoshes. A bathrobe tie was knotted around her waist. "Are you cold?" she asked.

"I'm rather warm actually," Mrs. Heckler said.

"So why are you wearing all those clothes?"

Mrs. Heckler spoke in a whisper. "Because she said when I went away I couldn't take everything. These are my favorites."

"You're moving?"

"Oh, no. Kathryn is taking me on a trip."

"Where are you going?"

Mrs. Heckler shook her head. The beret slipped off, unnoticed. "She said it was a surprise." The old woman smiled happily for a moment. Then her face fell. "But I can't take the Citron."

"I'll bring you some before you go," Phee said.

"Oh, I only want one." Mrs. Heckler grasped Phee's hands. "You are such a sweet girl. And generous, just like your mother." She patted the lab coat. "Your mother gave me this. She was going to throw it away but I told her I liked it. The next day she brought over this one, brand new." She dropped Phee's hands and reached for the doorknob. "Come in, come in."

Phee followed Mrs. Heckler into the house. She parked her backpack behind the coatrack. "My mom gave you a lab coat?"

Mrs. Heckler was on her hands and knees, her bottom stuck in the air, reaching under a china cabinet in the living room. "She's done many nice things for me over the years," she said, her voice muffled. "Here they are!" She pulled a bright orange bag from under the cabinet.

Phee helped her up and onto the sofa. Mrs. Heckler tore open the bag and offered it to Phee.

"Thanks," Phee said, taking a handful of the Day-Glo snack. Her mom would have freaked if she knew Phee was eating them—"food is not supposed to be neon"—but her mom wasn't there. Phee stopped eating. She didn't feel like Cheetos anymore.

Mrs. Heckler kept chewing. "Do you ever wonder how they came up with the idea for these?"

"Not really."

Mrs. Heckler ate another Cheeto. "Whoever did is a genius."

Phee thought about Mr. Duffy's lecture on inventions. Maybe she could invent a snack. Should it be salty or sweet? Salty, she decided. What color and shape should it be? What flavor? She ran through her favorites—guacamole, barbecue, sour cream and onion, sweet potato, salt and pepper.

She couldn't come up with a flavor that hadn't been taken or a new shape and color. Maybe all the salty snacks already had been invented.

There were cardboard boxes with a moving company's name on them stacked in a corner. Phee nodded at them. "Are you giving stuff to Goodwill?" Once a year, Phee's mom had everyone go through their books and clothes and stuff. Anything they hadn't used in a year got put into the donation pile. Except for last year, when Zane sold everything on eBay. He'd given Phee thirty-seven dollars. "Your share, minus my commission," he'd said.

"No, those are for what I want to take on my trip," Mrs. Heckler said.

Seeing the moving company's name reminded Phee of Rusty's refusal to tell her where he'd moved. Time to practice her interrogation technique. "Where does Mrs. Ris—Kathryn live?"

"When she and Tom were first married, they lived in Denver." Mrs. Heckler looked out the window, but Phee could tell her mind was seeing something in the past. "They had the sweetest little house you ever saw, white with blue shutters. I gave her my blue striped placemats." Mrs. Heckler paused. "She said they were the wrong shade of blue, so she never used them."

"I meant where do they live now?"

"After the blue house they moved to Lakewood, and then they had Rusty and moved to Golden. When Tom filed for divorce, Kathryn and Rusty came to live with me."

"And then where did they move?" Sometimes Mrs. Heckler took a really long time to get to the point.

Mrs. Heckler frowned in concentration. "I-I don't know," she said after about ten seconds. Her face was pinched.

It was bad enough to get old and lose your memory, Phee thought. But it was much worse to know you were going batty. "It's okay," she said quickly. "Where does Rusty go to school?" If Phee could find out that, maybe she could identify the town.

"He doesn't. His mother homeschools him. Since the divorce and the accident, she's become a bit overprotective, but Kathryn's a good parent. She has to be—she's the only one Rusty has."

"What happened to his dad?"

"Tom? He married someone else and has a new family. He never sees Rusty, and Kathryn is always taking him to court for the child support." Mrs. Heckler bit down hard on a Cheeto and chewed furiously. "I'm sure there were several fine things about him, but I can't think of any at the moment."

"Rusty's mom was in an accident?" Phee told herself she wasn't being nosy, just practicing her spy interrogation techniques.

"She was rear-ended by an SUV and hurt her back. Makes it hard for her to sit and stand for very long, so she had to stop working full time. There aren't a lot of jobs where you don't have to do one or the other."

"So how does she make money to live on?"

"The guy who hit her had a little insurance, but most of it went to doctor bills. I help her out, and she's able to work a few shifts at the hospital."

Phee wondered what it'd be like to have a mom like Mrs. Risborough. Not the crabby part, but one who homeschooled you and took you with her on trips. Would Phee feel smothered or loved? She'd always thought her mom was pretty cool, even if she was gone a lot. She was smart and not afraid to show it. She didn't tell Phee what to think, like Kimiko's mom did to Kimiko. Phee's mom listened and talked to Phee like she was a grown-up. Everybody argued with their mom, but Phee and her mom didn't do it too often. Talking with her usually made Phee feel better or helped her understand something.

As though reading her mind, Mrs. Heckler said, "You know your mother loves you and your brothers and sister more than anything." Orange crumbs dusted the front of her lab coat.

Something stirred in Phee's chest. Ever since Monday, when she'd found out about the tsunami, there'd been an uncomfortable feeling there, like something was pressing down on her heart. Now it expanded into a full-on ache.

"Why did she even go to Australia? Why couldn't she stay here?" Phee knew they were stupid questions but she couldn't help it.

"Because her job is really important to her. She once told me that if she didn't work, she didn't think she would be a very good mom."

The hurt got worse. For a second Phee thought she might throw up. No, she was going to cry. "No one can find her. I think she might be dead," she choked out before giving in to the sobs.

Mrs. Heckler wrapped her arms around her. "I don't think so, sweetie. Your mom is really tough and smart. Like you are. I'm sure she's going to come home."

Phee pulled away so she could look into the faded denim eyes. "Really?"

Mrs. Heckler's gaze was steady. "Really."

Phee wiped her cheeks and felt better, even though it made no sense to take the word of an old lady who was losing her marbles.

The night before she'd watched more YouTube videos of the tsunami. Waves of angry, dirty water roared through the streets, carrying furniture, cars, boats, trees, all sorts of junk, and even a cow as it smashed into buildings, pushing some off their foundations, and flattened light poles, parking meters, fences, and anything else in its way. Phee skimmed through the news stories, looking for tales of survivors. One woman had hugged a tree. She was there for three days before being rescued. A man had clung to a radio tower. Another had used a door as a raft. He was swept out to sea and picked up by a military ship miles offshore.

Phee's mom would be able to do something like that. Once when she was working on an Indian reservation in Arizona, she slipped off a rock formation and broke her arm. There was no cell phone coverage, so she hiked forty-five minutes back to the car and drove herself to the emergency room. Mrs. Heckler was right. Phee's mom was smart and tough.

Phee caught sight of the clock on the mantel—4:15. She stood. "I'd better get going." She reached for her backpack but stopped when she saw her fingertips. Her tears had mixed with the Cheetos coating and turned her skin orange. "Do you mind if I go wash my hands?"

Mrs. Heckler giggled. "Smart girl. Get rid of the evidence." Mrs. Heckler folded over the top of the bag and tucked it under the sofa. "The bathroom is at the end of the hall."

Phee walked down the hall, passing an array of framed photos on both walls. The shots were mostly of Rusty and his mom and Mrs. Heckler. It was like a timeline, with the people becoming younger the farther she walked. About halfway down the hall, a tall man, usually in a hat, began to appear in the photos, often standing with his arm around Mrs. Heckler. Her husband, Phee guessed. The photos right in front of the bathroom showed a pretty teenage girl. In one she rode a pony. In another, she stood on the deck of a boat in the ocean. The last shot showed her on a swing, her heels thrust to the sky, her hair streaming behind her. Phee recognized Mrs. Heckler in her smile and the tilt of her eyes.

Phee had never really thought about the lives grown-ups had before they were, well, grown-up. Mrs. Heckler looked like someone she would be friends with if they were close in age. Phee had never seen any photos of her mother when she was a teenager. She resolved to look for some. Would they show her mom being serious, like hanging out with the chess club at school? Or would she be doing something fun or even bad, like smoking or drinking beer?

Phee let herself into the bathroom while amusing herself with the mental picture of her mother gulping down beer and then throwing up, like Zane had done the night her parents had left them with the world's dumbest babysitter.

The bathroom was bigger than most, with a large window overlooking the yard and, in the distance, the Denver skyline. On the glass shelf over the sink was an unzipped toiletries bag with things spilling out—a comb, a pot of makeup, mascara in a pink-and-green tube. Next to the toiletries bag, two toothbrushes leaned away from each other in a cup. Hanging over the shower bar were a bra and several pairs of white tights. This must be the bathroom Mrs. Risborough and Rusty used.

She washed her hands and reached for a towel embroidered with yellow and pink flowers, but decided it looked too nice to use and wiped her hands on her pants instead.

Phee was about to open the door when she glimpsed the top of a pill bottle in the toiletries bag. She knew it was wrong to snoop. On the other hand, once she got a question in her head, she couldn't stop until she knew the answer. Her mom once caught Phee prying the back off the mirror in the front hall to find out where the reflection came from. "You inherited my scientific curiosity," her mom had said. "Be careful it doesn't get you in trouble."

Phee picked up the pill bottle. It might help her figure out why Mrs. Risborough had acted so weird at the grocery store and why there'd been someone else's name on her prescription.

She squinted at the tiny print. The patient's name was NANCY BILSON. The drug name was too long to remember. She'd just found an eyeliner pencil to write it down on a piece of toilet paper when a door opened and shut somewhere in the house.

"Mother, I'm home," called Mrs. Risborough.

Chapter 32

Phee froze.

"Mother?" Mrs. Risborough said, louder this time.

Phee heard the clomp of Mrs. Heckler's boots. "Is it time to go?"

"No. The man is here to watch you sign the papers. Remember when I told you about him?"

Phee peeked out from behind the door, which was ajar. She could see down the hall into the living room. Mrs. Heckler was sitting on the couch. Mrs. Risborough stood over her, a sheaf of papers in her hand.

"Put this book in your lap to write on," Mrs. Risborough said. "What is that orange stuff all over your front?"

Mrs. Heckler patted the top of her head, then the sofa cushion. "Have you seen my glasses? I had them right before Phee stopped by."

Mrs. Risborough straightened up. "The Mahoney girl was here?"

Mrs. Heckler stopped patting the cushions. "Why, yes. She's such a sweet thing."

"Mother, you know you're not supposed to have guests when you're alone. I don't want you to . . . to . . . get tired."

Mrs. Heckler picked up one of the sofa pillows. "They were right here . . .

"You don't need your glasses. I told you—I read everything. All you have to do is sign next to where the stickies are."

Mrs. Heckler set the pillow down. In a firmer voice than Phee had ever heard her use, she said, "Kathryn, have you been in my Citron again?"

Mrs. Risborough took a step back. "What? I never—"

"I may be old, but I'm still your mother. I know when you're not telling the truth."

Mrs. Risborough leaned in close to Mrs. Heckler. "This is not the time," she said in a harsh whisper. "Mr. Lyall is waiting. You need to sign these papers *now*."

Mrs. Heckler's shoulders slumped and she dropped her head, wilting like Phee's daisy plant did when she forgot to water it. Her voice became tremulous again. "If I could just find my glasses—"

The front door opened. Phee ducked out of sight.

"Hey, Mom." Rusty's voice.

Phee chewed on her bottom lip. The little house was getting pretty full. Sooner or later someone would need to go to the bathroom.

She knew she could walk out of the bathroom and down the hall, say hello to Mrs. Risborough and Rusty, and thank Mrs. Heckler for her hospitality. But the way Mrs. Risborough was acting, something told Phee she should avoid her. Seriously—who would steal candy from her mother?

Remember: you're always a spy. That was the first line in *The Master Spy Handbook*. The book had a chapter called "Rules to Spy By." Rule #1 was *Don't get caught.* Rule #8 was *Always have an alternate route.* Rules #12 and #13: *Plan ahead* and *Always have at least two alternate plans*. Phee was annoyed with herself for being unprepared. She should have thought about what she would do if Mrs. Risborough or Rusty showed up.

There were three ways to get out of the house—through the front door, the back door off the kitchen, and through the garage. All of them meant crossing paths with Mrs. Risborough. Maybe Phee could make it to a closet in one of the bedrooms and hide there until everyone went to sleep. No, she'd have to go to the bathroom before then and her dad and Aunt Helen would be concerned when she didn't come home. They might already be worried.

Phee looked at the window—dark except for except for a faint glow in one corner from the beam of the streetlight shining through the frosted glass—and realized she had more than three ways to get out of the house. There were as many additional exits as there were windows. Windows that opened, that is. She blew out a relieved breath when she saw the bathroom window was the type where the bottom pane of glass slid up over the top one.

She backed away from the door and gently pushed it shut. When the hinges squeaked, she froze. The group in the living room continued talking, Mrs. Risborough's voice louder than the others.

She flipped open the side latches, hooked her fingers under the bottom edge of the window, and pulled up. It didn't move. Phee lowered the toilet seat and stepped onto the lid. It had one of those fuzzy covers on it and she wobbled for a second as it slid to one side. Her fingers found a latch along the top of the window. She released it and pushed against the frame. The window slid open. A draft of cold air blew into the room, making her shiver and reminding her that her jacket and backpack were in a corner of the living room. Well, she'd have to figure out how to get them later.

Phee looked out the window. She saw two cars parked in Mrs. Heckler's driveway—the rental Mrs. Risborough drove and a white minivan with a magnetic sign on its door. Mobile Notary Public. Under that in smaller print was AVAILABLE 24/7, followed by a phone number. She knew what *mobile* meant, of course, and *public*. But the notary stumped her. Phee filed the words away in her memory to ask Ms. Vlachos about later.

She looked down. Under the window was a row of small shrubs, with the lawn just beyond. Like other houses on the block, Mrs. Heckler's had a walk-out basement. Her yard sloped down toward the street. That made the first-floor windows two and a half stories off the ground. Thinking about jumping gave her vertigo.

Bolted to the wall beside the window was a wooden trellis. Horizontal strips of wood were nailed to two vertical slats. There was just enough space between each slat for her foot, or at least her toes, to fit.

The longer she waited the more likely it was she'd be caught. Decision time—out the window or out the door. It didn't take much thought for Phee to decide she would rather go out the window than face Mrs. Risborough.

Option one: jumping to the ground. Probability of success: high. Probability of humiliation: low—no one was watching. But there was another risk to consider: probability of broken bones. That was high, bordering on certain.

Option two: climbing down the trellis. Same probabilities of success and humiliation, with a lower chance of broken bones. Option two it was.

She flipped off the bathroom light, put her palms on the window track, then pushed herself up like she was going to mount a balance beam. Not that she'd ever taken gymnastics—it was a sport for Tinker Bell-sized girls—but she'd seen enough of the Olympics on TV to get the general idea.

Her feet were in midair and the metal ridges bit into her hands. She twisted her body and plunked her bottom onto the windowsill. *Ophelia Mahoney of the United States—5.0 for style, 9.9 for execution.* She looked down again. A blanket of snow was draped across the bushes below her, which should help cushion her if she fell.

Phee brought her knees up to her chest and rested both heels on the sill. Then she straightened the leg closer to the street so that it dangled outside. She had to hurry. Thanks to the streetlight, anyone who drove up the street or looked out a window might think she was a burglar. She rotated toward the street so she could lower the other leg. Now she was sitting with both feet out the window.

The bushes below suddenly looked very tiny, with hardly any snow covering them. If she fell off the trellis, she could hit her head on the way down and get amnesia. She wouldn't know who Kimiko or Joshua-Alex were. She might not even recognize her mom when she came home. Although not knowing Joshua-Alex had a certain appeal, she didn't want to lose all her other memories.

According to Rule #17 in *The Master Spy Handbook*, a good spy knew when to abort a mission. *If the likelihood of success diminishes, it's better to withdraw and return another day.*

Phee figured the odds of avoiding injury were about point-one percent. She should go back inside and figure out what to do. She grabbed the edges of the window and raised her knees until her heels once again rested on the sill. Good thing she'd done crunches in gym class. She was about to twist around and climb into the room when the bathroom door began to open.

Phee thought she glimpsed a thatch of red hair. Rule #1 flashed through her mind—*Don't get caught.* She pushed herself off the windowsill toward the trellis.

Chapter 33

Phee grasped the wooden frame with both hands while her feet scrabbled to find a toehold. The trellis bowed under her weight and slivers dug into her palms. After ten long seconds, she had both sets of toes balanced on a slat. She forced herself to breathe through her nose and pulled her body close against the house. Rusty had to have seen her. She stared at the window, waiting for his head to appear.

Instead, she heard the sounds of him peeing (gross), flushing the toilet (unlike Brooklyn half the time), and washing his hands (phew). There was a squeak that sounded like it came from the hinges of the medicine cabinet, then some more noises she couldn't identify.

As soon as he left, she'd climb back inside and make a new plan of escape. She glanced down and immediately regretted it. The small bushes underneath her looked even smaller. Her stomach heaved and she bit back the pre-barf taste of egg salad. She pinned her eyes to the wall in front of her and mentally sang the song she and the other Brownies always sang on long car trips to take her mind off the nausea. *Ninety-nine bottles of beer on the wall, ninety-nine bottles of beer; take one down, pass it around, ninety-eight bottles of beer on the wall . . .*

Around *ninety-four bottles of beer* she heard the hinge squeak again and the bang of the medicine cabinet closing. Her fingers were starting to cramp and the rest of her was freezing. She pressed her lips together to stop her teeth from chattering and strained to hear the *ka-chunk* of the door handle. *Ninety bottles of beer on the wall, ninety bottles of beer . . .*

The window slammed shut, startling her so much she almost let go of the trellis. As she stared with dismay at the pane of glass, it went dark as Rusty switched off the bathroom light and shut the door behind him.

Rule #13: Always have at least two alternate plans. She looked up. The trellis went all the way to the roof. Once she got there, what could she do? Wait until everyone went to sleep and climb down? Not only would it be a long, cold wait, her dad would probably freak when she didn't show up for dinner and call the cops. She imagined Sheriff Allerd standing beside the Heckler house pointing his flashlight up at her on the roof, a squad car parked on the street with its red-and-blue flashing lights and all the neighbors staring. Probability of success: medium. Probability of humiliation: high. So much for alternate plan #1.

The other way was down, of course. She could climb down the trellis like it was a ladder. Probability of success: high. Probability of humiliation: low, assuming no one saw her. There was her fear of heights, but real spies didn't worry about that. She thought about Jason Bourne swinging between buildings on a cable. Instead of making her feel braver, the thought made her nauseated again.

This is just like the climbing wall, she told herself. Okay, the trellis was twice as tall. And there was no safety rope or Ms. Sobel to talk her down.

Phee took a deep breath. She thought of a poster she'd seen in the yoga place her mom went to sometimes. *A journey of a thousand miles begins with one step.* She lifted one foot off the trellis, straightened her arms a bit to lower her body, and stuck her foot onto a lower slat. Not too bad. She did it with the other foot, faster this time. No dizziness, no panic attack—maybe she was getting over her fear of heights!

She lowered herself a few more feet. The night air still chilled her and the spot where the splinter had poked her was beginning to really hurt, but at least she was on her way down. Why had she ever been afraid of the climbing wall?

A low creak sounded overhead. Phee froze. Had someone come into the bathroom? Was the person opening the window?

She looked up, straining to see. The window was still dark. Probably tree branches rubbing together. She felt for the next slat with her toes. Another creak, longer this time. Phee felt the trellis move slightly, the top pulling away from the house. She stretched her leg down and found a place for her foot to rest, accompanied by a loud squeal that tapered off to a groan. If she believed in ghosts, that was the sound they'd make.

This was worse than ghosts, though. The sounds she heard were from nails pulling out of the wood. The trellis was peeling away from the house.

Phee stood still. The trellis moved slightly, as though swaying in the wind. But there was no breeze. Now that some of the nails were loosened, her weight—even when she wasn't moving—was enough to pull them out. The only way to save herself from falling was to get down before the trellis peeled off.

Phee started down again, moving so fast she missed a toehold and had to cling to the frame while her foot searched frantically for a slat. She was almost halfway down. She estimated in two minutes, she'd be on the ground.

She made it there a lot sooner.

Chapter 34

Accompanied by a chorus of squeaks and groans, the trellis fell away from the wall like a tree toppling over in the forest. Phee landed on her back hard on a shrub, the wooden frame on top of her.

Phee lay without moving, blinking up at the stars. She was pretty sure they were real stars, and not the ones that whirled around cartoon characters' heads whenever they got injured doing something dumb—like fall off a trellis. Branches jabbed into her ribs and tangled in her hair. The snow, which hadn't cushioned her fall, soaked into her clothes, making her even colder.

Between the screeching nails and her landing thud, someone must have heard her fall. She looked up, expecting to see Rusty's head appear over the windowsill any moment.

But it didn't. No one's did. She waited several more seconds, then heaved the trellis off her. The torquing motion broke it in half. She tried to sit up, but couldn't; she was wedged in the shrub. Every time she moved, she only sank in deeper. It was the plant version of quicksand.

Quicksand . . . . The contestants in the reality TV show Zane watched once had to get out of quicksand. Phee didn't think it was real quicksand. Still, it was impossible to walk through. The contestants got stuck as soon as they were in over their knees. The winners figured out the only way to get across was to pull themselves along on their bellies. That way their weight was spread out instead of being in one place, where it would sink.

Phee straightened her body out as much as she could, extended her arms over her head, and rotated onto her stomach. This hurt more than lying on her back; there were more soft places for the sticks to dig into. She seized two branches and, moving her hips like a dolphin, started to pull herself across the top of the shrub.

"Ow," she muttered. "Ow, ow, *ow*!"

With a final wriggle, she tumbled off the top of the shrub and onto the ground. She lay for a moment, looking up at the stars, then rolled onto her side. Something fell out of her shirt pocket. She pushed herself up into a sitting position and patted the shadowy ground, searching for whatever it was. Her fingers touched a plastic bottle. Mrs. Risborough's pills! She must have dropped the bottle into her pocket without thinking when she heard Rusty's mom walk into the house. She put them in her jacket pocket. She'd figure out how to return them when she picked up the stuff she'd left in Mrs. Heckler's house.

Phee flexed her arms and legs. Nothing appeared to be broken. And she didn't seem to have amnesia.

The front door to Mrs. Heckler's house opened. Phee shrank back against the shrub. Mrs. Risborough and a man stood on the porch.

"I'm sorry, Mr. Lyall," Mrs. Risborough said. "She has her good days and bad days."

"I understand," Mr. Lyall said in a sympathetic tone. "That's the tragedy of Alz—"

"My mother is perfectly competent. I mean, she's fine. She's just tired. The neighbor girl was over earlier, bothering her."

Phee scowled. *I was not.*

"We can reschedule if you'd like," Mr. Lyall said. "I have other appointments tomorrow, but we can meet first thing next week. Perhaps we should schedule in the morning, when your mother is a bit . . . fresher."

"No! That is, I'm busy during the day. That's why I called you—your ad said twenty-four/seven." Mrs. Risborough looked pointedly at the sign on the minivan.

"O-kay," Mr. Lyall said, drawing out the word.

"Here's a check for today's wasted trip. I'll see you on Sunday, ten o'clock. Next time don't park on the street. Take the driveway to the rear of the house and leave your car there. Knock on the back door and I'll let you in."

"Uh, sure." Mr. Lyall turned away from the door. Phee shut her eyes. The *Master Spy Handbook* said to do that when hiding in the dark. Otherwise whoever was looking for you might spot the white parts of your eyes.

She heard Mr. Lyall walk down the steps, crunch through the snow on the driveway, click the minivan unlocked, open the door, and get in. Only when he'd started the engine and backed onto the street did she open her eyes again.

She rubbed her hands together; her fingertips were numb. Every other muscle in her body was cold, stiff, and/or sore. She peeked around the edge of the bush. On the other side of Mrs. Heckler's front yard sat her house, its windows lit up like a picture on a Christmas card. There was nothing she wanted more than to be in that warmth right now. She thought about taking a bath in her parents' bathroom, the tub filled with hot water frothed with bubbles that smelled like flowers. But she didn't move. *Don't get caught.*

Phee peered through the gloom at the shadowed front porch of Mrs. Heckler's house. She didn't see Mrs. Risborough. No big surprise; it was freezing out. But she hadn't heard the front door open. Maybe the sound of Mr. Lyall's car engine had drowned it out. Phee made herself count to twenty-five in her head. *Twenty-three, twenty-four* . . . . Her right calf was cramping. If she didn't move soon, it would get worse. She massaged the muscle and counted to twenty-five again.

She drew her legs under her, preparing for the sprint home. It was absolutely quiet. The air was sharp and crisp, tinged with the scent of pine—and smoke.

Phee stared at the shadows draped around Mrs. Heckler's porch. A glowing speck moved through the darkness, like a firefly.

A car started up the street. Was Mr. Lyall coming back?

A pickup truck pulled into Mrs. Heckler's driveway. Mrs. Risborough stepped out of the shadows on the porch and walked down the steps to the truck.

The driver opened his door, the cab light illuminating Mrs. Risborough. She flicked her cigarette butt toward the Mahoneys' yard. *Nice.*

"What are you doing here?" Mrs. Risborough said.

The driver pushed past her and headed for the bed of his pickup truck. Phee couldn't see his face, partly because it was dark and partly because his baseball hat was pulled low.

Mrs. Risborough stood with her hands propped on her hips, staring after the driver. She probably wasn't used to people walking away from her when she was telling them what to do. After a moment, she joined the driver at the rear of his truck, where he'd unloaded a tarp-wrapped bundle about three feet long and half as wide.

"I told you, you can't just show up here whenever you want," Mrs. Risborough said as the driver started across the lawn in Phee's direction with the bundle under his arm. Phee ducked behind the bush. "My son is home and my mother is awake!"

The driver stopped and turned to face her. "You did not seem to mind your son being home and your mother being awake the other night," he said in a German accent. Phee started. It was the man from the Trent factory, the one they called Jungen.

"That was different," Mrs. Risborough hissed. "We'd made arrangements."

Jungen fished something out of his shirt pocket and shook it back and forth. Phee heard a faint rattle. "Here," he said as he tossed the object to Mrs. Risborough. "I trust this will make up for my . . . rudeness," he sneered. Phee couldn't tell what he'd thrown but Mrs. Risborough scrambled to catch it like it was a football in the end zone.

Was Jungen Mrs. Risborough's boyfriend? They were both icky and bickered like lots of people who were together. Phee's parents didn't talk to each other that way. Her mom might boss around the kids, but she never did that to Phee's dad. And even though he was disorganized, he never forgot Phee's mom's birthday or their anniversary, and they still held hands when they thought no kids were watching. Phee didn't know how her dad would cope if her mom didn't come home. Even if Aunt Helen stayed, he would fall apart.

Lost in her thoughts, Phee only now noticed that Jungen had continued to the rear of the house and was about to pass right by her hiding spot. Taking care not to rustle any branches, she lowered her head further and held her breath. She listened to the swish of his pant cuffs against the grass, the slight creak and rub as whatever he was carrying under the tarp shifted in his arms. When she was sure he was past her, she counted to five then let out her breath and looked up.

Jungen was out of sight. Mrs. Risborough hadn't moved from beside his truck. Phee could tell from her stiff back and folded arms that she was still mad.

The front door opened. Rusty stood outlined in the light spilling out from the foyer.

"Mom! Are you out there?" He leaned forward, peering into the darkness. "Whose truck is that?"

"The neighbors are having a party. I said their guests could park in our driveway. Now go inside. You're letting all the heat out."

Rusty hesitated. "Grandma wanted me to find you."

Mrs. Risborough sighed. "Fine. Go inside and tell her I'm coming."

Phee's heart, which had been throbbing as fast as a hummingbird's, slowed a few beats as Rusty disappeared into the house and Mrs. Risborough climbed the front steps. Phee's heart sped up again when Mrs. Risborough paused on the threshold and swept her gaze across the yard and street like a lighthouse beam. Phee closed her eyes again, waiting for the command to come out of her hiding place. But all she heard was the nighttime quiet, followed by the sound of the door closing.

Chapter 35

Phee opened the door to the kitchen, breathless from the dash across Mrs. Heckler's yard. She'd decided not to wait for Jungen to come back to his truck. It was getting colder and who knew how long he'd be? She thought about what might be under the tarp. Snowboards maybe? But why would he be bringing those to Mrs. Heckler's garage? *More weirdness from weird people*, Phee thought as she closed the door and felt her heart slow.

Wafting through the room was the aroma of garlic, tomatoes, and herbs. It smelled so good, her stomach growled. She thought about changing out of her damp clothes, but ended up beelining for the dining room, where she could hear the sounds of the family at dinner.

Her dad sat at the head of the table with a twin at each side. If the twins sat next to each other, Brooklyn would tease Scout, Scout would retaliate by poking him, Brooklyn would yell that Scout had hit him, and the dinner rolls would be flying. Zane always sat beside Scout, and Phee's place was beside Brooklyn.

Tonight, Zane's chair was empty. Aunt Helen was jammed between Phee's dad and Scout at the table's corner. It would have been more comfortable for her to sit where Phee's mom usually sat at the opposite end of the table. Phee's dad had suggested Aunt Helen sit there the first day she arrived, but she'd declined, saying she preferred the corner next to one of the twins. Phee was glad Aunt Helen hadn't sat in her mom's place. The chair was angled away from the table as though Phee's mom had just gotten up and the chair cushion was still dented in the shape of her bottom. Phee squeezed her eyes shut for a moment then took her own seat.

"Sorry I'm late," she said.

"Another child present and accounted for," her dad said as he handed her a bowl of vegetables over Brooklyn's head. An empty wineglass was in front of him, with dribbles of red inside. A half full bottle stood beside it. Her dad didn't drink much, usually only on holidays and celebrations. He said wine gave him a headache.

"You look cold, sweetie," Aunt Helen said.

"I ran outside to check the mail," Phee said.

"You were looking for your lover boy," Brooklyn said. He made kissing noises.

Scout studied her sister. "You have a branch in your hair."

"I know. It's for decoration."

"I want one!" Scout said. Phee patted her head until she found the twig. She pulled it out and handed it to her sister. Scout stuck it behind her ear.

"Can I have dessert first?" Brooklyn said.

"No," Aunt Helen said.

"It's got four vitamins," Phee said. "C, A, K, and E."

"You're not helping," her dad said.

Phee took a spoonful of carrots and peas. There used to be broccoli in the mix, too, judging from Brooklyn's plate. He'd arranged about fifteen flowerets into a little forest. A toy knight was balanced on the plate's rim.

"Look, Phee," Brooklyn said. "It's King Arthur and Sherwin Forest."

"Sherwood," their dad said, refilling his wineglass. Aunt Helen reached for the bottle but he moved it out of her reach.

"Sherwin," Brooklyn insisted.

Phee's dad drank some wine, grimaced, and drank some more.

"Phee, do you know where Zane is?" Aunt Helen said.

"Nope." Most evenings her older brother didn't eat dinner with them—sports practice, a friend's house, or the library, he said. (Phee always rolled her eyes at the last one. She knew *library* meant hanging out with Carly Heppleson.) Their dad usually didn't eat with them, either, unless their mom was away on one of her trips.

Phee helped herself to a slice of lasagna. Meals had improved with Aunt Helen's arrival. She took a bite. "What's in this?" she asked.

"Tomatoes," Aunt Helen said. "Cheese, herbs, olive oil . . . " She waved her hand. "It's your mom's recipe."

"There's something wrong with the hamburger part," Phee said. She took another mouthful. "It's soft and mushy."

"It's not hamburger. I used tofu instead."

Phee stopped chewing. The mouthful of lasagna felt like a lump of papier-mâché paste. She forced herself to swallow and took a drink of water.

"Don't you like it?" Aunt Helen said. "It's healthier than hamburger."

"Healthy? Ew!" Brooklyn said. He galloped the knight through the broccoli forest and into the wedge of lasagna. "Help, I'm stuck!" he said in a high voice.

Phee thought about her escape from the Hecklers. "It's quicksand," she said.

"Quicksand!" Brooklyn crowed. The knight was immediately submerged in a tomato-and-tofu quagmire.

"Quicksand!" Scout echoed. She mashed her hair twig into her dinner.

"Brooklyn, Scout, Phee—that's enough!" her dad said.

"Sorry," Phee said. Her eyes fell on the toy knight. His horse had its nose stuck in Brooklyn's lasagna and there was a piece of broccoli tree on his head.

Phee's insides started to shake—another laugh attack. They always hit at the worst times, like at church or in front of the boy you liked. Or the dinner table when her dad was mad.

She clenched her jaw shut. *Don't laugh. Don't don't DON'T—*

Giggles burbled up, quickly turning into guffaws. Brooklyn and Scout gaped at her.

"Phee's going crazy!" Brooklyn announced. He hit his fork against the table. "Cra-zy, cra-zy."

"Cra-zy!" Scout echoed.

Phee clutched her stomach and howled. Tears ran down her face. She didn't know what was so funny. The food-encrusted toy certainly wasn't. But as she laughed, she felt some of the tension and fear—about her mom, Chord, Kimiko—evaporate.

"Phee! Stop it!" her dad said in that voice again, the one that had astonished them before. It worked. The twins quieted and looked at him with wide eyes.

"It's not me, it's Brooklyn!" Phee said. She felt the urge to cry again, but not happy tears.

Her dad shook his finger at Phee, something he'd never done before. "You're supposed to set an example for your little brother. With everything that's happening, I expect you—"

Aunt Helen laid her hand on his other arm. "It's my fault, Brad." Phee's dad looked at his sister as though he'd just noticed she was there. "I should have remembered not everyone likes tofu."

Phee's dad lowered his hand. His shoulders slumped, making his shirt look too big. Aunt Helen patted his arm. "It's going to be okay," she said softly, then looked around the table. "Who's ready for dessert?"

"Meeeee!" chorused Brooklyn and Scout.

Phee heard the outside door to the kitchen bang open. A moment later Zane ran into the room. His shirt was half tucked in and his usually carefully gelled hair was mussed. Tears streaked his cheeks. *Drama day at the Mahoneys*, Phee thought.

"Zane! What's wrong?" Their dad stood and grasped Zane by the shoulders. Phee had never seen her tough big brother cry, not even when he was twelve and broke his wrist snowboarding.

"I can't believe it, Dad," he said. "They said he might die!"

Chapter 36

"Who might die?" Phee's dad said. "What are you talking about?"

Chord, Phee thought. *They found Chord.* She pushed her chair away from the table. She had to call Kimiko. Her brother's next words stopped her in her tracks.

"Johnny," Zane said.

"Johnny Mercer?" she said.

"Who's that?" Scout said.

"Phee's boyfriend," Brooklyn said.

"Shut up!" Phee snapped at her little brother. "He's not my boyfriend!"

Tears welled up in Brooklyn's eyes. Phee yelling at him was more unexpected than his dad raising his voice.

Aunt Helen rose. "I heard there's peppermint ice cream in the freezer. Brooklyn, isn't that your favorite?"

He nodded, his face still scrunched up as he struggled with the decision whether or not to cry.

"I like peppermint, too," Scout announced.

"Then let's go get some," Aunt Helen said.

Aunt Helen took Brooklyn's hand and led him and Scout out of the room.

Phee felt bad about yelling at Brooklyn, but she'd make it up to him later. "What happened to Johnny?" she said as soon as the twins were out of earshot.

"They found him in a ditch beside the road. He'd crashed his hand bike," Zane said. His words poured through Phee like boiling water, scalding her heart.

"Where is he now?" their dad said.

"At the hospital. I guess he couldn't get out of the ditch by himself and he couldn't reach his cell phone. He lay there a long time before someone finally came along and called nine-one-one."

"I want to go see him," Phee said.

"Me and Austin tried to, but the nurse wouldn't let us in." Zane's voice was thick. "She said he was in a coma."

"I don't care. Dad, will you drive me?"

"Honey, I'm not sure that's a good idea. Why don't we wait and—"

"No! I'm sick of waiting, sick of not doing anything!" As soon as she saw the expression on her dad's face, she wished she could take the words back. She wanted to say she wasn't talking about her mom, she really wasn't.

Her dad was quiet for a moment, then said, "Get your coat. Zane, stay here with Aunt Helen and the twins."

"But he's my friend!" Zane said. "I want to—"

Their dad's voice was firm. "I'll call you if there's any news."

Phee and her dad drove to the hospital in silence. In addition to her coat, Phee wore her pom-pom hat. She gazed out the side window, her eyes unfocused. Snow, bushes, mailboxes all went by in a blur.

The hospital waiting room was crowded. Phee saw several members of Zane's baseball team and some of his friends from school. There was a man wearing a red-white-and-blue jacket with USA PARALYMPICS stenciled on the back. She didn't recognize most of the people, but from their whispered comments and questions, she knew they were there for Johnny.

A man and a woman about the age of Phee's parents sat in chairs in the middle of the room. Their faces were drawn and their clothes rumpled. There were half a dozen empty Styrofoam coffee cups on the table beside the woman. Her eyes were shut and she had her hands clasped in her lap. Phee thought she might be praying. The man sat hunched over with his elbows on his knees, tearing one of the cups into bits that he let fall onto the floor.

A nurse came through the door beside the reception desk. "Mr. and Mrs. Mercer?"

The woman's eyes snapped open. She got to her feet. The man dropped the cup and joined her. A hush fell over the rest of the room.

"How is he?" the woman said in a voice raw with eagerness and dread.

"Would you please come with me? The doctor would like to speak with you."

Mrs. Mercer gave an anguished cry and sagged against her husband. "Oh, God. Is he—"

"Oh, no, ma'am," the nurse said quickly. Everyone else had stopped talking and was listening to the conversation. "Would you come with me, please? It's more private in here."

After the Mercers left with the nurse, conversations picked up again. *I heard his dog got help . . . why would he go out when the road . . . swelling on the brain . . . .* Phee tried to eavesdrop on them all. Her head ached.

"I don't think you'll be able to see Johnny tonight," her dad said. Phee was inclined to agree. But she wanted Johnny to know she'd been there.

"I'm going to leave him a note," she said. Her dad produced a pen and she got a piece of paper from the receptionist. She sat in a corner and thought about what to write. She didn't want to sound too mushy or like she was crushing on him. She finally scribbled, *Hope you and Kirby are OK. Phee.*

She took the note to the receptionist. "Could you give this to Johnny Mercer?"

The receptionist smiled at her. "I'll be sure to put it with his chart."

Phee rejoined her dad. *Hope you and Kirby are OK*—could she have sounded more lame? She was debating whether or not to ask for her note back when the automatic doors to the ER wheezed open. Sheriff Allerd walked in. He spoke to the receptionist, then walked over to the water cooler and poured himself a cup of water.

He glanced around the waiting room as he drank, his eyes stopping when he came to Phee and her dad. He drained the last of the water, lobbed the cup into the wastebasket, then walked their way. People asked questions as he passed. He brushed them all off: "I know what you know, probably less . . ." ". . . a time to respect the family's privacy . . . "

When he reached Phee and her dad, he said, "Brad, may I have a moment with your daughter?"

Phee's dad frowned. "What's this about, Curtis?"

The sheriff lowered his voice. "She may have information about what happened to Johnny Mercer."

Chapter 37

Phee and her father followed Sheriff Allerd down a corridor, past a doctor dictating into his smartphone and an orderly pushing a boy with a leg cast in a wheelchair. They stopped at a nurse's station, where half a dozen people in hospital uniforms filled out paperwork or typed on computers. One nurse talked on the phone, facing away from Phee, knuckling the small of her back like it hurt.

Sheriff Allerd introduced himself to the woman behind the ALL VISITORS CHECK IN HERE sign on the counter. She wore pink scrubs and a nametag that said CHERRY. Phee wondered what it would be liked to be named after a color. Or did the women's parents just like the fruit? She was glad her dad hadn't yet discovered mangoes were his favorite by the time she was born.

"I understand there's an empty conference room I can borrow near here," the sheriff said.

Cherry pointed. "Two doors down on the left." The nurse on the phone finished her call and turned around.

Phee's dad said, "Kathryn?"

The nurse who'd been on the phone went still, her eyes darting between them. It was Mrs. Risborough.

"It's Brad, Brad Mahoney," Phee's dad said.

Mrs. Risborough smoothed the front of her white uniform. "I'm sorry, I didn't recognize you."

"It's been a while. My daughter tells me that you and Rusty have moved back to Bristlecone."

"We're just here for a little while." Mrs. Risborough propped both hands on her hips and grimaced. "Long enough to make the arrangements for my mother to go into assisted care and sell the house."

"I'm sorry, I didn't know."

"She's been fading for a while. It just isn't safe for her to live by herself any longer."

Phee frowned. Mrs. Heckler was doing fine. Maybe she couldn't drag the trash cans out to the curb and occasionally mixed Phee up with her mother, but that didn't mean she had to move into a nursing home.

"When are you leaving?' Phee said.

"Phee!" her dad said.

"It's all right," Mrs. Risborough said. "Sometime next week. Depends on how fast the lawyers can finish things. The hospital's been good about letting me pick up a few shifts in the meantime."

Was a lawyer the same thing as a notary public? Phee didn't think so.

Sheriff Allerd cleared his throat. Phee's dad started, as though he'd forgotten the sheriff was standing there.

"Kathryn, do you know Sheriff Allerd? Sheriff, this is Kathryn Risborough. She lives—used to live—next door to us."

"You're Irene Heckler's daughter? Sorry to hear she's not doing well. If you're out of town and ever concerned, we're happy to stop by and do a welfare check. Just give the station a call."

"Um, yes, but that won't be . . . she's moving . . . with us, I mean." Mrs. Risborough took a breath. "Thank you."

Another nurse approached. "Kathryn, I'm sorry to interrupt. I noticed you were busy so I did the hourly check on your patients. Mrs. Liu and Mr. Grimaldi are both complaining of pain."

"Did you check their charts? Their doctors ordered pain meds for both of them."

"I saw them. And when I *read their charts*, I also saw you'd administered the meds two and a half hours ago. They have to wait another ninety minutes before their next dose."

"Right. Sorry. I'll leave a note for their doctors about increasing the doses." Mrs. Risborough turned to Phee's dad. "Brad, it was nice to see you. I'd better get back to my patients."

"Of course." Phee's dad and the sheriff said their good-byes to Mrs. Risborough, then continued down the hall. Phee stayed where she was.

"I found your glove," she said to Mrs. Risborough. "The red one."

Mrs. Risborough frowned. "My glove? I wasn't aware I'd lost it." She shifted her weight from one foot to the other.

"At the store near the pharmacy section Wednesday night."

Mrs. Risborough put on a puzzled look. "I wasn't at the pharmacy on Wednesday."

First the guy at Trent and now Rusty's mom. Did they think just by telling Phee she hadn't seen them that she'd believe them? "Whatever. I'll drop it by later."

"You don't need to do that. I'm happy to come by." Mrs. Risborough backed away from the counter. "Just leave the glove on the bench by your front door and I'll pick it up." She retreated to the far end of the counter and began flipping through patients' charts.

"Phee? You coming?" Her dad stood in front of an open doorway.

"Yeah."

She walked down the corridor to where he waited. At the doorway, she looked back. Mrs. Risborough had stopped reading charts. She was staring at them—more precisely, at Phee.

Chapter 38

The room the sheriff had chosen was furnished with a fake wood table and teal plastic chairs that had seats molded in the shape of a person's bottom. There were no windows. With the three of them in there and the door closed, Phee felt slightly claustrophobic.

She sat in one of the chairs, her dad in another. The sheriff propped a hip up on the table, facing them, and folded his arms.

"What could my daughter possibly know about what happened to the Mercer boy?" Phee's dad said. He put his arm around Phee's shoulder and squeezed. He did it too tightly, but Phee didn't shrug him off. "What *did* happen, anyway?"

"Johnny Mercer was found near the top of Deer Mountain Road in the ditch. Looks like a car hit him."

Phee gasped. "Again?" she whispered.

"Afraid so. He might still be lying out there if his dog hadn't found some hikers and herded them over."

"I still don't see how this involves Phee," her dad said.

"I understand she talked to him this morning," the sheriff said.

"Phee?" her dad said, turning to her.

"Zane did, too!" she said, feeling defensive.

"And neither of you did anything wrong," Sheriff Allerd said. "I was just wondering if you saw which way he went after he left your house."

"He went to the corner, then turned up Deer Meadow."

Deer Meadow Road wound its way up the mountain that rose behind the Mahoneys' neighborhood, dead-ending at the top. It was a strip of asphalt so tilted, skiers often schussed down it after a fresh snow. It had lots of blind curves, hardly any shoulder, and no pullouts. Other than cyclists who used it to practice climbing and people who lived in the half dozen houses hidden among the trees, hardly anyone ever went up there. Even the mailman didn't; at the bottom of the hill was a collection of mailboxes where he deposited the residents' mail.

"Did you take the bus this morning?"

"Yes," Phee said.

"Do you remember any cars going up Deer Meadow while you were waiting for the bus?"

"No."

"So you think this is a hit-and-run?" Phee's dad said.

"Looks that way. One of my deputies found some metal and glass that may have come from the vehicle that hit Johnny." The sheriff wiped a hand over his face. There were bags under his eyes and he needed a shave. "Well, I'd better let you two get home."

Phee's dad stood. He and the sheriff shook hands, then he looked down at Phee. "Let's go, honey."

Phee didn't get up. "This was a crime, not an accident," she said.

"Technically, you're right," the sheriff said. "Even if someone didn't intend to hit Johnny, it's illegal to flee the scene."

Phee folded her arms. "I mean, someone hit him on purpose."

Chapter 39

"Honey," her dad said. "I'm sure the sheriff doesn't need—"

"It's okay," Sheriff Allerd said. "I'd like to hear her theory." He took a notebook and small pencil from his shirt pocket.

Theory, Phee thought, pleased. That's what detectives said on TV. She waited while he opened the notebook to a clean page, then said, "First you'd have to be blind not to have seen Johnny on the road." She described his fluorescent green jacket and bike helmet, Kirby's neon booties, the neon orange flag attached to the hand bike. "There is no way someone driving a car would miss seeing him, especially against all that white snow."

The sheriff regarded her with eyes bluer than Peter's—the blue of Arctic icebergs, and just as chilly. "If someone looks away for just an instant, texting or changing the song on their cell phone, that's all it would take," he said.

Phee pressed her lips together and shook her head like Scout did when anyone tried to feed her applesauce. "No way. The ditch is at the end of the road."

"And . . .?" the sheriff prompted.

"The road is flat and straight for a long way before it goes past the ditch. Even if you read a text *and* changed a song, you still would've seen Johnny ahead of you. It wasn't even snowing today. Someone hit him on purpose."

The sheriff's cell phone rang. He unclipped it from his belt and checked the display. "Excuse me for a minute." He moved toward the door to take the call.

"Allerd," he said, then listened. "Send Deputy Ramos to check it out." Another pause. "I've got a hit-and-run victim here." His voice was louder than it was before. "Deputy Ramos is more than qualified to take a burglary report. I don't care if Kolata is a campaign supporter. Give him back his contribution if he wants! I can't leave here for a few stolen auto parts!"

Phee shifted in the chair. She felt funny eavesdropping but it wasn't like she had a choice. Kolata, she guessed, was Mel Kolata's dad, who owned the auto parts store in town. Mel had one of those cardboard pine trees hanging in his locker and his bike was covered with NASCAR stickers.

"Fine," Sheriff Allerd said. "I'll call him as soon as I'm finished here." He ended the call, returned the phone to his belt, and resumed leaning against the table.

"Do you know anyone who would want to hurt Johnny?" the sheriff asked.

"No," Phee said. "But I barely know him. You should ask his friends."

"Who are they?"

"Well, my brother knows him. And I guess everyone else on the baseball team." She spread her hands. "I don't really know his friends, either."

The sheriff closed his notebook. He hadn't written anything down.

"We'll certainly look into all possibilities. Thank you for your time." He got up, opened the door, and waited for them to walk out.

Phee knew from his attitude he hadn't believed her, but it was stupid for her to keep sitting there. She got up and walked out. Her dad stopped at the door and spoke to the sheriff in a low voice. Phee caught a few words.

Still no word . . . hard on the kids . . . overreaction . . .

Phee's cheeks got warm, like she was sitting too close to a fireplace. She wasn't being a drama queen because her mom was missing. The sheriff was *under*reacting.

That was the trouble with living in a place like Bristlecone, the "safe, family-friendly gateway to the Colorado Rockies," according to the billboard off the highway on the Denver side. Bad things weren't supposed to happen there. So teachers, parents, even the sheriff got in the habit of expecting the good and overlooking the bad.

And when something bad did come along, nobody could see it.

Chapter 40

Her dad's cell phone rang when they were in the lobby.

"Helen, they know they're supposed to take turns. Put Brooklyn on." A passing nurse pointed at the No Cell phones sign and frowned. Phee's dad nodded and started for the automatic doors. "Brooklyn? Friday is your sister's night to choose which movie to watch." He tipped the phone away from his mouth. "I'll take this outside, then we can go," he whispered to Phee. "Wait in here. It's warmer."

She leaned against the wall and tucked her hands into the pockets of her jacket. Her fingers found a round plastic bottle—Mrs. Risborough's pills. She'd acted so weird about Phee finding her glove, she would have probably freaked out if she knew Phee had been in her house looking through her stuff.

After making sure no one was watching, she took the bottle out of her pocket and looked at the label. OxyContin. She walked to the reception desk, where a large-sized woman in a blue nurse's top printed with bears sat behind a desk, typing.

Without looking up from her computer screen, the woman said, "Have your mom or dad fill out the intake form and bring it back here." On the counter in front of Phee was a stack of clipboards with forms attached.

"Oh, I don't have to see a doctor."

The woman continued to type. "Visiting hours are from ten to two. This area is for waiting patients only. There's a lounge—"

"Do you have a book on drugs?"

The woman stopped typing and shifted her gaze to Phee. "Drugs?"

"I need to look something up."

"Our reference library is for doctors only. Is this a drug you're taking?"

"No. A, um, friend is."

The woman regarded her. "What do you want to know about this drug?"

Phee shrugged, feigning nonchalance. "What you take it for, and if there are side effects."

The woman frowned. "Is your friend having problems?"

"No, she's fine." Phee backed away from the counter a few steps. "I think I'll just google it."

"What's the drug called?" the woman said.

Phee made a show of remembering. "Oxy, Oxy . . . Oxy-something."

"OxyContin?"

"That's it!"

"How old is your friend who's taking this drug?"

"She's, um, forty."

The woman got up and moved to the counter. Her electric blue nails were the same color as her top. "Are we talking about your mom?" she said in a low voice.

"No!"

The woman plucked a pamphlet from a rack beside her. "There's a number in there for your *friend*"—Phee heard air quotes around the word—"to call if she wants to get help. Even if she doesn't, there's a number for a group that might be helpful for you."

Phee stuffed the pamphlet into her pocket. "Um, thanks." She turned and hurried to the exit doors.

Outside the smell of burning wood was in the air. Phee paused in front of the building to look for her dad. He stood beside their car. He waved.

"Coming!" she called.

She dropped to one knee beside a trash can to tie her shoe—rather, pretended to. Instead, she took out the pamphlet. At the top of the front page was a logo—the letters N and A surrounded by a circle. Below was printed NARCOTICS ANONYMOUS. She tossed the pamphlet into the trash and sprinted for the car.

Chapter 41

Her mom would have believed her theory about what had happened to Johnny, Phee thought as she and her dad headed home. Or at least she would have given it more than ten seconds' consideration. Her mom said scientists looked at facts objectively before drawing their conclusions. They didn't pretend things were one way when they were really another, even if it meant admitting that things—or people—weren't too nice.

Phee's dad didn't think that way. He looked on the bright side, gave people the benefit of the doubt, and thanked store clerks like they'd meant it when they told him to have a good day. He believed the captions on the inspirational posters in the doctor's office.

Phee glanced over at him. He looked like he could use one of his own pep talks. He was staring at the road, shoulders tensed, fists gripping the steering wheel, knuckles white.

She felt a stab of guilt. She'd been thinking only about what it would be like for her to be without her mom. What about for her dad? He was sensitive like Brooklyn, enough that this might change him in a bad way. Phee looked out at the houses flashing by, lit like lanterns, the mountains behind them not really shapes, just a blackness where the stars weren't. Everything sucked right now.

Right before they turned onto their street, her dad said, "I was proud of you for telling your idea to the sheriff."

"Yeah, well, he didn't believe me."

"That isn't the point. You reminded me of your mom. You've got her intelligence, her determination, her independence—all the best parts of her."

Warmth spread through Phee's chest, making her feel better than she had the whole week.

"What about the bad stuff?" she asked, sort of kidding, sort of not.

"There isn't anything bad about her. She marches to her own drummer, and that's a good thing."

When they were home Phee went directly upstairs. She didn't feel like talking to Zane or Aunt Helen about what had happened at the hospital. She changed into her pajamas and went to the bathroom to wash her face and brush her teeth. She closed the door behind her. A fluffy white bathrobe hung on a hook on the back of the door. The robe had always been there, but this was the first time Phee had paid attention to it.

The name of a resort and a gold palm tree were embroidered on the front of the robe. It was her mom's, a souvenir from her trip to Hawaii with Phee's dad. Phee had wanted to go, too, but she, Zane, and the twins had to stay home with Aunt Helen. "It's a second honeymoon," Aunt Helen had told Phee. "No kids allowed."

Phee fingered the material, soft as Homicide's fur when he was a kitten. She stroked her cheek with a sleeve, then gathered the robe to her face and inhaled. It smelled like her mom—the shampoo she liked, the perfume Phee's dad had bought her—at least Phee thought it did. Was she already forgetting how her mom smelled?

Phee closed her eyes and tried to imagine her mom's voice, saying good night, wishing her sweet dreams. After a minute, she opened them. She couldn't do it. Phee thought the memory was there, but it felt like it slipped into a corner of her brain that was just out of reach. She closed her eyes and tried again. Nothing.

She went to bed without brushing her teeth or washing her face.

Chapter 42

Phee woke up early Saturday morning. She rolled up her sleeping bag and stuck it in the closet. She slept in it on top of her furry rug. She hated making her bed, which was one of the few chores her mom was kind of picky about. When her mom was gone, she slept under the covers and left them messy. She'd made her bed Monday morning when she thought her mom was coming home. Since then, she hadn't wanted to sleep in it.

She went to the window. Even though spring was a week away, you wouldn't know it. There was no color anywhere. The tree branches were bare and the snow on the ground was grungy-looking under the pigeon-colored sky.

As though reading her thoughts, a flash of red swooped past the glass and came to rest on a branch in Mrs. Heckler's front yard. A cardinal. As Phee watched the bird preen its feathers, the door to Mrs. Heckler's house opened. Mrs. Risborough emerged, followed by Rusty and Mrs. Heckler. Mrs. Heckler wore her plaid coat and beret. She leaned on Rusty's arm and he walked slowly so she could keep up.

Mrs. Risborough led the way to her rental car parked in the driveway. She unlocked it with the remote and opened the passenger door.

Mrs. Heckler stopped short. She shook her head and pointed at her house while saying something. Mrs. Risborough shook her head, too. She walked up to Mrs. Heckler. Rusty reluctantly let go of his grandmother's arm before Mrs. Risborough seized it.

Mrs. Heckler tried to wriggle out of Mrs. Risborough's grip, but Mrs. Risborough held firm. She pulled Mrs. Heckler forward, the older woman now crying and twisting her body, trying to escape.

Mrs. Risborough didn't shove Mrs. Heckler into the rental car, but she came pretty close. She clipped Mrs. Heckler into her seat belt, shut the door, gestured Rusty into the backseat, and walked around to the driver's side. She was about to get in when she spotted the fallen trellis.

At first she just stared, then she arrowed through the yard, her spine stiff and her step angry. She picked up one of the broken pieces, looked it over, then tossed it back onto the ground. Phee watched, feeling guilty.

Mrs. Risborough returned to the car, her lips pinched. She opened the door to the backseat and said something to Rusty. He slowly got out of the car and stood at the edge of the driveway. Mrs. Risborough got in and backed the car onto the street. Phee glimpsed Mrs. Heckler's pale face at the window. It looked like she was still upset.

The car lurched as Mrs. Risborough shifted into reverse. She backed into the street and sped off, the car's tires slipping on the ice. Rusty gave a little wave as he watched the car go.

After the car turned the corner and was out of sight, Rusty went around the side of the house, returning with the remains of the trellis. He broke the pieces into smaller ones, then broke those into sticks, and stacked them in a neat pile in the driveway. Next he got out some garden stakes and used them to prop up the bushes Phee had squished when she fell.

Phee turned away from the window, thinking about how much it had hurt to fall onto the bushes. She couldn't imagine what it would feel like to be hit by a car. She still believed someone had intentionally run Johnny off the road. How was she going to convince the sheriff?

Her mom's voice whispered in her head. *Investigate. Find the evidence.* At first Phee was so happy to remember what her mom sounded like, she didn't pay attention to the message. When she'd calmed down, she repeated it out loud.

"Investigate. Find the evidence."

It was like her mom had turned on a light in her brain. Before, Phee had been letting other people tell her what to do and what to believe, and spies didn't do that. They found out things for themselves.

Phee rubbed the face of her watch. She was going to figure out who hit Johnny.

Her iPod Touch dinged, signaling the arrival of a text. HAVE 2 BAIL 2DAY ON SCI PRO. PARENTAL UNIT-THING. MEET L8R. K.

Kimiko was bailing *again* on their science project. Annoyed, Phee typed back. MEET 2NITE!! She waited for a response but none came. Kimiko's mom had a fit if Kimiko texted when she was with them, so maybe she was telling the truth—she had to go somewhere with her parents. Or she was figuring out how to tell Phee she didn't want to be Phee's lab partner.

Phee went to her closet to get dressed. Draped on the doorknob was her blue-striped T-shirt, the one she'd been wearing when Peter Allerd kissed her. Thinking about him made her stomach feel funny. She thought about tossing the shirt into her dirty clothes pile but instead hung it in the back of her closet. After pulling on a pair of navy jeggings and a Broncos sweatshirt, she stood in front of the mirror on her door and braided her hair. Scotch-taped to a corner of the glass was a photo of her and Kimiko. They were eating cotton candy at the state fair. Kimiko had her mouth open wide and Phee was feeding her a chunk of the spun sugar. Phee took a pen and turned two of Kimiko's teeth into fangs.

Feeling a little better, she opened her bedroom door and ran smack into Brooklyn.

Chapter 43

"Ow!" he said as he sat down hard on the floor.

Brooklyn and Scout loved to invade Phee's room. "It's what little brothers and sisters are supposed to do," Brooklyn had said the last time she caught the twins playing dress-up with her clothes. Phee explained that real-life brothers and sisters weren't supposed to act like the obnoxious ones on TV, but the invasions had continued. Maybe she should ask her dad to install a lock.

"What did I say about going into my room?" Phee said.

Brooklyn looked up at her. "Where's your baby?"

"I gave him back."

His eyes grew wide. "Why? Didn't you like him?"

"I only had to take care of him for a little while. Now it's someone else's turn."

His brow went crinkly. "Do you think Mom wants to give me and Scout back?"

Phee kneeled beside him. "No. Why would you say that?"

"Because she doesn't want to come home!" Tears rolled down his cheeks.

"Oh, Brooklyn, she wants to come home. She just can't yet."

"Is Mom dead?" His words sliced through the air, taking Phee's breath—and voice—away. The twins were growing up faster than she'd thought.

"I don't know. I hope not."

Phee watched the emotions flicker across his face—denial, anger, sadness—and for a moment regretted not telling him a lie. But truth was better in the long run. She hugged him and smelled his boy smell—sweat and dirt and milk and cereal. He pulled away and stood.

"If she comes home, do you think she'll bring me a kangaroo?" he said.

Phee laughed. "I don't know. Maybe."

Brooklyn held his hands in front of his chest, elbows bent, and hopped down the hall. Phee watched him go. She wished she could switch her brain from sad to happy like that.

Aunt Helen sat at the kitchen table with Scout. Pancake rims were stacked on the plate in front of Scout, who didn't eat the edges of pancakes, waffles, or bread. She tore out the middle and ate only that.

"Your dad left early this morning," Aunt Helen said.

"He's going to get Mom!" Scout said.

"He's going to Australia," Aunt Helen corrected.

"Why didn't he say good-bye?" Phee said.

"It was the middle of the night when he decided to go. He didn't want to wake you all up." Aunt Helen stood and began clearing the table. "He wanted me to tell you there's a candlelight vigil for your friend Chord tomorrow. It's up on the mountain after some snowboard thing."

"The championships," Phee said, remembering what Chord had said. "He wanted to compete."

"I'll drive you if you'd like. Let me have that, sweetie," Aunt Helen said to Scout, taking the squeeze bottle of maple syrup from her.

"But I was making art!" Scout said, pointing at the flowers drawn in syrup on her plate.

"Why don't you use a crayon and some paper? That way we can hang them up."

Scout slid off her chair and headed for the cupboard where the art supplies were kept.

"I don't know if I want to go," Phee said.

The door to the garage opened and Zane came in. He was dressed in his snowboard gear—oversized lime green and orange jacket, orange turtleneck, and olive cargo ski pants. White earbud cords snaked up through his jacket collar and were draped around his neck.

"Go where?" he said as he opened the refrigerator and grabbed four cans of Mountain Dew.

"Chord's candlelight vigil," Phee said.

Zane looked at her. "Did they find his body?"

"I don't know."

"But they're sure he's dead."

"I don't know!"

"Fine, Miss Cranky. By the way, Johnny woke up. They think he's going to be okay."

Phee dropped the pancake rim she'd been nibbling. "When? What does *okay* mean?"

"Do I look like a doctor?" Zane said as he headed for the pantry.

Phee barred his way, arms folded. "I want to go see him."

"You can't. Austin and me checked—no visitors." Zane reached around Phee and took a bag of Chips Ahoy! cookies from the shelf. "Gold had some big power failure overnight," he said to Aunt Helen as he added two bananas to his haul. "Nationals were moved to Silver. They're doing boardercross today. Austin and I are going up."

"What time will you be back?" Aunt Helen said.

"I dunno," Zane said. "Five maybe? If it's about dinner, I'll eat on the mountain." Carrying his provisions, he shouldered through the door, leaving it open.

The garage door was open, too, and Phee could see Austin's pickup parked in their driveway. Austin stood beside the truck, lifting Zane's snowboard into the bed. Someone sat on the passenger side of the front seat. The glare made it impossible for Phee to recognize who it was. But there was something about the hair . . . .

Kimiko.

Chapter 44

Zane and Austin were adjusting the bindings on a snowboard at the workbench in the garage.

"We got more girl's stuff from that house," Zane said. "Lots of pink."

"I hate pink," Phee said.

"Fine. Just wanted to give you first pick before it went on eBay. I'd give you the special sister price."

"You mean more than you'd charge everyone else?"

"I'm trying to be a nice brother and this is what I get?" Zane said with mock indignation.

"Hey, Phee," Austin said.

"Um, hi," Phee said. Zane's friends usually ignored her.

"You riding with us?" Austin said.

Zane looked at Austin like he'd just announced he'd decided to skip snowboarding and read math textbooks instead. "She doesn't know how."

"Thanks, but I gotta work on my science project." Phee said the last two words extra loud for Kimiko's benefit.

If Kimiko wasn't her friend anymore, who was Phee going to talk to about Peter? About how to let a guy know you liked him back without becoming all clingy and stalkerish? *Teen Vogue*, which she only read at Kimiko's house because Phee's mom said it Photoshopped the models to look too thin, said if a guy likes you and you like him back, at the beginning you should ignore him. But how did the guy know if you were fake-ignoring or real-ignoring? How long were you supposed to do it?

She stalked up to Austin's car. If you didn't have a BFF, it didn't matter if a guy liked you or not.

Kimiko had pulled her ski hat over her face and scrunched down in the seat. Phee tapped on the window. "I'm not blind, you know."

Kimiko pulled off the hat and sat up.

Phee opened her door and eyed Kimiko's clothes—white Ed Hardy jacket decorated with skulls, and red pants. "I didn't know your mom was a Betty, too. Or does your dad ride? You guys meeting him on the mountain?"

Kimiko didn't meet her eyes. "The thing got cancelled."

Phee held up her phone. "You were in the car with Austin when you texted me!" She wasn't shouting, but pretty close. Austin looked up at the mention of his name. Phee lowered her voice and said, "Why don't you just say it?"

"Say what?" Kimiko kept her head down, seemingly engrossed in zipping and unzipping the backpack on her lap.

Phee's whisper was fierce. "That you hate me!"

Kimiko's head jerked up. "What are you talking about?"

"You blew off hanging out, tubed the science project, and lied about being with your parents. I get the hint."

Kimiko's face went tight. "I don't hate you." The backpack slipped from her fingers and tipped over. Energy bars, sandwiches, and cans of Mountain Dew spilled through the unzipped opening onto the dirty snow. Kimiko got out of the car and scrambled to stuff everything back in. Phee watched, too mad to help her but feeling a little mean about it. When the pack was zipped up and re-stowed in the car, Kimiko stood in front of Phee. She was almost five inches shorter, so she had to tilt her face up and squint against the sun.

"I don't hate you," she said again. "There's stuff going on, stuff you don't know about."

"So tell me."

"I can't!"

"Why not? I'm your best friend!"

Kimiko dropped her eyes. "Maybe we need to take a break."

Phee felt as though an icicle had stabbed her in the heart. She tried to speak but couldn't.

Seeing Phee's expression, Kimiko added quickly, "Just, like, for a few days."

Phee found her voice. "A few days? Why not a few weeks? A few months? Tell you what—let's make it forever." She started down the driveway, then stopped and turned. "In case you were wondering, you're gonna look bad in pink." She resumed walking.

"Phee, wait!" Kimiko said.

"And I hope you eat all that food and get fat," she yelled over her shoulder.

Phee turned right when she hit the street. She didn't know where she was going. But she couldn't go back through the garage, at least not when Austin and Zane were there. She didn't want them to see her crying.

Chapter 45

Phee broke into a run, partly to keep warm but mostly because she wanted to be as far away from Kimiko as possible. She wished she were a boy. Or back in fifth grade. If two guys were friends, they pretty much stayed that way—*mean boys* wasn't a hot topic in *Seventeen*, another magazine her mom disapproved of. And girls got along when Phee was in elementary school. She and Ashley had their spats and arguments, but they didn't stop being friends.

Everything changed in middle school. Mean girls, cliques, gossip. If you weren't a target, you were worrying about how not to be. It was like every move you made—the clothes you wore, how you answered questions in class, what movies you liked—were graded on a scoreboard that everyone could see. Your score determined how popular you were. But you never knew which choices would add points and which would take them away. And high school was only going to be worse. Phee wondered how her parents felt about homeschooling.

She kept running, circling the block until she was back home. Austin's pickup was gone. The only person she saw was Rusty, trimming Mrs. Heckler's bushes with clippers. She walked to the bottom of his driveway. "Hey," she said.

Rusty stopped trimming and wiped his forehead with his sleeve. Even though it was cold out, he was sweating. "Hey."

Phee hoped he hadn't heard her fight with Kimiko. "What're you doing?"

Rusty gestured with the shears. "A bear tried to break into our house last night. He ripped down the trellis and tore up the garden. My mom told me to fix it."

"A bear?" Phee didn't know if she should laugh or be insulted.

"A big old fat one! It sat on our bushes and crushed them. You should've seen its butt marks."

Definitely insulted. "All the bears are hibernating," she said. In the summer, the occasional brown bear made its way into town. Last summer one got into the Zaleny's house and somehow opened the freezer. Mrs. Zaleny found the bear snoring softly on her kitchen floor surrounded by empty Haagen-Dazs cartons.

"Not this one," Rusty said. He snipped some more branches then stepped back to view his work.

"Now the bush sort of looks like a bear," Phee said.

"It's supposed to look round." He grimaced. "My mom is going to be mad."

"I like it," Phee said.

"Thanks." He set the shears down. "Do you want your backpack and coat?"

Her stuff! She'd forgotten she'd left it at Mrs. Heckler's. "Um, yeah. Thanks."

She followed Rusty inside the house. Her roller backpack and coat were in the front hall closet. She put on the coat and wheeled the pack onto the porch.

"When I saw it, I knew it was yours. I didn't want my mom . . ." His voice trailed off. "Things haven't been all that great for her since my dad left."

Phee thought about Jungen. "Doesn't she have a boyfriend?"

Rusty's eyebrows shot up. "My *mom*? No way."

"I thought I saw a guy come over."

"Last night? He was just here to watch Grandma sign some stuff. My mom doesn't have a boyfriend."

Phee tried to imagine what it would feel like to have someone you thought you'd spend the rest of your life with say he didn't love you anymore. She couldn't. Divorce was one of the grown-up things she was not looking forward to.

"I think being back here reminds her more of the breakup," Rusty said. "It's making her act really weird. Like she has a fit if I go outside, and we have to go to all these different stores to buy groceries."

Phee nodded. Adults did a lot of things that were impossible to understand.

Rusty fidgeted and pursed his lips. "Um . . . ."

"What?"

"I heard about your mom—"

"My dad flew to Australia today to get her," Phee said quickly.

"Cool." Rusty jerked his head toward the garden. "I'd better finish before my mom gets back."

"I can help, if you want." She felt guilty about the carnage caused by her bear-like rampage.

"Well, you could put those sticks next to the trash cans," Rusty said.

Phee gathered up the trellis pieces and carried them into the side yard. Apparently neither Rusty nor Mrs. Risborough knew when trash day was. The cans were filled to overflowing and there was stuff in several movers' boxes stacked against the fence. Phee opened one of them. It was filled with clothes, stuffed into the box haphazardly. Phee shook out several garments. One was a sunny yellow dress she'd seen Mrs. Heckler wear during the summer. Another was a blue dress she wore to church. Under the dresses was a straw hat Mrs. Heckler liked to wear while gardening. Phee tried it on. It was too small and the straw made her head itch.

The next item was a white jacket. Phee held it up. Not a jacket—a lab coat. Phee stared at it. She glanced over her shoulder to make sure Rusty wasn't coming, then rolled up the lab coat and tied it around her waist under her parka.

Phee closed that box and opened the next one. It held greasy rags, some plastic clamshell packaging cut into pieces, a really big lightbulb with a crack in it, and some metal pieces, including a ring about the size of a dinner plate and a handful of screws. She jammed the trellis sticks into the box, then wove the flaps shut with the sticks protruding through the gaps on top.

Rusty would need more cardboard boxes for the branches he'd pruned. Mrs. Risborough would probably want him to use old ones. Phee walked to the back of the house and tried the door to the garage. Locked. She walked around to the front and tried to pull up the overhead door. It wouldn't move.

"Hey, Rusty! How do I get in the garage?" she yelled. A moment later, he appeared at the side of the house. His eyes were wide.

"You can't go in there!" he said.

"I was looking for some more box—"

"I mean it. My mom will have a fit. The garage is off-limits."

"Why? Is there a dead body inside?"

"You'd better get going. My mom and grandma are going to be home any second."

"Rusty, I was just kidding."

"I wasn't." He herded her to the front of the house, with Phee keeping her arms folded over her middle so the lab coat would stay put. When they reached the porch, Rusty thrust the handle of her backpack at her.

"See ya," he said tersely. "Thanks for the help."

"Look, I'm sorry if I—"

"I have to finish here."

"Got it. Later." She dragged the wheeled bag down the driveway, one hand still pressed to her middle.

Rusty watched her go. "Later," he echoed without much enthusiasm.

Chapter 46

Phee dumped her backpack on the floor of her room and took off her parka. She untied the lab coat from around her waist and laid it on her bed. It reminded her of her mom. After smoothing out some of the wrinkles, she carefully refolded the garment and slid it between the top and bottom mattresses. Someone like Sheriff Allerd could find it but she hoped Scout and Brooklyn wouldn't.

She sat at her desk and doodled with her new gel pen. She drew a sports car with no roof and a girl wearing a pom-pom hat behind the wheel. It would be fun to drive a convertible when it was snowing, to feel the flakes falling on you. Could you get covered with the stuff so it'd look like a snowman was driving? She wrote PHEE in fancy script and PETER under it, then drew a heart around both names. Appalled, she immediately erased everything, tore it into bits, and threw them into the trash.

How was she going to prove to Peter's dad that someone had hit Johnny intentionally? *The Master Spy Handbook* was on the blotter in front of her. Beside it was a photo of Phee and her mom, taken in Wyoming. They wore matching archaeological hats—that's what Phee called the khaki floppy brims—and smears of white sunscreen on their noses. Phee and Zane had been brought along to see a dinosaur skeleton that was found when the company their mom worked for was drilling for oil.

"How do you know where the oil is?' Phee had asked. The barren land stretched away in every direction, all looking pretty much the same.

"We study the geography, do soil tests, research the geological history," her mom had said. "After all the evidence is in, we decide if it's enough to start drilling."

Spies, scientists, sheriffs—they all looked for clues. If Phee was right about what had happened to Johnny, she had to find the evidence to support it.

Phee went downstairs. Aunt Helen was tidying up the family room, putting the twins' toys away.

"Mom makes them do that," Phee said.

Aunt Helen straightened up and blew her bangs off her head. "I don't mind. Makes me feel useful."

"Do you think you could drive me to the hospital? I want to see if Johnny's okay."

"Sure, sweetie. Mrs. Barrows just picked up the twins for a playdate so we could leave right now."

Phee gave Aunt Helen directions as she drove. A little after twelve thirty, they pulled to the curb beside the front entrance.

"Do you want me to wait?" she asked.

"That's okay. I can catch the shuttle home." A free shuttle bus roamed the streets of Bristlecone, stopping at the downtown shopping area, each of the schools, the library, the hospital, and the park before heading up the hill toward the residential areas. It was slow because of all the stops, but Phee didn't know how long she'd be at the hospital and didn't want to make Aunt Helen wait.

"Give me a call if you need a ride." Aunt Helen drove away.

Phee went to the reception desk.

"I'd like to see Johnny Mercer," she said to the woman sitting there.

"Are you family?"

She hesitated for only an instant. "I'm his cousin."

They nurse consulted her computer. "He's still in ICU. Your aunt and uncle are in with him now. Only two visitors are allowed at a time. Why don't you have a seat and I'll call you when it's your turn."

Phee sat in the far corner of the waiting room, facing away from the receptionist's desk. She hoped she could avoid seeing her "aunt and uncle."

Phee heard her name called and swiveled in her chair. The receptionist was beckoning her forward. Behind her, Johnny's parents got off the elevator and walked toward the lobby.

Remembering Vinushu's avoidance tactic in gym, Phee stood, pointed to the bathroom, and held up her finger in the universal *just a minute* gesture. She went into one of the stalls, counted to one hundred, washed her hands, and came out. The Mercers were gone.

Following the receptionist's directions, Phee got off the elevator on the third floor. She caught a glimpse of herself in the shiny metal doors. She'd worn the pink hat, taking extra care to arrange it like the Donner Partiers wore theirs. It looked like pink frosting was running off one side of her head. She stuffed the hat in her pocket and walked down the corridor to room 314.

The door was ajar and she peeked in. Johnny lay on the bed, his right leg in a cast. Wires ran from under his hospital gown to various machines that beeped and wheezed. An IV bag dripped something into his arm. He seemed smaller than he had on the ski slope, his cheekbones cutting sharp ridges under his skin. His shock of thick spiky hair looked like a Japanese cartoon character's.

Phee didn't want to wake him up. She was composing a new note in her head, something not so lame this time, when his eyes flickered open and focused on her.

"Hey," he said.

Phee ventured into the room. "Hey."

Johnny looked so pale, she almost expected to see blood pushing through his veins. He had a black eye and a cut on his forehead.

"I hope you brought me some Twizzlers," Johnny said.

Phee frowned in confusion. "No, but I can go get—"

"I'm just kidding. I've only eaten breakfast and already I'm sick of the food here."

"It's bad?"

"Except for the Jell-O. Green's the best."

"No, red rules!"

"I'll order us some." A wire was pinned to his bed with a button on the end. He picked it up and pushed it. A nurse appeared in the doorway a moment later.

"How are we doing?" she said.

"I'm kind of hungry," Johnny said.

"I can get you another breakfast. You didn't eat much of the first."

"I'm thinking Jell-O." He winked at Phee. "One red and one green."

"Coming right up." The nurse left.

"Thanks for coming by. Is Mahoney No Baloney here?"

"He and Austin went to watch nationals," Phee said.

"I forgot they were this weekend. Funny—stuff like that used to be the center of my life." He shifted his gaze to the window and Phee got the sense he was looking at something she wouldn't be able to see.

"I'm sorry," she said quietly.

Johnny turned back to her. "For the first hit-and-run, or the second?" Seeing her expression, he added, "I'm just kidding you. This time hurt a lot less." He gestured at the cast. "I didn't even know I broke my leg until they told me."

"If you don't mind me asking, what happened?"

"I was cruising along on Ridge Road, just past Thistle Lane. Kirby was chasing a squirrel down the center line. One minute I was yelling at him to get out of the road and the next, *bam!* Lights out for me."

"Is Kirby—"

"He's fine. My neighbor is taking care of him. If it weren't for him, I might've frozen to death in that ditch." Johnny grinned. "One of the cops told me the mayor will probably give him a medal."

"Did you hear the car coming?"

"Barely. It sounded more like a scooter. Anyway, I wasn't really looking for cars. Not many use that road, and you'd have to be blind not to see me."

That's what I told the sheriff. "Did you hear the brakes squeal?"

The two creases between Johnny's eyebrows told Phee he was thinking.

"I don't think so, but my attention was on Kirby. I might have pulled away from the shoulder a little bit when I was trying to get him to come. If the sun got in the driver's eyes—"

"It couldn't. That road runs north-south."

"Then maybe the driver swerved to miss Kirby and hit me instead." He spread his hands. "It was an accident. Whoever did it probably freaked out and took off."

Phee took a breath. "Or maybe they hit you on purpose."

"Why would anybody want to do that?"

"Make anybody mad lately?"

Johnny shrugged. "No more than usual."

The nurse returned with Johnny's Jell-Os. She set them on the table beside his bed. "Time for Mr. Mercer to eat and get some rest."

"Five more minutes," Johnny said and flashed the nurse a smile.

"Only five." She looked at Phee. "I'm counting on you to keep track."

"I will," Phee said.

When they were alone again, Johnny handed a red Jell-O to Phee. As they scooped up the jiggly sweetness, he said, "Would you ask Zane to do me a favor?" He pointed at the closet. "My car keys are in my backpack. I left it at the trailhead at the bottom of the hill. I don't want to get a ticket or have it towed. If he could get Austin to drive it to my place or keep it at yours, that'd be great."

"Okay." Phee went to the closet and retrieved the keys. "I'd better go."

"Thanks for coming by." When she was at the door, he called to her. "Phee? This really was just an accident."

Phee forced a smile. "You're probably right." She shut the door behind her, unconvinced.

Chapter 47

Phee caught the Bristlecone shuttle and took a seat in the back. She pulled out her pink hat and put it on. As the bus rumbled among its stops downtown, she thought about what Johnny had said. Was it really an accident? She hadn't spent much time in the area where he was hit. Deer Mountain Road led to Thorne, a small mountain community of shabby houses, old apartment buildings, and double-wide trailers. The residents were aging hippies, people who worked in Bristlecone but couldn't afford to live there, and ski bums. Pot growers, too. Last year two guys from the high school tried to steal a few plants from a patch hidden in the forest that surrounded Thorne. One of them got a face full of buckshot when he hit a tripwire. There were rumors of poisonous snakes tied to trees and bear traps and hidden pits filled with sharp spikes used to guard the plots. Bristlecone parents warned their kids to stay away, which most of the kids were happy to do.

The shuttle approached the trailhead. Johnny's van was parked in the far corner of the mostly empty lot. A yellow piece of paper under a windshield wiper flapped in the breeze. *A parking ticket.*

The shuttle driver called out, "Trailhead?"

"Yes," Phee said. A minute later she was in the parking lot, watching the shuttle leave. It would be another half hour before the next one showed up.

A pair of stroller-pushing fitness moms passed in near-matching workout clothes, talking nonstop. When they were gone, Phee was alone. She walked to the van and pulled the ticket out from under the wiper. The print on the ticket was so tiny, she could barely decipher what it said in places. She couldn't find any references to towing, but that didn't mean it wasn't there in the legal mumbo-jumbo.

Phee started to put the ticket back under the wiper. What if it blew away? Could you go to jail if you didn't pay it? She unlocked the van, climbed in on the driver's side, and stuck the ticket in the middle console. She'd tell Zane it was there.

She pulled the door shut, confident no one would see her because the window tint was so dark. The van's dashboard didn't look all that different from the driving simulation software Zane used to practice. She'd tried it a couple of times, scoring fairly high on steering and speed regulation, less so on reversing, and pretty much a D- when it came to parallel parking.

The software came with fake brake and gas pedals that were plugged in via USB cable to Zane's laptop. Phee wondered what it would be like to drive using only her hands. She stuck the key into the ignition slot and twisted it. The van turned over smoothly but a bell began to ding incessantly. Phee scanned the dashboard for warning lights until she realized it was the seat-belt indicator. She put the belt on and the sound stopped.

She remembered what Johnny had said about the chromed levers extending from the base of the steering column: "Green is the gas and red is the brake."

She shifted from Park to Drive—just like on the software—and pushed on the green lever. The van surged forward. Panicked, she pulled on the red lever. The van slammed to a stop. She killed the ignition and sat, gripping the steering wheel and feeling her heart pound, relieved there hadn't been anything in front of her.

When her pulse slowed, she started the van again. This time, she slowly pushed the green lever forward. The van rolled across the parking lot. Delighted, she grabbed the knob mounted on the steering wheel with her left hand and guided the van in a sweeping circle. She motored to the end of the lot and smoothly pulled on the red lever, bringing the van to a gentle halt.

Phee sympathized with her brother's impatience to drive. It wasn't all that hard. She did some quick math in her head. If she walked up the hill to see where the hit-and-run had happened, it would take her about forty-five minutes each way. If she got Aunt Helen to drive her, that meant waiting fifteen minutes for the shuttle, a ten-minute drive home, then a half hour round-trip. And that was supposing Aunt Helen was free. But if she drove from here, she could get to the accident site and back in less than ten minutes.

She pushed the green lever. The van glided forward. She steered left and then right, the van tracing perfect S's in the unplowed snow. She braked and shifted into park.

Phee knew she was at one of those points where she could make a good decision or a bad one. Even though there were a lot of good reasons to borrow the van, it still fell into the latter category. What had making the "right choice" done for her lately? She'd lost Kimiko as a friend, been ridiculed by the Donner Partiers, and chased out the window by Mrs. Risborough. Besides, her mom wasn't here to find out. Come to think of it, since Phee began middle school, it seemed like her mom's work took her away more than ever.

A mom couldn't get mad at her kid if she wasn't there to set an example, Phee decided. A mom got to be the boss only if she was present to boss her kids around. Now Phee's dad was gone, too, and it was her mom's fault.

There was a pair of neon green-rimmed sunglasses on top of the middle console. Phee put them on. Although the dark-tinted side windows would obscure her identity, she wanted to be sure anyone who saw her through the windshield wouldn't recognize her. She guided the car to the parking lot entrance. There was no traffic in either direction. Phee pushed the green lever and pulled onto the street.

The drive up the hill was anticlimatic. Staying on the road was pretty much like running the driving software. She kept her eye on the speedometer, making sure she stayed five miles under the limit. The lanes were relatively wide, which gave her room to weave a bit as she got used to steering while holding on to the knob mounted to the wheel.

A car passed in the opposite direction and Phee quelled the urge to laugh. She was driving a car!

Almost too quickly, the road leveled off as it traveled across the mountain ridge. She passed the weathered wooden sign that read THORNE—POPULATION 147 (UNLESS WILBUR FORGETS TO CHANGE THE SIGN WHEN HE LEAVES FOR FLORIDA EVERY WINTER). Up here there was more snow on the road. Phee pulled on the green lever, slowing the van to fifteen miles an hour.

It wasn't hard to find where Johnny had gone into the ditch. Just past Thistle Lane, tire tracks cut through the snow, and a discarded flare from the emergency vehicles lay in the middle of the road. Phee slowed even more and guided the van to the edge of the road. The right front wheel thumped off the pavement onto the soft shoulder. She yanked on the red lever and the van stopped. She parked, turned off the engine, and got out.

The van was tilted, the passenger side noticeably lower than the driver's. The right front tire had sunk into a patch of snow. Her dad had done this a time or two in their SUV. All he'd had to do was shift into reverse and the car pulled itself free.

A ditch ran beside the road about ten feet away. Just ahead of where she'd parked, a set of tire tracks showed a car had veered off the pavement into the snow. The driver had stomped on the brakes—the tracks got deeper—and then reversed, the outgoing set of tracks nearly matching the ones that led in.

Phee pushed the sunglasses on top of her head and squatted beside the set of tracks. A thin line ran between them, ending at the ditch. *From Johnny's bike tires.* There was a deep depression where the bike tracks met the ditch, and the snow there was torn up. She walked over to take a closer look.

Footprints, a flat spot—maybe from one of those boards firefighters used?—a bandage wrapper, and dog tracks. Lots of dog tracks, Kirby's frantic circling of his injured master. Something orange showed in the churned-up mud. She scraped away the snow and dirt, uncovering the orange pennant that had flown from the aerial attached to Johnny's hand bike. She wiped it against her pants, leaving a brown-red stain from the mud and—a bitter taste rose in Phee's mouth—*Johnny's blood.*

Phee dropped the flag as though it had burned her. She looked away and forced herself to swallow. Keeping her eyes averted, she backtracked a half dozen steps and baby-stepped down into the ditch, arms extended for balance. The ditch's floor was a good three feet lower than the surrounding ground. Passing traffic wouldn't have seen Johnny lying in the ditch. Phee thought about how scared she had been in the tree well, and Chord had arrived after only a few minutes. She couldn't imagine waiting for hours as it got darker and colder. If she were Johnny, she'd be feeding Kirby steak—or whatever his favorite food was—for the rest of the dog's life.

Phee clambered out of the ditch, walked back to the van, and got in. She grasped the steering wheel and stared down the road toward the buildings and trailers of Thorne half a mile away. It was early afternoon, almost the same time the accident had occurred. The sky was the color of a white T-shirt that had been washed too many times. No doubt about it, no doubt at all—a driver wouldn't have missed seeing Johnny rolling along the side of the road.

Phee started the van, put it in gear, and pushed on the green lever. The van lurched forward and stopped. Phee pushed harder on the green lever. The van didn't move. A high whirring sound, like a chainsaw cutting through wood, whined through the cabin. Remembering her dad's trick, Phee shifted into reverse and pushed the green lever again. The van inched backward. She kept pushing. Suddenly the van roared butt-first onto the pavement.

Zane's driver-training software talked while you were driving, as if you didn't have enough to think about without a mechanical voice yapping away. Where was the robot lady when Phee needed her? *When reversing, turn the wheel the direction you want the vehicle to go.* Or was it the opposite way? Flustered, Phee cranked the wheel to the right.

The van veered in that direction. Phee felt the bump as both rear tires went off the pavement, followed by the front one on the driver's side.

"No, no, no!" Phee wrenched the wheel back to the left. The van zigzagged toward the ditch. Phee let go of the steering wheel. She pulled on the red lever while shifting into drive. The van bucked to a stop. She pushed on the green lever. More whirring. The van didn't budge.

Phee released the green lever, shifted into park, and turned off the engine. She rested her forehead against the steering wheel, closed her eyes, and listened to the tick of the engine in the quiet. One more fail when driving in reverse. But this time it was more than game over.

Johnny's van was stuck.

Chapter 48

The cold cut through her thin jacket as she walked along Ridge Road toward Thorn. *The Master Spy Handbook* listed items that no spy should be without, especially one who might be marooned. Flashlight, hand warmers, space blanket, energy bars—all things Phee would have really appreciated as her toes went numb and her stomach complained of hunger. Rooting through her backpack had turned up only hair bands, some quarters, Chapstick, a dusty half-eaten roll of LifeSavers, a friendship bracelet Ashley had given her—a *long* time ago—and Ms. Vlachos's Koosh ball.

She squeezed the ball, the jelly-like plasma center squirming pleasantly in her hand. She had to figure out how to return it—assuming she didn't die of exposure first. She pulled the pink hat low over her ears, crunched on a LifeSaver, the spearmint stinging her lips, and continued to walk, swinging her arms to try to keep warm.

There was the sound of a car behind her. Phee didn't turn around. After all the stranger-danger lectures, hitchhiking was out of the question and she didn't know anybody in Thorne. As the car passed her, she couldn't help looking over. Staring back at her from the passenger seat was Veronica Swingle.

Without thinking, Phee raised her hand like she was hailing a taxi. She'd never done it but had seen it a million times on TV. To her surprise, the car stopped. As Phee approached, she saw that Veronica and her mother were talking. Actually, it looked like they were arguing, with Veronica waving her hands and her mother shaking her head.

Phee stopped beside the passenger door. Veronica shot a dirty look at her mother before lowering the window.

"What you doing out here?" she said.

Phee wasn't about to tell her the truth. *Investigating Johnny's hit-and-run.* She was tempted to say, *I was out driving and had car trouble.* The coolness of driving would cancel out the dumbness of ending up in the ditch. If only Veronica were there and not her mom, Phee would've said it. Maybe.

"Walking," she said.

"Told you," Veronica said over her shoulder to her mother. The car window started to rise.

"Wait," Veronica's mom said. She leaned toward the window. "It's Ophelia, isn't it?"

Phee nodded. "Hi, Mrs. S-s-swingle," she said, her teeth chattering.

"It's freezing out there and that jacket isn't keeping you warm. Get in and we'll drop you where you're going."

Phee ignored Veronica's glare and climbed into the back.

"The seats are heated," Mrs. Swingle said. "Just push the button."

Phee saw a black dial and cranked it to 5. Moments later warmth rose from the leather, making the backs of her legs tingle. Right then Phee decided any car she bought would have heated seats. Mrs. Swingle's car was a Mercedes, but Phee was pretty sure you could get that feature in less expensive cars, too.

"Where are you going?" Mrs. Swingle said.

Good question. "My brother was supposed to pick me up but I think he forgot. I was going to call him."

"Do you have a cell phone?" Mrs. Swingle said.

Phee caught Veronica's eye roll in the side mirror. "An iPod touch."

"Why don't you come home with us and get warm. You can text him from there," Mrs. Swingle said. She seemed oblivious of her daughter, who was glowering at her. "It's been a while since Veronica had anyone over."

This last statement didn't make sense to Phee. What about the Donner Partiers? If she lived in Veronica's house and had Veronica's bedroom, she'd have friends over all the time. "Sure. Um, thanks."

They drove into Thorne. It wasn't much of a downtown—a tired strip center fronted by a Chinese restaurant in an A-frame, followed by a row of shabby office buildings that included a medical marijuana dispensary. A VW bus with decals was parked behind a Subaru speckled with rust. The people Phee saw on the street looked as out of date as their cars—gray messy beards, tie-dyed maxi skirts, and Day-Glo ski jackets. What were Mrs. Swingle and Veronica doing in a place like this?

Instead of finding a parking space on the street, Mrs. Swingle drove through the town. Phee was about to ask where they were going when Mrs. Swingle flipped on her signal and turned right into an apartment complex. *Complex* was too grand a word for the two-story, sixteen-unit building. *Dump* was more accurate. The building was made of red brick that had once been painted a pinkish color. There was no lobby. The doors to the apartments on the ground floor opened onto the parking lot. A metal staircase in the center of the building led to the second-floor apartments.

Mrs. Swingle pulled into a slot opposite from the building. *She's probably dropping something off*, Phee thought, *like for a charity thing*. She imagined a Junior League project that brought groceries to old ladies who wore cardigans over printed dresses with uneven hems. Phee wondered if she'd be one of those old ladies—living in a small apartment, worried about money, with only a fat cat for company. How did you end up like that? She pushed the thought from her mind as Mrs. Swingle pulled the key from the ignition. Veronica made no move to get out of the car. She sat low in her seat with her arms folded, scowling.

"Well," Mrs. Swingle said, forcing cheeriness into her tone. "We're home."

Chapter 49

Phee hadn't said anything to Veronica. Not when she'd trailed Mrs. Swingle and Veronica up the metal staircase to Apartment 207, not when Mrs. Swingle had handed her the phone to call Zane, not when Mrs. Swingle poured them glasses of milk and put some store-bought cookies on a gold-rimmed china plate so thin you could practically read through it. "Finally getting some use out of the Wedgewood," Mrs. Swingle had said with a laugh that petered out when she saw the look on her daughter's face. Since they entered the apartment, Veronica had stood stock-still beside the fake-granite countertop, clutching her pink backpack to her chest.

"I'm going to my room," she said. She walked down the short hall through a doorway and slammed the door behind her.

Mrs. Swingle looked at the closed door. "It's been hard on her," she said in a soft voice. Her hair wasn't the soft honey-streaked blond Phee remembered it to be. Now it was the same color all over and more yellow except for the dark roots.

"I'm, uh, going to call my brother," Phee said. "And thanks for the cookies."

The conversation with Zane was brief.

"You did *what*?" her brother said when she'd finished explaining.

"Just come in Austin's truck, okay? And bring, I don't know, a rope or something."

While Phee talked to Zane, Mrs. Swingle went into the room at the end of the hallway and closed the door. Soon came the sound of a shower. It reminded Phee she had to go to the bathroom.

She found the powder room beside the front door. Embroidered linen towels hung on the towel bar and soap embossed with a seahorse sat in a gold dish on the counter. Phee dabbed at the bottom of the soap with her fingertips and dried her hands on the back of the towels. She always felt funny messing up people's guest bathrooms. Even though you were supposed to use this stuff, it was usually arranged to make you think the owners didn't want you to.

She returned to the main room. A dining table too big for the space was in the corner with six chairs crowded around it. A sofa with carved wooden legs and a glass-topped coffee table were in the middle of the room. The kitchen was tiny, just a sink, a refrigerator, and a stove separated from the rest of the room by a counter.

Phee had pretty much figured out the Swingles got divorced and Veronica and Mrs. Swingle were living here temporarily. Usually when divorces happened in Bristlecone, the mom and the kids got to stay in the house. She wondered why it hadn't happened this time, and why Mrs. Swingle had chosen to live in Thorne.

There were three placemats on the table. Veronica didn't have any brothers or sisters. Did Mrs. Swingle have a boyfriend? Was this his place? People like Mrs. Swingle usually didn't live with their boyfriends, or even have boyfriends, after getting divorced. Phee walked down the hall and knocked on Veronica's door.

No answer.

Phee tried the knob. It was unlocked. She cracked open the door.

"Veronica?"

"Go away."

Phee pushed the door open and entered. Veronica's pink bed and desk and beanbag chair were crammed into the space. The walls were bare, except for a pair of pink-framed prints of a skinny girl walking a poodle. There were no horse-show ribbons, ballet slippers, vacation pictures, posters, or other stuff that Phee remembered from her prior visit to the Swingles.

Veronica lay on her bed looking out the window. She had earbuds in, a cell phone on her stomach. Beside her was a sketch of the gym floor. Written on it were things like *pink balloons* and *punch bowl table*. The Donner Partiers were in charge of the graduation dance. Not surprisingly, the theme was *Pretty in Pink*. Phee would rather watch an endless loop of *Frozen* than attend.

"Hey," Phee said.

Veronica gave no sign she'd heard.

Phee tried to think of what to say. *When did your parents decide to get divorced?* No. *Why are you living in this crummy apartment in Thorne?* Nope.

"So, have you met Wilbur yet?"

Veronica didn't turn her head. "What are you talking about?" she said in a flat voice.

"You know, the guy who forgets to change the sign."

Veronica blew out a dismissive breath.

Phee stepped over a pair of Uggs and sat on the desk chair. "Thanks for the ride. Zane'll be here any minute."

"Great. Someone else to witness my humiliation."

"Everyone gets divorced. I mean, not everyone, but I read somewhere like half—"

"Is that what you think is going on here?" Veronica sat up, pulled out the earbuds, and looked at Phee for the first time. "You are so clueless."

Chapter 50

"I assumed, I mean, I thought that. . ." Phee let her voice trail off.

"You know, they call it losing your house. What a stupid thing to say. Our house isn't lost. It's right where it's always been."

Phee said nothing. She now had a good guess who the third placemat was for.

"They also call it losing your money in an investment. That's stupid, too." Veronica's mouth twisted into a fake smile. "We all know where my dad's money went: to his stupid friend who was going to buy stupid foreclosed houses and make lots of stupid money from them." Her laugh was bitter. "But he didn't. He took the money and left. Now our house is one of those stupid foreclosed ones."

Several kids at school had to move away when their houses were foreclosed. Phee's mom had explained that most people borrowed money from banks to buy houses, and that if they couldn't pay the money back, the bank took the house.

"I'm sorry," Phee said. She knew she'd leave the house on Fir Lane someday, but she couldn't imagine her parents not living there. No matter where she went, she wanted to know she could always come home to her room with the notches on the doorjamb that showed how much she'd grown, to the swing her dad had made for the tree in the backyard, to the white curtains in the kitchen that were still stained light pink from the time her science-project volcano had blown up. She thought about where they used to live in Denver, the house she couldn't remember. Had her parents "lost" that house? Is that why her mom still drove by it? She filed the question away for future reference.

Veronica's tone was bitter. "It's not like you didn't know."

"What? I didn't."

"Right. Like your dad didn't tell you."

Was that what her dad did all day at his job? Took people's houses away when they couldn't pay? Of all the jobs Phee could imagine having, that would never be one of them.

"I didn't know. And I won't tell anyone else."

Veronica's eyes narrowed. "You'd better not. You will totally ruin my life if you say anything."

"I get it." *No one will know that the Golden—make that Pink—Girl is living in a rundown apartment in Thorne.*

"No, you don't. If anyone finds out I'm living here, I have to change schools. The middle school here has, like, thirty kids and they're all dumb. All their parents do is smoke pot and drive snowmobiles."

Phee would've laughed if Veronica hadn't looked so serious. She wanted to tell her Thorne was just a place where ordinary people lived who didn't have as much money as Veronica's parents had—make that used to have.

"The high school is worse. No SAT prep, no AP classes, no extracurricular activities," Veronica said. "You need that stuff to get into a good college, which I'm not going to do if I have to go to school here. My dad says I'm going to need a scholarship to pay for college."

Hui doing Veronica's math homework now made sense. "I won't tell anyone, I promise," Phee said again, at the same time wondering if she were the only eighth grader not worried about higher education.

Veronica scowled. "What are you doing out here anyway?" Her look implied only the demented would voluntarily come to Thorne.

Phee considered making up a story. But there was something about how, well, sad Veronica looked that made her decide to tell the truth.

"I wanted to see where Johnny's accident happened."

"Why would you do that?"

"Because I don't think it's an accident. I think somebody hit him on purpose."

Veronica rolled her eyes. "You're crazy."

"I don't think so." Phee described what she'd observed about visibility and the lack of skid marks.

"And you walked all the way up here to find this out?" Veronica said.

"I didn't exactly walk. . ." Phee told her the story of driving Johnny's van and getting it stuck in the snow. Veronica's eyes went wide and Phee thought she saw a hint of admiration in them.

"So now what are you going to do?" Veronica said when Phee had finished. "Call the police?"

"I don't know."

"First Chester and now Johnny—again. That sucks."

"Who's Chester?" Phee said.

"It's what we used to call Chord. Before he. . ."

"Grew up and got cute?"

Veronica's mouth twitched. "Something like that." She became serious. "I can't believe he's dead."

A horn sounded outside. Phee saw Austin's truck out the window. She rose. "Thanks again for the ride."

"Wait," Veronica said. She stood and reached for Phee's hat.

Phee realized Ashley had been right—the hat *was* Veronica's, left behind with a lot of other stuff in the foreclosed house that was subsequently emptied out by Zane. "I didn't know it was yours," she said, flushing with embarrassment. "Here, take it." She started to pull off the hat.

"What is everyone's problem? For the last time, this stupid hat isn't mine." Veronica tugged on one side of the hat and smoothed the other side down. "There. Now you don't look like such a dork." She moved back so Phee could see herself in the mirror. The hat looked just like the beret Missy Fairheitz brought from Paris for her sister Rachel.

"How'd you do that?"

"It's easy. Watch."

Two minutes later, Phee knew how to arrange the hat so it looked like a fancy *chapeau*—another Missy word—and less like a pizza slice draped over one ear. She also knew Veronica wasn't telling the truth. The hat *had* been hers. Phee understood why Veronica didn't want it back.

The horn sounded, longer this time.

"Oh, and you don't have to worry. I won't tell—"

"I'm not worried. And don't think today makes us friends. Because we're not."

"'Course not."

The last thing in the world Phee wanted to be was a Donner Partier. So why did she feel a tiny prick of pain? Nobody likes to be rejected, even by someone they'd rejected.

Veronica had put her earbuds in and resumed looking out the window.

Phee raised her voice. "Well, I'd better go."

When Veronica didn't respond, Phee navigated through the Uggs and other stuff strewn on the floor. She closed the door to the pink-trimmed bedroom behind her. The color didn't look quite as rosy as when she'd walked in.

Mrs. Swingle wasn't in the living room or kitchen. The shower had been turned off but the door to the bedroom at the end of the hall was still closed.

"Good-bye, Mrs. Swingle," Phee called. "Thanks again for the ride."

She let herself out. As she clattered down the metal stairs, she imagined Veronica's hot stare on her back. She wondered if it was worse to have nice things and then have them taken away, or never have them at all.

Chapter 51

Austin was alone in the truck.

"Where's Zane?" Phee said as she opened the door. Austin's rescue patrol pack was on the seat. She pushed it over and climbed in.

"Driving Johnny's van to your place."

"How did he—"

"You left the keys in the ignition."

"Oh," Phee snapped on her seat belt. "Um, how'd you guys get it unstuck?"

Austin patted the steering wheel. "Dallied a line on Ariel's trailer hitch, tied the other end to the van's chassis, and hit the gas. Two hundred horses did the rest." He shifted into gear.

"You named your truck after the Little Mermaid?" Phee said as the truck's tires crunched on the gravelly pavement.

"No!" Austin looked offended. "Ariel Winter. She's hot."

"Oh, sure." Phee said, not sure if he was talking about a celebrity or a girl at school.

"Who do you know up here?" Austin said.

"What? Um, no one."

"So whose apartment was that?"

"Oh, just someone I know."

Austin glanced over at her. "I thought you said—"

"Of course I know them. I meant they're not a friend or anything."

Change the subject, change the subject, change the subject. "Was it hard for you guys to figure out how to work the van?"

Austin pulled onto Ridge Road. "We couldn't. Zane had to call Johnny."

Phee closed her eyes, a habit left over from when she was the twins' age and trying to undo something bad by wishing it away. "Is he mad?"

"Nah. I think he thought it was funny. And kinda cool."

Relief washed over her. Of course there were still her dad and Aunt Helen to deal with, but at least Johnny wasn't mad.

They passed the spot where Phee had gone off the road. The snow was churned from the boys' efforts to retrieve the van. The Thorne sign flashed by. On this side it read, HOPE YOU ENJOYED YOUR VISIT AND REMEMBERED TO TURN OFF THE LIGHTS.

"Are we going home?" Phee said.

"Yeah. Zane had to get the van back ASAP before anyone saw him. If he gets caught driving without a license. . ." Austin grimaced. "Anyway, we were supposed to go to Silver for boardercross today. Now it looks like we're going up tomorrow."

The snowboard championships, Phee remembered. So much had happened since Zane had talked about it that morning.

Austin was a faster driver than she was. Before she knew it, they were slowing for the T-intersection at the end of the ridge. A turn to the left would take them past the old quarry where the rock climbers practiced, up to the back entrance to Silver Mountain. Right would take them down into Bristlecone. Austin turned right.

Phee traced the outline of the black-and-white triangle on the front of Austin's pack. An idea had started to come to her.

"How much food do you have in here?" she asked, patting the pack.

"If you're hungry, I'd wait until you got home. All that's in there is survival stuff—energy bars, nuts, dehydrated meals."

"Enough for how many days?"

"Two. My C pack has enough for three."

"Can I go with you tomorrow?"

"To nationals? Aren't you going to be grounded or something?"

"Not if Zane didn't tell."

He shrugged. "If it's okay with Zane, it's okay with me."

Phee slumped in her seat. Probability of her brother not telling she'd "borrowed" Johnny's van: low. Probability he'd let her come with him and Austin to nationals if she weren't grounded: no way in heck.

Chapter 52

When they arrived at Phee's house, Johnny's van was parked at the curb. Austin pulled in behind it and headed for the house, texting as he walked. Phee let him get a few steps ahead before she cut across the lawn to Mrs. Heckler's. No way would Zane not tell Aunt Helen what she did. Phee wasn't looking forward to that discussion.

Phee rang Mrs. Heckler's doorbell. She heard shuffling that approached the door and then stopped. She waited for a moment. "Mrs. Heckler? It's me, Phee."

The door opened. Mrs. Heckler seized Phee's arm, pulled her into the house, and shut the door.

"You have to help me!" Mrs. Heckler said. Normally the older woman dressed neatly and her hair was combed. Now her shirt was untucked and her hair looked like Einstein's in the poster in science class.

"What's wrong? Do you need to go to the doctor?"

"I need to go to a lawyer," Mrs. Heckler said, swaying slightly. Phee took her elbow, afraid Mrs. Heckler was going to fall. She remembered what Mrs. Risborough had told her dad in the hospital.

"If this is about selling your house, Mrs. Risborough is taking care of that."

"She's trying to, but I'm not going to let her!" Mrs. Heckler was slurring her words. Phee wondered if she had been drinking.

"Let's sit down," Phee said, leading her to the sofa in the living room. "Can I get you some water? Maybe tea?"

"You can get me a lawyer." Mrs. Heckler enunciated each word with effort. They still came out strung together. Phee surreptitiously looked around for a wineglass or open bottle but didn't see any. She didn't smell alcohol on Mrs. Heckler's breath, either, but that didn't mean anything. Some of the kids at school were already into partying, and the Internet was full of ways to hide it.

"Why do you want a lawyer?" Phee said.

"To take my side! My daughter said she's going to have the judge say I'm crazy and then she's going to sell my house and stick me in a nursing home!" Tears rolled down her cheeks, finely wrinkled like saved tissue paper. "Do you think I'm crazy?"

"Of course not," Phee said, feeling sorry for Mrs. Heckler. Who wanted to hear they're too old to live on their own? "She thinks it would be better if you were in a place where there were people around to take care of you. Look at the bright side—you'll make a lot of new friends."

"Old people like me? No, thanks. I've been taking care of myself since I was on my own at sixteen, and that was over sixty years ago." She fixed Phee with bright eyes. "Do I look like I need somebody taking care of me? I know I sometimes forget things and call you by your mother's name, but that doesn't mean I need to be locked up in some home."

"Maybe if you talked with—"

"It won't help. This isn't about me—it's about her. Her and the Citron. She thinks I don't know her secrets, but I do."

Phee frowned. Did Mrs. Heckler think her daughter was stealing her candy? Phee felt a stab of guilt. Maybe Mrs. Risborough had taken the Citrons away because they weren't good for Mrs. Heckler. At the same time, eating candy was hardly a reason for getting put in a nursing home.

Phee heard voices outside—Zane and Austin. "I'm sorry, but I have to go. I promise I'll come back later and we can talk about this then."

Mrs. Heckler took Phee's hands in hers. "Later is going to be too late. As soon as she gets rid of the Citron, I'll be next!" Mrs. Heckler tightened her grip. "Why else do you think she moved away?"

Phee gently pulled her hands free. "I'm sure that's not true." She stood. "What's your second favorite kind of candy? If it's okay with Mrs. Risborough, I'll bring you some of that."

Mrs. Heckler scrunched up her face in puzzlement. "Candy? What's that got to do with anything?"

A car door slammed. "I'm sorry, I really have to go," Phee said. She darted to the front door and opened it. Austin sat behind the wheel of his truck. Zane was climbing in the passenger side.

"Wait!" Phee called. She dashed to the truck. "Can I go with you tomorrow?"

Zane gave her a look that suggested she'd asked to borrow his kidney. "Do you know how much trouble you're in?"

"Tons." Something in his face clued her in. "You didn't tell yet, did you?"

He gave her a smug smile. "I can be bought."

Phee sighed. "How much?"

"Chores for two weeks."

"And a ride tomorrow?"

"No way, José."

"P-l-e-e-e-e-e-a-s-e! It's really important."

"Why don't you steal another car and drive yourself?" With a smirk, Zane reached to pull the door shut.

Phee moved to block him. "I didn't steal Johnny's van!" Her foot hit an icy patch. She slipped and sat down hard on a patch of snow along the edge of the curb.

"Hey!" she yelped.

Still grinning, Zane closed the door. Austin backed out of the driveway.

"You're just jealous I've driven more miles than you. And not just in the alley behind the house!" Phee yelled as the truck rolled down the street. She got up and brushed snow from the butt of her jeans, then looked over at Mrs. Heckler's house. She wanted to go back and figure out how to help her. But she had another problem to solve first.

How was she going to get to Silver Mountain tomorrow?

Chapter 53

"Hey, dude, you seen my phone?" Austin said.

It was Sunday morning around ten o'clock. He and Zane were loading the truck with their snowboard gear en route to nationals. Phee was hiding in the backyard within earshot. She'd gotten up early in order to be there before Austin arrived, and had told Aunt Helen she was spending the day with Kimiko. Grand theft auto, lying to her family—at this rate drugs would be her next step on the road to ruin.

Austin zipped up his backpack. "It's not here. I think I left it in your room."

"I'll get it," Zane said. "I want to get my other jacket anyway."

Phee peered around the corner of the house at the truck. Austin sat with his head against the headrest and his eyes closed. Maybe she could get him to let her come along. After all, it *was* his truck. Zane wasn't the boss of it.

A sharp wind blew. Shadows cast by clouds alternated with intervals of cold raw sunlight across the lawn. Phee tiptoed across the snow-crusted grass to the driveway, stopping just behind the driver's door. She was about to rap on the window when she saw the tarp crumpled in a corner of the truck bed. It looked to be about five feet square and was made of heavy green canvas. Zane and Austin's snowboards lay beside it.

Better to ask forgiveness than permission, Phee thought as she walked as quietly as a cat to the rear of the truck. Not that it mattered—thumping music pounded through the closed windows. Austin wouldn't have heard her if she'd arrived by elephant. She stepped onto the bumper, grasped the tailgate with both hands, and pulled herself into the truck's bed. Seconds later she was under the tarp.

The ride to Silver Mountain was bumpy and cold. The boys' playlist was all hip-hop. The heavy bass vibrated through the truck's body into her bones. Phee tried to brace herself as they careened around the bends in the road, but she still ended up sliding across the bed. It could be worse, she told herself. It could be snowing. As though on cue, white flakes drifted down when she peeked out.

By the time they arrived at the resort parking lot, Phee was stiff and sore. Enough snow had fallen that the tarp lay heavy on her shoulders. She waited curled in a ball, hugging her backpack and listening to Zane and Austin don their helmets and goggles.

"How much trouble is your sister in?" she heard Austin say.

The truck bed tilted as one of them jumped in. "A lot," Zane said, his voice close.

Great, Phee thought as she concentrated on keeping her breathing slow and shallow. She heard a scraping noise and then a clang as Zane picked up the snowboards. The truck bed bounced like a trampoline when he jumped out again.

"You have to admit, it was a pretty ballsy move," Austin said. Phee felt a little glow of pride.

"Idiotic, more like it," Zane said. Phee frowned.

"Why'd she do it?"

"Who knows why my sister does anything?"

Phee wanted to stand up and say, "I did it because someone ran your friend over on purpose and I'm trying to find out who." Instead, she held her knees tighter and tried to stop from shivering.

"What time do finals start?" Austin said.

"Fifteen minutes," Zane said. "Let's take Half-Dollar up, then ride down to the top of Gung Ho and watch from there." Snow crunched under their boots as they walked away. Phee made herself count to thirty—in case one of them forgot something and came back—before easing out from under the tarp. She swung her arms in circles and stamped her feet to get her blood circulating, then climbed out of the truck bed and headed for the lodge. The wind dogged her footsteps, filling her prints almost as soon as she made them.

The resort was a lot more crowded than it had been on field-trip day. Phee climbed up the lodge's stone steps and wove through the people until she found the room where she and Chord had waited. The couches and chairs were filled with skiers and boarders talking on cell phones, eating snacks, lacing up boots for another go.

Phee looked around—no obvious hiding places for what she was seeking. Trying to be as inconspicuous as possible, she circled the room and peered under each piece of furniture. Nothing. Next she went into the women's room. She doubted what she was looking for was in there, but she figured it would be good to do *preliminary reconnaissance*, as *The Master Spy Handbook* called it.

The bathroom was pretty basic—tile floor, painted walls, and ceilings. A long counter with three sinks stood across from three stalls. Two of the stalls were occupied. Phee checked in the empty one. Nothing. She waited until the other stalls were empty and checked them, too. The far one had a metal grill against the wall. Phee looked through its slats into a long tunnel about eighteen inches square. It was an air conditioner or heating duct, big enough to hold what she was looking for.

Phee examined the screws holding the plate in place. They were speckled with rust and loose enough to turn with her fingers. She pulled the grill off and looked in. The space was empty. The fine layer of dust inside told her nothing had been there, at least not recently.

She re-screwed the grate, left the stall, washed her hands, and returned to the hallway. It was getting to be late afternoon and the crowd had thinned. Phee stood outside the entrance to the bathrooms, keeping track of the traffic.

One in, two out, one out, one in . . .. She couldn't wait any longer. She stuck her hair up inside the pink hat, hoping it made her look more boy-like. *One out.* She was pretty sure only one person was left inside, and he should be washing his hands by now. *It's now or never.* Keeping her head down, she walked into the men's room.

Chapter 54

She'd forgotten about the urinals. One man stood in front of them as she sped, head down, to the far stall. Thankfully it was empty. She locked the door behind her, leaned against it for a moment, breathing hard.

The grate was there. She peered through the slats. The space beyond looked empty, but she had to be sure. She twisted the first screw loose. The second one was more of a problem. She looked in her backpack for something she could use as a screwdriver. A penny, a quarter—both too thick. She found a dime in a side pocket. Its edge fit the slot of the screw perfectly. Two quick turns and the screw came out. The others weren't any trouble. In less than thirty seconds, the grate was off.

Phee looked in. *Empty.* And the duct was just as dusty as the one in the women's room.

Disappointment welled in her. She'd been so sure it was here. She screwed the grate back into place and walked out of the men's room, oblivious of the startled man washing his hands.

Two teenage guys sat on the floor leaning against the side of an empty chair. Phee dropped into the chair without asking if it was free. The two guys didn't seem to notice.

"Finals start in a half hour," the one in the navy jacket said.

"Cool. I'll chow my burger and we'll go back up," the one in the orange hat said. "I wanna see that guy in the flower jacket again."

"What's with the flowers?" Green Jacket said.

Orange Hat snickered. "Looks like he's wearing his little sister's jacket."

"Yeah, but did you see that air on his last trick? And what was with that triple twist?"

"He's doing some sick stuff. What's his story?"

"Dunno. No one's heard of him before. He just, like, showed up from Kansas, I think."

Phee looked glumly around the room. She'd been so sure she was right. It had to be stashed here somewhere.

"Oh, crap!" Navy Jacket exclaimed.

"Wassup?" Orange Hat said.

"My lift ticket. It's gone." He fingered the zipper on his jacket "It got torn off somewhere."

"You're going to have to buy another one," Orange Hat said.

"Double crap!"

"Maybe they'll make an exception today 'cause of the finals and everything. You still got the receipt?"

Navy Jacket felt in his pocket and produced a piece of paper. "Yeah!"

Orange Hat stood. "Let's go find out. Hurry up, I wanna see that flower dude." The two loped off.

Phee arranged herself more comfortably in the chair, figuring she could grab a nap and stay warm until the snowboard thing was over and she'd have to hide in the pickup truck again for the ride home. The lodge was emptying as people either called it a day or went out to the slopes to see the final runs.

As she squirmed in the chair, trying to get comfortable, something crinkled underneath her. She stuck her hand between the cushions and came out with a wadded-up piece of paper. She smoothed it out. Across the top was printed SILVER MOUNTAIN LIFT TICKET. Underneath was that day's date.

This was probably Navy Jacket's lift ticket. She thought about stuffing it back between the cushions. No one would know.

Except for her. From overhearing Zane and Austin, she knew lift tickets were fairly expensive. And she was pretty sure if you lost it, you couldn't replace it, even with a receipt. Maybe she could get it back to Navy Jacket before he bought a new one.

She got up and slung her backpack over her shoulder. "Excuse me, could you tell me where you buy lift tickets?" she asked the girl sitting in the couch across from her. Without looking up from her phone, the girl said, "Go out the main doors and turn right. Can't miss it."

"Thanks."

She walked toward the entrance, stopping short of the doors to brace herself for the blast of frigid air that awaited. Dusk had fallen. Through the large windows on either side of the front door, she saw the lights had been turned on along the half pipe. Bundled-up people lined the course, puffs of breath hanging near their heads.

On the wall beside Phee were signs with arrows after them: Rentals, Day Lockers, Lost & Found, Ski Shop, Cafeteria. Phee considered the Lost & Found sign. She was cold. Maybe she could claim a jacket as hers, then turn it in right before she left or on a subsequent visit. She followed the arrow to the left down a corridor, stopping in front of the door under a sign that said Lost & Found Hours 9 am-4 pm.

Even though it was after four o'clock, the half top of the door was still open. A woman in the ski-resort uniform at the far end of the room. She was hanging up a white parka on a rod filled with others of various sizes and colors.

Phee stood on tiptoe, trying to guess which jacket would fit her best. The green striped one looked like it was her size.

"Can I help you?" the woman said. Her nameplate read YOLANDA.

"Yes. I was wondering if a . . ." Her voice died as her gaze fell on a rack of backpacks.

Chapter 55

There it was, on the top shelf. Phee could hardly believe it.

"Yes?" Yolanda said.

"A turquoise backpack." Phee pointed. "There it is."

Yolanda walked over to the rack. "This one?"

"Yes!" Phee said.

Yolanda brought the pack to her. "May I see some ID, please?"

"ID? I'm too young to drive." *Make that, I'm too young for a driver's license*, she thought a little smugly.

"Can you tell me what's in the backpack? I have to make sure it's yours."

Phee tried to remember if she'd ever seen Chord take anything out of the pack. She hadn't.

"My hat . . .school notebooks. . . snowboard stuff. . ." she said as she nudged her own backpack closer to the wall so Yolanda wouldn't see it.

Yolanda opened the pack and frowned. "What color is the hat?"

Phee guessed the universal guy color. "Navy," she said as another resort worker approached the counter.

"Hey, Yolo, a bunch of us are going up to watch the finals. You coming?"

"Yeah. Just give me five." Yolanda retrieved a form from under the counter and gave it to Phee. "Sign here."

Phee scribbled *Chord Oakeson*. Yolanda took the form and handed her the pack.

"Thanks," Phee said. "Oh, and there's my coat." She pointed at the green striped parka. Yolanda gave her another form to sign.

Phee took the coat, slung the turquoise pack over her shoulder, picked up her own pack, and dashed down the hall.

The main room in the lodge was nearly empty. Phee found a chair in the corner. She opened the turquoise pack.

"I knew it," she muttered as she pawed through the contents. Her list hadn't been that far off the mark. There was school stuff, snowboard stuff, a Ride sweatshirt, and a hat in another universal guy color: black. There was no wallet, but she found Chord's name written in marker on the inside lining near the zipper.

She closed her eyes and thought back to the day of the field trip. When Chord had walked away from her, he'd been carrying a red pack, not this one. A red pack with a triangle on the front. Chord had left his turquoise pack in the lodge. Either that, or he'd hidden it and someone had found it. Where had the red pack come from? It didn't matter. What was important was why he'd switched packs.

Phee pulled out the lift ticket and smoothed it flat. In the excitement of finding the turquoise pack, she'd forgotten to turn it in. She didn't want to go back to the Lost & Found with her "borrowed" coat. Plus, it sounded like Yolanda was closing for the day.

Phee pulled on Chord's sweatshirt and hat, zipped into the parka, and picked up the two backpacks. She followed the signs to the ticket windows. The clock on the building read 4:30. Normally, the lifts closed at four. Today they were staying open later to carry spectators off the mountain after the snowboard championships were over.

Phee took her place in line, wearing the turquoise pack in front and hers in back. She stuck her bare hands into the parka's pockets and was pleased to find a pair of wool gloves there. They were crusted with what was probably nose juice but she didn't care. She stamped her feet to keep warm as she worked her way to the front of the line.

"I found this." She gave the ticket to the ticket seller.

"It's a day pass."

"I know who it belongs to," Phee said. "There were two guys—one had on an orange hat and the other, a navy jacket. It belongs to the guy in the navy jacket. I wanted to turn it in so if he had to buy another ticket, he could get a refund or something."

"Do you know how many guys I've seen just today in orange hats and navy jackets?" the ticket seller said. "Besides, I told you—it's a day pass."

"I don't know what that means."

"It means whoever has it can use it to go up the lifts today. Technically, you're not supposed to share it, but today's nationals." She returned the ticket to Phee. "It's yours to use or toss." She looked over Phee's head at the person behind her. "Next."

Phee moved out of the way of the next customer. Now that she'd found the pack, she was pretty sure she knew what had happened to Chord. Her eyes went to the mountain. That was probably where she'd find proof.

She fingered the lift ticket as her gaze went to the ski lift.

Her stomach muscles clenched.

Chapter 56

Phee joined the lift line feeling a little self-conscious. She was the only one not on skis or a snowboard. Her heart beat faster after the resort employee scanned her lift ticket. It was walloping against her ribs by the time she arrived at the loading point. She really was terrified of heights.

She decided the best way to carry the packs was to sling one over each shoulder. Four skiers to go, now three . . . too soon it was her turn. She tightened her grip on the packs' straps.

"Miss, it's better if you carry your packs in front. You don't want to get hung up on the chair while getting off," said the lift operator, who was sweeping snow off the waiting platform. Phee shrugged off the packs and clutched both to her chest.

"Ready?" said the other operator as he held a chair still. Phee sat on the cold seat.

"Hey, can you drop the bar? My hands are—"

"Sorry," said the lift operator as she sailed upward out of his reach.

"Just put one of the packs on the seat," called the other. "You can do it!" He threw her a thumbs up, but she had no intention of moving at all until she made it to the top. She pressed her back against the metal rails and closed her eyes.

I'll count to a hundred and I'll be there. One, two . . .. The air brushing her cheeks got colder. *Thirty-two, thirty-three* . . . . Below her, above the thump of the bass, she heard the *oohs* and *ahs* of a crowd. She must be over the half pipe. Curious, she opened one eye and looked down.

She glimpsed a long upside-down snow tunnel cutting through the trees, each side lined with people. In the middle of the half pipe, a snowboarder was suspended in air, one hand gripping his board, the other extended skyward as though he wanted to shake hands with Phee. It was weird looking down at treetops.

The snowboarder touched down, slid across the width of the pipe, and launched himself into the air on the opposite side, this time spinning his body two full revolutions. The lift was carrying Phee in the opposite direction. She twisted in her seat to watch the boarder land. Her chair passed a lift tower, which quickly became smaller as she moved away from it.

The diminishing lift tower reminded her how far up she was and how fast she was going, and that there was no restraining bar in front of her. She faced forward again, leaned back, squeezed her eyes shut, and began counting again.

"Hey, wake up!" said a voice.

Phee wasn't opening her eyes until the last minute. The voice said, "Yoo-hoo, time to get off!" Phee kept her eyes closed.

When the voice shouted, "RISE AND SHINE!" Phee figured it was safe to open her eyes. The chair was almost at the top of the mountain. The disembarkation platform—a flat place in the snow before the chairs hooked left for their return trip down the mountain—rushed toward her.

On field-trip day, Phee's skis had glided along the snow platform and down the little hill on the far side. Now she'd have to walk. Or run, fall, and slide, as it turned out. The momentum from the moving chair was like a shove in the back. It sent her stumbling across the platform and onto the hill, where she tripped and fell forward. Cushioned by the two backpacks, she slid down to where the hill flattened out again. Two teenaged boys who'd been strapping on their boards stopped and applauded. Phee got up and gave a clumsy bow. For a change, her cheeks were red from the cold, not embarrassment. Or maybe anger. She was about to find out if she was right.

"Where's the snowboard thing?" she asked the two boys. They pointed down the hill to where a crowd was gathered. Pennants were stuck in the snow, snowboard companies manned booths, and a DJ was set up between two giant speakers that were pumping out music. Phee saw the Trent logo above the closest tent.

"That's where they start," one of the boys said, pointing.

"Thanks," Phee said. She slung the packs onto her shoulders and walked across snow etched with board and ski tracks toward the area. The sun had nearly set and the shadows pushed out long from under the trees. She tripped on a rut, nearly falling again.

One of the teens glided up beside her on his board. "Wanna ride?"

"Um, sure." He had Phee stand behind him on his board and hold on to his waist. With his left foot secured in the binding, he paddled along with his right. They coasted down the gentle slope toward the crowd.

A leaderboard was on the left, lit by two spotlights. Competitors' names ran down one side, across from their scores. One of the names jumped out at Phee. She'd barely registered its implications when she glimpsed a familiar pink-and-tan plaid jacket in the crowd.

"Stop!" Phee said.

The teen leaned back and the board cut to the left. Phee tumbled off.

"Sorry about that," the boarder said as he helped her up.

"That's okay," Phee said as she got to her feet, still scanning the crowd. The plaid jacket had vanished into the darkness. It was almost impossible to recognize anyone or tell the color of their clothing unless they moved into a circle of light. One of the manufacturers had given out glow sticks, which turned everyone's face an eerie Martian green. "Thanks."

Phee took off at a jog. She wore her pack on her back and carried the turquoise one in front. She headed for the start area, pushing through the increasingly dense crowd. She kept bumping into people with her added girth, earning annoyed looks and *watch it!*s. When she dodged around a boarder in a Dr. Seuss-style hat, the pack on her back slammed into a man carrying an armful of snowboards. Several slipped out of his grasp and he swore.

"I am so sorry," Phee said, bending over to help pick up the boards. "I didn't see you." The pack on her back hit the man again, eliciting more swearing.

"It's okay. I've got it," he snarled in accented English as he collected the boards. A spotlight panned the crowd. Phee saw each board was painted a different bright color and had a sunflower decal on its nose.

Phee straightened up. So did the man, the snowboards now safely re-tucked under one arm. The spotlight passed over the crowd again as their eyes met.

"You!" the man said. "Are you following me?"

In the bad lighting it took Phee a minute to recognize the face under the baseball hat with the neon lime-green logo. It was the man from Trent Snowboards. *Jungen.*

"Uh, no." She was looking past him for a glimpse of pink.

"So what are you doing here?"

Phee saw a flash of pink plaid by the roped-off area labeled COMPETITORS ONLY. "There's my friend. I gotta go."

As she tried to brush by him, Jungen shot out his free hand and grabbed the front of the turquoise pack.

Chapter 57

He dragged Phee close until their faces were inches apart. "Whatever you think you saw, you didn't," he hissed. His breath stank of cigarettes. "So forget about it, understand?"

Phee clasped her hands together low in front of her. "I have no idea—" she began, then brought both hands up abruptly, breaking his grip on the pack and ending with a pretty solid punch to the underside of his jaw.

He staggered back a step. "*Du schlampe!*"

Phee burrowed through the crowd in the direction where she'd last seen the pink-and-tan plaid jacket, heedless of people's complaints as she jostled by them. It wasn't until she got to the announcer's table that she allowed herself to turn around to check if Jungen was following her. He wasn't in sight.

What was that all about? Phee pushed her hair off her sweaty face.

"Phee!"

She turned in a panic, thinking it was Jungen. Joshua-Alex jogged clumsily toward her, headphones around his neck and the metal detector held in front of him.

"I'll take People I Never Expected To See On The Mountain for one hundred," he puffed after he caught up with her. "And the answer is—"

"Long story."

"Who'd you come with?"

"Myself."

He raised an eyebrow.

"Even longer story," Phee said.

He studied her. "Chloe Fieffer has a jacket like that."

"Did she lose it?"

"I don't know. Why are you carrying two backpacks?"

"I got this one from the resort—"

"From the side, you look pregnant." Joshua-Alex held the handle of the metal detector up to his mouth as though it were a microphone. "Medical miracle, ladies and gentlemen," he said in his best imitation of a news announcer's voice. "Girl has baby Tron, then gets pregnant." He broke into laughter, stopping when he saw the look on her face.

"Sorry," he said in his normal voice. He lowered the metal detector. "You got what at the resort?"

Gratification from telling him her idea: medium. Odds he'd never let her forget it if she was wrong: sky-high.

"My lift ticket. That's how I got up here. No more fear of heights," she lied. She nudged the metal detector with her foot. "I don't have to ask why you're here."

"I'll take Things I Found for two hundred. The answer is—" He dug into his parka pocket then opened his fist. On top of his mitten lay two lighters, a pocketknife, a dozen coins, a silver hair clip, a mini iPod, an iPhone, a phone, and a watch.

Phee picked up the watch. "This looks like gold. And are those real diamonds?" She turned it over. On the back was inscribed a date: 6/15/09.

"I'm going to turn it in," Joshua-Alex said. "Maybe there's a reward."

Phee handed the watch back. "What about the iPhone?"

"That, too. I called the number and left a message on the voice mail." He regarded his haul. "If nobody claims this stuff, do you think I get to keep it?"

Phee didn't know if *finders keepers* was a law or just a really annoying playground rule. "I don't know." She shifted the backpack in her arms. "I gotta go. See ya."

"Wait." Joshua-Alex stuffed the handful of items into Phee's jacket pocket.

"What are you doing?"

"I'm running out of space in my pack—I didn't think so many people would be here. I'll get 'em from you later, ok?"

"What about turning the stuff in?"

"Will you do it for me? It'll take forever and I want to keep detecting. My mom's meeting me at the lodge in an hour."

"No! I have to . . . I have to do something else," Phee said.

"I'll give you the iPod," he said in a wheedling tone. "Assuming I get to keep it. I already got one."

"Fine."

Joshua-Alex grinned. "You rock!" He adjusted a dial on his headphones and walked into the crowd, swinging the metal detector back and forth in front of him as though it were a blind man's cane.

Phee zipped shut the jacket pocket, remembering too late Lost & Found was closed. She checked the leaderboard and found the name she'd spotted earlier. *Cute*, she thought as she walked up to the announcer's table. A man wearing a Hawaiian shirt over a parka sat behind a microphone, talking about the current rider on course. Beside him, a woman marked score sheets while she listened to the two-way radio pressed to her ear.

"Yes?" the woman said without looking up at Phee.

"How many more times do they go?"

The woman scribbled something on one of the sheets. "This is the last run."

"Are they going worst to best?"

"Uh-huh."

"Thanks," Phee said.

It was snowing again. The curtain of white flakes glittered when it passed in front of the lights. People waved glow sticks and yelled their appreciation for the riders.

Phee tramped to the competitors' area. Four boarders with race bibs over their jackets stood apart from the crowd and each other. Three of them listened to music, head bobbing or swaying to the beat pounding through their earbuds. The fourth, wearing a bandanna over his face bandito-style and a purple-flowered jacket two sizes too small, talked to a small figure in a pink-and-tan plaid jacket in the far corner.

A rope surrounded the competitors, separating them from everyone else like they were horses in a corral. A man in a Silver Mountain ski parka stood beside the opening. He turned away a teenaged girl in a camo parka holding a pen and piece of paper, then held up his hand to block her as she tried to take a photo of the competitors with her cell phone.

Phee turned back into the crowd. She found Joshua-Alex regarding a twisted piece of metal wire.

"Another roach clip," he said and tossed it away. "I must have found ten of them so far. How many stoners are up here?"

"You'e at a snowboarding competition. Anyway, come with me. I need a favor."

Three minutes later, Joshua-Alex was engaged in conversation with the man in the Silver Mountain parka. Joshua-Alex held up the watch, gestured toward the lift, then at the crowd. The man in the Silver Mountain parka held out his hand. Joshua-Alex looked to be handing the watch over, but Phee saw a flash of metal as the timepiece flew through the air and landed about ten feet from the competitors' enclosure.

Joshua-Alex and the man hurried to where the watch had landed. The man remained standing and scraped across the snow with his foot. Joshua-Alex dropped to his knees and dug vigorously, sending a flurry of snow into the air.

"Good job," Phee said under her breath as she slipped into the competitors' area. She dashed past the three snowboarders toward the couple. The girl in the plaid jacket had her back to Phee.

"Hey!" A man's voice behind her.

She ignored it, beelining toward her targets. Deep in conversation, they didn't notice her approach.

"Hey!" The man's voice again. A glance behind her confirmed it was Silver Mountain Parka. Joshua-Alex wasn't in sight. The resort employee jogged across the enclosure, pointing at Phee. "You can't be in here!"

Phee turned and raced to the couple. She grabbed a pink sleeve and spun the jacket's wearer around.

"Hey, what are you—"

"Hi, Kimiko," Phee said. Still holding Kimiko's sleeve, she turned to the snowboarder. "Hey, Chord." She nodded at the leaderboard. "Or do you prefer Chester?"

Chapter 58

"Phee!" Kimiko said. "What you doing here?"

"Cheering Chester on. It's a lot more fun than going to his candlelight vigil."

The man in the Silver Mountain jacket walked up to them. "Miss, you'll have to come with me."

"It's okay," Chord said, his voice muffled by the bandana. "She's my sister, too." The man glanced between Phee and Kimiko, shrugged, and left them alone.

"Are you guys insane?" Phee said. She thought about seeing Mr. and Mrs. Oakeson in the principal's office. "How could you let people think Chord was *dead*?"

"I told you it was a dumb idea," Chord said to Kimiko.

Kimiko held up her hands. "It's not my fault! How was I supposed to know people would assume the worst?"

"What did you expect them to think?" Phee said.

"We thought"—Chord gave Kimiko a look—"*I* thought people would just think he was missing and that everything would be okay when he showed up again."

"Well, I get why you tossed your bus ticket," Phee said to Chord.

"Kimiko told me that you'd found it." He nodded at the turquoise backpack. "Thanks for bringing that. Did you find it in the lodge?"

"Lost and found."

"And that's how you figured it out?" Kimiko said.

"There was other stuff, too. Your pack was always full of energy bars even though you hate them. Chord was wearing a rescue patrol pack when he pulled me out of"—Phee cleared her throat and Chord grinned—"when I saw him before I got on the bus." She looked at Chord. "Did you snowcamp?"

"Crashed in one of the yurts on the backside."

"This is crazy," Kimiko said. "No way could you know what was going on from just that."

"There's more. I found your snowboard tool near the lodge two days *after* the field trip. It only had a little snow on it, which meant Chord hadn't gotten lost two days before. The final thing was seeing CHESTER ELMDAUTER on the leaderboard. Even if the last name hadn't been so obvious—Elmdauter? Oakeson? Seriously?—Veronica told me about Chester. Plus *Chester* had more points than anyone else. Who else could it be?"

Chord grinned hugely under the bandana. Kimiko crossed her arms.

"*Veronica* told you about Chester? She your new BFF now?" she said.

Phee spread her hands. "What was I supposed to do after you kept blowing me off?"

"I did not blow you off! It was just one project, and I had to bring food to Chord. Are you really a Donner Partier now?"

Phee thought about yesterday at Veronica's. "Trust me—I am more de-friended than ever."

"Wyatt Lucheen, currently in third place, is next down the pipe," blared the announcer.

Chord had been holding his snowboard vertically, with one end resting against the snow. Now he began batting the top half back and forth between his hands, the first sign of nervousness Phee had seen from him.

"What about Chord's parents?" Phee said. "Did you guys even think about them?" She thought of Mrs. Oakeson crying in Mr. Sandoval's office.

"I know!" Kimiko wailed, looking miserable. "But it's not like he could just hitch a ride up the mountain the day of the competition and expect to do well. He was already behind on practice 'cause of being grounded. He needed the snow time!"

"Couldn't you have sent them a text or something saying you were okay?"

Chord shook his head. "They'd have figured out what I was doing and stopped me from competing."

"They think you're dead!"

Chord stared down the mountain as the snowboard flipped back and forth faster. It was electric blue with a sunflower on top, like the ones the guy from Trent had been carrying when Phee collided with him. "This is my one shot," he said. "I had to take it. Don't be mad at Kimiko. It was my idea."

"What's the plan when this is all over?" Phee tipped her head toward the half pipe lined with eager fans cheering Wyatt as he twisted and caught big air.

"You mean after he wins," Kimiko said.

"Get a big enough sponsorship offer so I can pay for college without a music scholarship. Have my parents realize I can snowboard *and* play the violin." The snowboard had become an arc of white and blue between his hands.

"Where did you get the board?" Phee said.

"Trent. After the first two rounds I was in first. For this to work, I had to stay away from people and keep my bandanna on. I couldn't wear any of my own jackets, either. Everyone knows them." He plucked at the one he wore, trimmed in lavender daisies. "You couldn't have borrowed one from a guy friend?" he said to Kimiko. "Or at least found one without flowers on it?"

"The board?" Phee prodded.

"Oh, yeah. After I did so well, Kimiko went to Trent. She said she was my sister and that if they had a proto board available, I'd like to ride it."

"What's a proto board?"

"A prototype," Kimiko said. "That's what the flowers mean."

Chord twirled his board. "I got lucky. They'd brought the one they made for me last month."

"Bridger Solon," said the announcer.

The boarder glided out of the enclosure. Chord was the only competitor left.

"Let's go," Kimiko said. "I want to get a good spot to watch." She bumped fists with Chord, followed by some complicated finger wiggling and other gestures. "Go tear it up, dude."

He hugged her. "Thanks for everything, Betty."

"Good luck," Phee said. She stayed on Kimiko's heels as she pushed through the crowd to a place near the top of the half pipe. Bridger was near the bottom of the four-hundred-foot long U-shaped trench. He slid up the near-vertical icy wall on the right facing backward, spun twice in the air, and landed. The crowd groaned and Bridger dropped his chin, obviously disappointed.

"Cab 720," Kimiko said. "Baby stuff."

"A cab-whatever is . . .?"

"A cab is a switch-frontside spin that goes all the way around. The number is the degrees rotated. So in a cab 720, you take off, switch, and spin twice frontside."

"Why was he bummed?"

"He needed to go at least three times or cork it to get on the podium."

"Forget I asked." A roar rose from the crowd. She looked over to see Chord standing at the top the ramp that led into the pipe.

Chapter 59

The spotlights were as bright as a million candles, making the snow sparkle and casting a halo around Chord's head. Phee felt as though all the people—the mountain itself—were holding their breaths.

Chord hopped his board forward and it began to slide. He crouched low and the board picked up speed.

Phee had watched snowboarding when the Olympics were on TV, but she'd never seen it live. Chord launched himself into his first aerial maneuvers, rotating, turning, soaring higher than any other competitor had over the lip of the pipe. Phee saw a flash of blue right before he landed and slid across the base of the pipe into the next trick.

"Front double cork 10, switchback 900, double-back rodeo . . ." Kimiko muttered the names of the tricks as Chord finished them.

Two-thirds down the pipe, he slid left into a twisting double flip in which he seemed to float in the air. The crowd cheered.

"Cab double cork 10!" Kimiko said and pumped her fist.

Chord started up the wall on the right for his last trick.

"Oh, no," Kimiko said. "He's losing momentum."

Chord launched himself into a spin at the same time rolling over backward. Phee gasped. He spun three and a half times while rolling twice.

"A Double McTwist 1260!" the announcer shouted as Chord landed and threw his arms in the air. All around them people were cheering.

"Look!" Kimiko pointed at the Jumbotron at the base of the hill. Chord stood beside the sports reporter from Channel 9. Before she could ask him a question, he pulled down his bandanna. The camera zoomed in on his face.

"Hey, that's Chord Oakeson!" the guy beside Phee said.

A girl with red hair standing in front of them turned around. "I thought he got lost in the mountains."

"He must've found his way home," the guy said. He began to chant, "Chord, Chord, Chord."

The spectators around him picked it up. Soon the whole hill was rocking. "CHORD! CHORD! CHORD!" The reporter asked a question, but her mike couldn't pick it up over the crowd noise. She waited while Chord, still grinning, made calming motions with his hands. When the noise subsided a bit, the reporter tried again.

"I'm here with the winner of the Junior National Snowboarding Finals, Chester Elmdauter. Or I should say, Chord Oakeson. That's your real name, isn't it?"

"Yes, ma'am."

"Why did you compete under an alias?"

Chord held up the blue snowboard. "I wanted to see if Trent would be awesome enough to lend a proto to a newbie." He held the board over his head and patted the sunflower decal. "They were!"

The crowd roared.

"Seriously, Chord, you entered the competition under a different name. Why would you do that?"

Chord ducked his head. "Personal reasons."

Phee tugged on Kimiko's sleeve. "We have to call them!"

Her eyes still on the Jumbotron, Kimiko said, "Who?"

"Chord's parents! Remember? They think he's dead. How do you think they're going to feel when they turn on the TV or get a phone call from someone who's watching?"

"Oh my God, you're right."

"Give me your phone," Phee said.

"No go. It's dead."

Phee turned to the guy who'd started the Chord chant. "Can I borrow your phone?"

"Sure." He took it from his pocket, hit a button, and the screen lit up. "There you go."

"Thanks. Kimiko, what's the number?"

"I don't know."

"Are you serious? Don't you have the number memorized?"

She scrunched up her face. "Why would I know his parents' numbers? Anyway, I don't even know his. I'm dyscalculic, remember?"

From their homework sessions, Phee knew her friend could read just fine. But when it came to numbers, they made as much sense to Kimiko as Japanese did to Phee. "Yeah, sorry." She returned the phone to its owner. "Thanks."

"The people at Trent might know!" Kimiko said. "They used to call Chord all the time when, well, he was Chord. His parents, too, about sponsorship stuff." She pointed. "Their booth is over there. That's where I got the board from."

"You have to come with me," Phee said. "Take this." She handed Kimiko Chord's pack then took her friend's wrist and led her through the crowd. "You're the one who has to tell them."

Phee realized she had to call someone, too. As she sidestepped through a bevy of boarders starting their slides down the mountain, she wondered how she would find Ms. Vlachos's number.

Chapter 60

"Let me talk to Trent," Kimiko said.

Phee stood beside her, trying not to get slapped in the face by the yellow Trent Snowboards flag. Each exhibitor had planted one in front of its booth. On her left flapped a big red A on white background for Avalanche Boards. To her right flew a green and purple frog representing some binding company.

"He's busy," the young woman at the Trent booth said. She was packing up the snowboard display.

"This is really important," Phee said, batting at the yellow flag.

The young woman wrapped a snowboard in bubble wrap and laid it in a carton. "In case you didn't notice, one of our riders just won nationals. He's doing press."

"This is hopeless," Kimiko said.

Phee agreed. "We have to go find Chord."

Kimiko started walking. "This way's shorter," she said as she cut behind the Trent booth. Phee followed her down the alley created by the exhibitor tents.

"You really should have told me," Phee said.

Kimiko stopped so suddenly Phee nearly ran into her.

"I wanted to! I tried a couple of times. But I knew you'd say it was a stupid idea, and you'd be right! Then your mom—well, anyway, I didn't want to stress you out more."

Phee felt tears in her eyes. "We'd better hurry," she managed to say.

Kimiko nodded at the Porta-Potty at the end of the alley. "I have to pee. I'll be just a minute."

Phee groaned. "Seriously? Hurry up!"

Kimiko opened the door and a blast of chemical odor assaulted their noses.

"You think I want to spend a lot of time in here?" Kimiko said as she went inside and latched the door behind her.

As she waited, Phee thought about what Chord had done. Was there anything she wanted to do badly enough that she'd let her parents think she'd died so she could do it? She couldn't come up with anything. She thought about her mother. Had she taken it one step further, spending so much time away from her family, risking death to do what she loved? Parents, teachers, sappy TV commercials all told you to follow your dreams. But what about the effect that had on the people in your life? If—when—her mom came back, they were going to talk.

A thick, calloused hand clamped over Phee's mouth. At the same time another hand yanked her hair back. Her pack slid off her shoulder and fell on the ground. Her attacker began dragging her backward. He pulled her behind the Porta-Potty and headed into the trees.

Phee flailed her arms and tried to dig in her heels, but her assailant didn't slow down. She switched to punching and kicking. Her blows glanced off his head and shoulders but she caught a shin with a donkey kick.

Her attacker stopped and jerked her upright. Something sharp pressed against her side.

His mouth was close to her ear. She smelled cigarettes. "Stop fighting or I will use the knife," he said in a German accent. He pressed the sharp point harder against her side and she gasped in pain.

"Okay," she choked out.

"Good," he said, pronouncing it *goot*. "Now we are going to walk. If you scream, I will cut you. If you fight, I will cut you. Understand, *ya*?

Phee nodded. Slowly he took his hand away from her mouth. Phee inhaled a big breath and cut her eyes toward her attacker. It was Jungen, the man from Trent. Was he kidnapping her? Was he going to rape her? Kill her? A shudder made her arms spasm.

Jungen stood close behind her, his left hand gripping her left shoulder and his right arm—the one holding the knife—pressed against her back.

"Walk," he said. *Valk.*

She took a tentative step.

"Faster!" he said. Phee complied.

The noise from the crowd receded as they followed a snowboard trail deeper into the trees. Anyone looking at them from a distance would think they were a romantic couple, or a father and daughter. Anyone wearing night vision goggles, that was. Dusk had become night. Shadows stretched long in the glow cast by a nearly full moon hidden behind snow clouds.

Jungen steered her downhill. Unable to tell obstacle from shadow, Phee tripped over a tree branch and would have fallen without Jungen's grip on her. As she fought to stay on her feet, the knife pricked her under the ribs, and she pressed her lips together to keep from crying out. She wondered what Kimiko had done when she left the Porta-Potty and saw Phee wasn't there. Would she think Phee had gone down the hill without her? No one at home knew where Phee was. It could take the only three people who did—Kimiko, Joshua-Alex, and Chord—hours to figure out she was gone. Phee blinked rapidly. She was close to crying.

They were at the edge of the trees. Before them was an access road, used by maintenance vehicles in the summer and skiers in the winter. Jungen steered her right. It was uphill, but the going was easier on the packed snow.

The road leveled off. They were at the base of one of the mid-mountain ski lifts. The metal conveyor was silent and unmoving. Jungen marched her over to the lift shack beside the boarding area. He pushed her face-first against the door, pinning her there with the flat of his hand against her back.

He's going to kill me, Phee thought, trembling.

She heard the sound of the doorknob rattling.

This is where he's going to leave my body. Phee shut her eyes.

She sensed Jungen get something out of his jacket pocket. Seconds later she heard broken glass tinkle onto the floor inside the shack. He pulled her off the door, pivoting her around so he could reach through the broken window and turn the inside knob.

The door open, Jungen shoved her into the shack.

Chapter 61

Jungen closed the door and switched on the flashlight Phee assumed he'd used to break the window. The shack was tiny, maybe twelve feet by twelve with windows on three sides. There was a student-sized desk, a chair, and a space heater. An old-style land-line telephone was on the desk. Snow shovels, brooms, and a rake stood in a corner beside a backboard used to transport injured skiers. Notices and announcements on Silver Mountain letterhead were pinned to the bulletin board on the wall.

Jungen put the knife in the sheath at his belt. "Sit," he said, indicating the chair. Phee moved cautiously away from him, afraid a sudden move would cause him to go after her with the knife. She pulled the chair out from the desk and sat on the cold wood.

You're not dead yet. Think. She concentrated on recalling the "When You Are Caught" chapter in *The Master Spy Handbook.*

Take stock of your surroundings. See what items you can use to your advantage. The tools in the corner—if Jungen came at her, she could use them to defend herself. Maybe she could hurt him enough to have time to call for help.

Jungen reached toward her. Phee cried out and shrank into her chair. He leaned past her, set the flashlight on the table. He picked up the phone, tore it from the wall, and used the wire to tie her hands behind her. Then he unthreaded the straps from the backboard and wrapped them around her ankles and the chair legs. He knotted the webbing, tugged on it to make sure it would hold.

It took all of Phee's willpower not to fight against being tied up. But she figured if he were going to rape or kill her, he wouldn't be lashing her to the chair.

"Why are you doing this?" she said as he finished securing her.

He didn't answer. He took out his cell phone and tapped a button. The backlight came on and he checked the screen.

"*Verdammt!*"

He put the phone into his pocket, then sourly regarded the telephone lying on the floor, useless without its cord.

"You work for a snowboard company and you don't know there's no reception on the mountain?" Phee said. "Pretty stupid to rip out the phone before making your call."

"*Halt's maul!*"

Phee was through being quiet. "Is this because your girlfriend hates me? All I did was talk to Rusty!"

"My girlfriend? What are you talking about?"

"Mrs. Risborough. I saw you at her house."

He barked a laugh. "Kathryn isn't my girlfriend. We do have a special relationship, though." He chuckled. Phee heard the nasty in it.

"Why are you doing this?"

"So you cannot talk to Mr. Trent, of course."

Phee felt like she was playing some dumb game with the twins. "Talk to Mr. Trent about *what*?"

"About the boards."

"I have no idea—"

"Stop lying." He picked up the flashlight. "I am not stupid. First you are snooping when I make the delivery last week. Then you come to the company and are telling that you saw me. Now your friend rides one of the boards and you want to see Mr. Trent. Too bad for you I will be on a flight to Germany tomorrow."

Phee thought back to the day of the field trip. She'd first seen Jungen coming out of the metal shed carrying the snowboards with the sunflowers on them. She lost sight of him in the storm. She next saw him talking with a man. They'd been standing beside a van with an *A* on the door.

Phee had seen that *A* earlier in the day—it had almost hit her in the face. It was on the flag stuck in front of Avalanche Boards. She thought of Chord holding his board overhead after his win. He'd patted the sunflower decal and thanked Trent for lending him a "proto."

"It's you! You're the one stealing Trent designs!" she said.

He slapped her. Pain exploded through Phee's head. Hot tears ran down her cheeks. Her ears rang.

"Yes. And that is for destroying my business," Jungen said.

Phee tasted something metallic and spat blood onto the floor. Already the side of her face was swelling. "Look, I won't tell. Not before you get on the plane. You can—"

Jungen opened the door and vanished into the night.

Chapter 62

The quiet pressed down on her. Phee's breath rasped loudly in her head. It reminded her of horror films she wasn't supposed to watch but had anyway at Kimiko's, when the ax murderer chases the dumb blonde and the camera makes it like you're the ax murderer, so you see the blonde running away from you and hear the *huh huh huh* of your breath while you're running. Even though she knew it was her imagination working overtime, she was scared.

"Relax," she said to hear something other than her breath. Usually when someone told Phee to relax, it just made her more tense. But telling herself that seemed to work. She stopped thinking that Freddy or Jason was going to burst through the door and decapitate her. Instead, she started to worry about how she was going to get out of the shack.

Probability someone would find her in the morning when it was time to open the lift: high. Probability she'd have hypothermia by then: equally high. She believed Jungen had only wanted to buy time so he could catch his flight out of the country, not freeze her to death.

Her head ached. The slap had been a hard one. Phee wasn't a big *if only* person when things went wrong—if only she hadn't gone to Mrs. Heckler's she wouldn't have had to climb out the window; if only she hadn't taken Johnny's car she wouldn't have gotten it stuck—but in this case, it was hard not to go there. If only Kimiko knew Chord's phone number they wouldn't have gone to the Trent booth, Jurgen wouldn't have freaked out and grabbed her, and she wouldn't be tied up in the shack.

By now Chord's parents must have heard about his reappearance. Maybe Ms. Vlachos had, too. Phee hoped so. She also hoped Kimiko would notice Phee was gone—not just somewhere-else-on-the-mountain gone, but *gone* gone. More likely, Kimiko was caught up in the celebration of Chord's win and return from the land of the dead and it would be hours before she realized Phee wasn't there.

Phee wished she could remember more from the spy handbook on how to escape. There had been a page on how to hold your hands when being tied up so later you could move your hands a certain way and get free. Unfortunately she'd skipped that page, along with the ones on lock-picking and Morse code.

A motor rumbled somewhere down mountain. It was joined by another, and then another. *Snowcats.* The shack and the lift beside it sat in the middle of a grooming run. If she could draw the snowcat driver's attention to the shack when he went by, he might stop and investigate.

Take stock of your surroundings. See what items you can use to your advantage. Phee looked up. A light fixture was attached to the ceiling. Jungen hadn't turned it on, using the flashlight instead. She peered at the wall where the door was and thought she saw a light switch there. All she had to do was go to it and flip it on.

She strained against the telephone cord and backboard straps. The knots seemed secure. She'd have to get to the switch while attached to the chair.

Phee grabbed the sides of her seat, tightened her stomach muscles, and jerked her butt forward. The chair hopped forward an inch. Tighten. Jerk. Hop. Tighten. Jerk. Hop. She was tired after eight of them. Plus her head really, really hurt. The skin on her left cheek felt tight where it was swollen.

Tighten. Jerk. Hop. Tighten. Jerk. Hop. If—when—she made it out of there, she would work harder on crunches in gym class. Tighten. Jerk. Hop. One more and she'd be inches from the wall. The light switch was at eye level.

Tighten. Jerk. Hop. Phee tucked her chin, leaned forward, and pushed up under the switch with the top of her head. It didn't move. She leaned forward and pushed harder. The light stayed off.

Phee gathered herself to spring upward as much as her restraints would allow. She ducked like a turtle retreating into its shell, closed her eyes, shot upward with all the force she could muster.

All four legs of the chair left the ground as the top of her head hit the switch. At the same time, Phee's right foot and knee collided with the wall. The chair landed at an angle, the impact throwing Phee backward to the right. For one moment the chair balanced on two legs, hanging in space. There was a crack, and the chair—and Phee—toppled to the floor.

Chapter 63

She yelped as she hit the ground. Now her shoulder and her hip hurt almost as much as her head did. To make things worse, the light was still off. She cried, more out of frustration than pain, but stopped after several gulping sobs. Snot from her nose was running down the side of her cheek and it was gross. Plus, she had to move.

The glass rattled in the windows as the wind howled, trying to get in. Or was she hearing a wolf?

She rocked her body from side to side. On the fourth try, she managed to roll onto her knees. The chair was still tied to her, forcing her face almost to the floor. But her legs didn't feel as tightly bound as they had before. She tried extending one. The backboard strap unspooled from around her ankle, and one of the chair legs, broken off in the fall, fell onto the floor and rolled away. She wiggled the other leg. Although the strap still attached her to the chair, at least it no longer dug into her shin.

Phee bent her free leg and drew it under her. Foot flat on the floor, she tried to stand. But the chair made it impossible for her to straighten up. Three times she tried, and three times she ended up falling over onto her side again.

Giving her bruised hip a rest, Phee craned her neck to look out the window. The snow clouds had cleared, and an overturned salt shaker of stars spread across the dark purple sky.

Something fell out of her parka pocket and clattered onto the floor. She twisted around to see what it was. More things dribbled out. The diffused moonlight streaming through the window glinted on metal.

The stuff Joshua-Alex found with his detector. She moved sideways—half scoot, half slide—until her fingers touched a disk. *A quarter.* She scooted over once more, this time skinning her knees.

She blindly groped through the objects. Elation surged through her when she found the cell phone—until she remembered there was no cell reception in the shack. She kept searching.

Her fingers closed around one of the lighters. Phee had never worked one except for the long skinny kind her dad used to light the barbecue. She felt for the spin wheel with her thumb. She'd seen dumb movies where the good guy was tied up and used a lighter to burn through the ropes. Probability of burning the telephone cord: unknown. Would it even catch fire? Probability of burning her skin or setting her clothes on fire: very high.

She could set something else alight. There were papers on the desk and stuck to the bulletin board. Of course, to reach them she would have to get loose from the chair. The shack itself was wood, but as she couldn't reach the door handle or even move much, most likely she'd go up in flames with it. Reluctantly, she dropped the lighter and felt for the next object.

Wood and metal, about four inches long—the pocketknife. She braced it against her chair arm and pried one of the blades open. She tried to saw off the telephone cord but the angle was too awkward. She either dropped the knife or couldn't apply enough force.

She rested for a moment. It was getting colder. She shivered all the time now, her teeth clicking together. She was having trouble seeing out of her left eye. She'd never had a black eye before. It would be kinda cool to go to school with it. Assuming she made it out of the shack.

If she died, would the school have a vigil for her? What if Chord had stayed away a few extra days and then just shown up at his vigil, like Tom Sawyer did? Phee realized her mind was wandering. *Focus. What would a master spy do?*

Take stock of your surroundings. See what items you can use to your advantage was pretty much all she had to work with. She went through the checklist.

She was in a lift shack during nighttime. No one other than the idiot who had left her there knew where she was. She had a cell phone, but no service. She had a lighter and a knife, too, but they were similarly useless. It was winter, she didn't have a hat or gloves, and the broken window in the door and the knothole beneath her in the floor were letting in a chilly draft.

Knothole.

Chapter 64

Phee wiggled sideways and down until the knothole was in reach of her fingers. She felt around the rim, wincing when a sliver stuck her. The size of the knothole seemed about right. She reached for the knife. The blade was still extended. Carefully, she maneuvered it upright and set the base of the handle into the knothole. She was worried it would fall all the way through, but it was a snug fit. She wiggled the knife back and forth, keeping her fingers away from the blade, until it was firmly stuck into the opening.

She scooted forward a little and rolled slightly onto her back, using her free leg to brace herself underneath. With the wooden chair underneath, she pressed her bound wrist against the knife and rocked gently back and forth. The knife tilted away from her, but stayed wedged in the knothole. She kept rocking for one minute, then another. The edge of the chair seat dug into the small of her spine and her shoulder joint ached from holding her arm at such an awkward angle.

Outside she heard a periodic beep, the warning signal a snowcat made when it backed up. The groomer was getting closer to the runs that surrounded the shack. Phee rocked faster. The grooming machine's headlights flashed through a window, making a kaleidoscopic pattern on the wall.

"Help! I'm in here!" Phee yelled, even though she knew she wouldn't be heard over the growl of the machine. Frantically, she sawed her wrist against the knife, not caring when the blade nicked her skin.

The groomer rumbled closer, shaking the floor.

"Help!" Phee screamed. The knife drew real blood. Through the pain, Phee worked her hands faster. The big machine rolled by without stopping and started up the ski run.

"No-o-o-o-o!" Phee wailed. She gave a last hard rub against the knife, resigning herself to the cold and possible hypothermia until the lift operator arrived the next morning. But as she rolled back onto her side and relaxed her shoulder, she felt a slight easing in the tie that bound her arm to the chair.

She bent her hand nearly in half, straining to reach her wrist. Her fingers bumped into the frayed end of a piece of telephone wire. Excitedly, she circled her wrist, loosening the wire wrapped around it. Soon she was able to pull her hand free.

"Yes!" She picked up the knife, stretched her hand over her head, rolled onto her stomach, then her side. She sawed on the telephone wire that trapped her other wrist. In thirty seconds, her other hand was also free.

She unbuckled the strap around her legs, pushed herself to her feet, and tried to stand. She was almost there when she collapsed again, pain shooting through her legs.

"Ouch, ouch, ouch!" She rubbed her calves, trying to restore circulation and make the hot pins-and-needles feeling go away.

Thirty seconds later she got shakily to her feet. She flipped up the light switch, savoring the resulting glow. She picked up the knife and put it in her pocket, along with the coins, the cell phone, and the iPod.

The space heater was in the corner. She turned it on. It made a loud whirring noise that didn't match the pitiful stream of warm air it emitted. But Phee was grateful for any heat. She put her hands next to the metal grill.

After her fingertips were partially defrosted, Phee went to the shack's door and opened it. Freezing air pushed against her. On the run above her, a set of white lights was moving away from her as the grooming machine made its way up to the top of the hill.

She shut the door and began to walk in a circle, swinging her arms, trying to stay warm until the groomer returned. After the seventh circuit, she felt dizzy, so she leaned against the desk. Her stomach growled. She slid open the middle drawer, hoping to find someone's snack stash. All it held was what looked like job-related papers. She opened the rest of the drawers. She found a first-aid kit, a dented snowboarder's helmet, and a headlamp. In the back of the bottom drawer she found a petrified Butterfinger.

Phee put on the headlamp and flicked the switch. The light worked. Gnawing on the stale candy, she opened the first-aid kit. A small square of what looked like aluminum foil was in the bottom of the kit. Phee knew what it was from snooping through her brother's rescue patrol pack. She unfolded the survival blanket and wrapped it around her like a shawl. Next she dabbed antibiotic ointment on her skinned knees and covered the deeper scrapes with Band-Aids, then used the tweezers to pull the sliver out of her finger.

Feeling slightly better, she started pacing again. The shack had gotten colder, and the survival blanket wasn't helping much. *Where was the groomer?* She opened the door again. Maybe he'd see her headlamp, or catch a reflection from the space blanket if she waved it in front of the windows.

The beam from her headlamp skittered across the parallel tracks cut into the snow. The ridges extended up and down the mountain. Far above, the white top lights of the groomer were barely visible.

Phee decided to wait until the groomer started down the mountain again before she signaled with the space blanket. She was about to shut the door when her headlamp caught the pattern of carved lines closest to the shack.

"Oh, no!" Phee dashed forward, then came to an abrupt stop. She pivoted on her heel, letting the headlamp's beam sweep in a circle over the sparkling snow—the perfectly groomed sparkling snow. The groomer wouldn't be coming back.

Chapter 65

Phee went back inside the shack, slammed the door, and slumped to the floor. She'd never been very good at swearing. Not only did her parents forbid it, but the words sounded funny, at least coming from her mouth. But now she said the word she'd heard her dad mutter when Homicide walked across the garage floor her dad had just painted. She said it again, and a third time. It didn't make her feel better.

She pulled the space blanket around her shoulders and checked her watch. It was nearly nine o'clock. The lifts didn't open for another twelve hours. She looked around the shack. The backboard lay where Jungen had left it after stripping off its straps. Maybe she could use it like a bed, with the space blanket as a cover. The heater had taken the chill off the room, but it was still very cold.

Phee considered walking down the mountain. She didn't have the right gear for a hike in the dark and wind. If she made it all the way to the bottom, she'd lose some toes and maybe fingers to frostbite. Plus, there was the wolf factor. Probability she'd run into wolves: low. Probability she'd end up like Red Riding Hood's grandmother if she did: high. So hiking down was out.

She got up and pulled the backboard onto the section of floor with the fewest knotholes. She squatted and climbed onto it, first one knee and then the other until she was lying on her back with the blanket pulled up to her chin. The sides of the backboard were curved. If she moved too much, it would tip her out.

Phee switched off the headlamp and stared up at the ceiling. She wished she had Ms. Vlachos's Koosh ball to squeeze. After a few minutes the cold seeping up from the floor drove her to her feet again. She began to pace to keep warm.

She made a circuit of the room, stepping over the backboard. It reminded her of the red sliding dish Zane had handed down to her after he got a sled with runners and a steering wheel. She and Ashley would pull the dish to the top of the little hill at the end of the street and take turns. Phee would lie on her back and watch the sky spin as she sped down the packed snow.

Phee stopped pacing. *Take stock of your surroundings. See what items you can use to your advantage.* She knew how she was going to get down the mountain—fast.

Chapter 66

Phee fastened one of the nylon straps into a makeshift set of reins, tying each end to one side of the nose of the board, and used them to pull the backboard out the shack's door. She went back inside, buckled the headlamp onto the helmet, and tried it on. It was too big, so she took an Ace bandage from the first-aid kit and wrapped it around her head, then put on the helmet. Carrying the rake, she went back outside. She pulled the backboard by its reins onto the ski run.

In the wavering beam of the headlamp, the hill fell away from her. It looked steeper than the run Johnny had taken her down. At the bottom, windows glowed in the houses and condos that surrounded the resort.

Phee kept the backboard perpendicular to the slope so it wouldn't take off. She laid the rake, tines down, on the snow, then stood on the toothy end, driving the metal points into the snow. She slid the backboard around until it pointed downhill in front of the rake. She held it in place with the reins in her left hand.

Phee straddled the backboard. Something yellow glinted in the trees. Probably the eyes of some creature looking at her. A wolf?

She looked over at the shack with its wimpy space heater. What used to be her prison now felt safe and warm. She touched her bruised cheek. She wasn't going to let Jungen get on that plane.

After digging her heels into the snow to serve as brakes, Phee tucked the rake handle under her right arm and slowly lowered herself onto the rear section of the backboard. Her wrist stung where she'd slashed it with the knife cutting through the wire. She'd pulled the collar of her shirt up over her mouth and nose, and the material felt damp from her breath. She began the countdown in her head.

Three . . . two . . . one.

Phee leaned against the rake. Holding the reins with her right hand, she swung her feet over the sides of the backboard and jammed them against the front edge.

The backboard didn't move. Phee scooted her bottom forward a few times. The board stayed where it was. Tentatively she leaned forward, taking some of her weight off the rake tines buried in the snow behind her.

The backboard started to slide. Phee immediately lay back, pressing down on the rake, and the backboard abruptly stopped. She let herself feel a small glow of satisfaction. Her braking system was working.

She eased up on the rake and the backboard began descending again. Phee let it run for fifteen feet then put on her brake. She was worried about picking up too much speed and careening down the hill out of control. Stop start, stop start. She jerked her way down a third of the hill.

She tried using the reins to steer, but they didn't really work. Phee found if she leaned slightly to the right or left, the board would turn that way. She maneuvered around the clump of trees in the middle of the run.

She knew now what the weather people meant when they talked about wind chill. Her face felt stiff and her eyelashes were stuck together with frozen tears. Snot crusted her cheeks and she couldn't feel her fingers.

Three-quarters of the way down, the hill plateaued for fifty feet. Phee braked beside a swath of snow fence, grabbing on to the orange plastic netting with her left hand to give her right a break from holding on to the rake. She swung her right arm in big circles, forward and then back, trying to force blood into the frozen fingers. She was close enough to the resort to make out individual buildings. The restaurants, the ski rental shops, and even the Starbucks were all closed. But she saw lights in what looked like maintenance buildings near the base of the mountain and away from the main part of the resort.

Phee gave her arm one last swing and reached behind her for the rake just as the backboard took off. She grabbed air instead of rake handle. The back of her helmet bounced against the backboard, the impact loosening the Ace bandage. Several loops of elastic drooped in front of her eyes. A length of torn snow fence was tangled around her left hand.

The backboard picked up speed. Phee screamed.

"Help! I can't see!"

She dropped her feet over the side and tried to dig her heels in. But the board was going too fast. One boot was sucked off, leaving only a sock to protect her skin. The pain of skidding across the diamond-hard snow was too much and she heaved both feet back onto the board.

Phee pulled the dangling bandage away from her eyes. The resort rushed toward her. Directly in her path was one of the metal maintenance sheds.

"I can't stop! Help!"

No one appeared from any of the buildings or cars in the lot. If they had, she wasn't sure what they could do for her, short of playing cowboy, galloping up the hill, and lassoing her as she sped by.

Phee figured she had thirty seconds before she crashed into the building. A vision of paralyzed Johnny flashed through her head.

She bailed off the board to the left. When she hit the snow she kept rolling, the snow fence wrapping around her and turning her into a human burrito. Behind her, a loud crack split the air like a gunshot when the backboard slammed into the building.

Phee kept tumbling. She was headed toward a small grove of trees, her arms and legs trapped in orange plastic. Helplessly she watched the trees get closer. *Three more turns . . . two more turns . . .*

Then she was falling, and everything went quiet.

Chapter 67

A siren roused her. Groggy, she moved to sit up, but her arms were strapped down. *Had Jungen come back?* She thrashed, kicking and trying to wrest her arms out of the restraints.

"Hey, take it easy," said a voice.

The siren wailed. Phee continued to fight.

"Pushing thirty ccs of . . ."

She drifted off again.

The jostling woke her the next time. She blinked her eyes open to find herself lying on what she thought was the backboard, except now a sleeping bag was wrapped around her. And she wasn't alone. A man and a woman ran alongside her, holding on to the backboard's metal rails, which she didn't remember it having. They wore white shirts with patches on the sleeves.

Phee blinked again. Garish fluorescent lights, not stars, flashed by overhead. She turned her head. She was several feet off the ground, speeding down a corridor lined with doors.

"Where am I?" she rasped. Her throat was dry and her lips were chapped.

"Hospital," the woman said. "You got pretty cold. The docs are going to warm you up."

The backboard—which was a gurney, she realized—jerked to a stop. The man and woman in uniform disappeared, replaced by a woman in a white lab coat with hair the same color. The woman leaned over her.

"What's your name?" she said.

"Phee . . ." She was so tired, it was hard to focus. "Phee Mahoney."

"Okay, Phee. I'm Dr. Glick. You were out in the snow without enough clothes. Your body got really cold. Too cold."

Phee's eyelids fluttered. "Sleepy."

"That's from your body shutting down. When you get too cold, your heart sends blood to only the most important parts to keep warm. We're going to work on getting your circulation going in your arms and legs again. Do you understand?"

Phee nodded.

"We'll get someone to call your parents in a little bit. But we need to start getting you warm now."

"My mom . . ." Phee's tongue felt thick. She was too tired to explain where her parents were.

"She'll be here soon," Dr. Glick said soothingly. She put on her stethoscope and pressed its cool disk against Phee's chest. "You have a nice strong heart," she said after listening for a few seconds. "That's good." She wrapped the stethoscope around her neck and began to probe Phee's stomach. "I'm going to check you over for other injuries. Tell me if something hurts, or if you feel pain anywhere."

As Dr. Glick examined Phee, a nurse joined them. She was an older woman wearing a blue smock with teddy bears on it.

"I'm going to change your IV," the nurse said.

An empty clear plastic bag hung on a pole above Phee's head. Phee watched the nurse pull the tube out of the bottom of the empty bag and stick it in one full of clear liquid. She took the empty bag down and hung the new one up. Phee's eyes followed the tube down to a needle stuck in the back of her hand. *When did they do that?*

Dr. Glick continued her examination. "You've got a heck of a bruise on your cheek. And this looks swollen." She touched Phee's left wrist. A bandage was wrapped around Phee's right wrist where she'd cut it sawing through the telephone wire.

Phee drew in a sharp breath. "Hurts," she said in a rough voice.

"We'll take an X-ray. It may be broken."

The nurse began placing what looked and felt like hot water bottles along Phee's sides.

"We're starting the warming process," Dr. Glick said. "You're going to feel a prickling sensation as blood flow resumes in your arms and legs. It can be uncomfortable, so we put something in your IV to help you relax."

Phee was too tired to nod. She felt so comfy under the sleeping bag, nestled among the bubbles of warmth the nurse had packed around her. She let her eyes close.

"How'd the poor thing get up on the mountain?" The nurse's voice sounded far away.

"There was that big snowboard race. She probably wandered away from her friends and got lost in the dark."

Phee's eyes flickered open. *I didn't get lost*, she tried to say. All that came out was a croak.

"Phee?" Dr. Glick said. "Are you doing okay? The medicine should kick in any moment. You'll be asleep before you know it."

Pins and needles pricked her arms, rousing her. "Jungen," she rasped.

Dr. Glick leaned over her. "What was that?"

"Call . . . Sheriff . . . Allerd."

"*Sheriff*? Phee, did someone—"

Phee didn't hear what Dr. Glick said next. She was asleep.

Chapter 68

When Phee woke up, her mouth felt like she'd swallowed a handful of dust. She was still in the hospital but had been moved to a regular room. There was another bed but it was empty. A plastic bag still dripped into the needle in the back of her hand. Her other hand was encased in a narrow cast over the wrist area. The cast was wrapped with purple tape.

Aunt Helen sat in the chair beside her, with eyes closed. When Phee stirred, Aunt Helen's eyes immediately opened.

"Ophelia!" Her aunt had never used her full name before, but for some reason it didn't bug Phee. "How are you feeling?"

"Okay. Thirsty."

Aunt Helen picked up a juice pack from the rolling table beside the bed and jabbed a straw through the top. "The nurse said you could have as much juice as you wanted. Jell-O, too. Are you hungry?"

Phee, sucking on the straw, shook her head.

Aunt Helen watched her, eyebrows crinkling. "How did you end up by yourself on the mountain?"

Phee sucked in a breath, sending some juice down the wrong pipe and herself into a coughing fit.

Aunt Helen stood and gently patted Phee's back. "You won't get in trouble. Everyone just wants to know what happened."

Phee stopped coughing and gulped some more juice. "Didn't anyone call the sheriff?" she said when she could speak again.

Aunt Helen's expression changed. The worry was still there, but now there was sadness, too. "The nurse said you asked for someone to call the police." She lowered her voice and took Phee's hands in her own. "What happened, honey? You can tell me. And if you don't want me to tell anyone else, that's okay."

"But I want you to tell. You need to call the sheriff right now. Otherwise Jungen is going to get away to Germany."

"Jungen?"

"He's the one who locked me in the lift shack."

Aunt Helen's grip tightened. "What happened in the shack?" Her tone was as sharp as a knife's edge.

"He tied me to a chair with telephone wire and straps."

Aunt Helen flexed her jaw. "Go on," she said through barely parted teeth. Her body was tense, as though she were waiting for something heavy to slam into her.

"And he left me there! He said he was going to fly to Germany. That's why you have to call the sheriff!"

Aunt Helen took her cell phone from her bag. She pushed a few buttons then stopped. "He didn't hurt you or . . . do anything else to you?"

"He hit me. Once. Jungen is the one who's been stealing the Trent prototypes. He thought I'd figured it out. I didn't, at least not until after he locked me in the shack. But you need to call the sheriff so he can . . ." Phee wasn't sure how cops stopped people from taking off on a plane. "Call whoever so he doesn't get away."

Aunt Helen called 911 and got the operator to connect her to Sheriff Allerd's office. "I'll be right back," she said to Phee and walked out into the hallway. Phee heard parts of Aunt Helen's side of the conversation.

"She's awake . . . . Doctor said it was a close call . . . . Apparently someone locked her in a shack . . . thought Phee found out he'd been stealing snowboards . . . plane to Germany . . . . Okay." Aunt Helen returned to the room.

“He’s on his way,” she said.

Phee settled back onto her pillow. “Good.” She was feeling sleepy again.

Aunt Helen sat down. “You said he left you in a lift shack. But the resort employees found you on some ski patrol rescue board at the bottom of the mountain. How did you get from the shack to there? For that matter, how’d he get you into the shack in the first place?”

“It was after we went to the Trent booth to ask for Chord’s phone number . . .”

Phee recounted what had happened, pausing often to drink more juice. Toward the end, she had trouble keeping her eyes open. “The last thing I remember is heading toward the trees.” She stifled a yawn. “I couldn’t stop. Then I had the feeling I was falling and everything went white.”

“One of the groomers was late coming in. He saw you—rather, he saw your headlamp—coming down the mountain. When it disappeared, he went to check it out. He found you in a tree well.”

“Again?” Phee couldn’t believe it.

“What do you mean?”

“Private joke. Sorry.” She raised her left hand, the one with the purple-taped cast. “Is that how I broke this?”

“It’s a hairline fracture. The doctors think you hit your wrist against a tree or something on the way down.”

Phee examined the cast. She’d never had one before. At least she didn’t have to worry about any more school ski trips that year.

“Kimiko came by this morning to see how you were doing. She found your pack outside the bathroom. She said you were pretty amped about getting in touch with Chord’s parents, and thought you had forgotten it.”

Phee saw her rollie backpack in the corner. “What about Mom and Dad?”

“I talked to your dad this morning. He’s taking a boat to the island where your mom was working. I didn’t tell him what happened. I thought he had enough to worry about and there wasn’t much he could do from over there. But you were *kidnapped*. I should—”

"Don't. It will freak him out. It can wait until he's back." *With Mom, I hope.* "So when can I go? Home, I mean."

Aunt Helen indicated the plastic bag. "As soon as your IV is empty."

"What's in it?"

"Saline solution, basically salt water. You got really dehydrated and almost got hypothermia. The doctor had to warm up your insides."

Phee wiggled her fingers. "My hands and feet still feel funny."

"She said you might have some numbness in your toes and fingertips but otherwise no permanent damage."

"Good thing they didn't have to cut off your nose or something," Zane said as he entered the room.

Chapter 69

The twins crowded in behind him. Scout wore a pink cast on her wrist. Brooklyn had a green one. Both headed for the bed, jostling each other as they tried to climb in beside Phee.

"Careful of your sister's IV," Aunt Helen said.

"We didn't have to go to school because you were lost," Scout said.

"Yeah!" Brooklyn said. He looked at the tube that connected Phee's hand to the plastic bag. "What's in that?"

"Smart juice. Now I'm going to be even more intelligent."

Zane leaned against the wall and crossed his arms. "Makes up for the stupid juice you must have been drinking when you got lost."

"I didn't get lost! I was—" Phee caught Aunt Helen's glance at the twins and slight shake of the head. "I'll tell you later."

"At least you didn't freeze your face off or anything. Though it was nice not to have you hogging the bathroom this morning."

"You're the one who takes forever to shave the twelve hairs on your chin."

"Snap!" Zane said. His smile was small but Phee loved it. Her parents may not be there, but her brothers and sister were. There were times she'd envied Kimiko and Rusty's only-child status—no arguments over who gets to ride in the front seat of the car, no babysitting duties, no parent missing your swim meet because your brother's baseball game ran late. But if she had a choice, she'd keep her siblings. Although she wouldn't mind lending out Brooklyn now and then.

"Brooklyn said they were going to have to cut off your leg," Scout said. She was nestled under Phee's arm. She wore a white sweater over a blue tutu and leggings. The tulle skirt was scratchy but Phee didn't care.

"Nope. I still have both of them." Phee flexed her toes under the covers. Her sister giggled. "I think I saw a wolf," Phee said.

"A *wolf*?" Brooklyn said, wide-eyed.

"I got away on the backboard. So what's with the casts?"

"Zane brought the twins by earlier when you were still asleep," Aunt Helen said. "When they saw yours, they wanted their own, too. Dr. Glick obliged and put on temporary ones."

Brooklyn had wormed under the IV tubing and now lay alongside Phee on top of the covers, his cast thrown over her stomach. "Don't go away anymore. I don't like it."

"Okay." Phee blinked back tears.

A nurse entered the room, the same one who had packed Phee in hot water bottles. "Look who's awake," she said. She took Phee's temperature, checked her pulse, and made some notes on her handheld computer. "You have two more visitors," she said when she'd finished. "I told them five minutes max. I don't want you to get overtired."

After she left, Sheriff Allerd appeared in the doorway. He wore a crisply ironed uniform and held his hat under his arm. "Hello, Phee."

Aunt Helen introduced herself, then said, "Zane, it's time to take the twins to school now."

"No!" Scout said, clinging to Phee like a barnacle.

"No-o-o-o-o-o," Brooklyn said. "I don't want to go!"

"If you go to school now, you can play in my room later," Phee said.

Brooklyn stopped wailing. "Really?"

"Really."

"Cool!" He scrambled off the bed. Scout stayed where she was and gazed up at Sheriff Allerd, focusing on the badge pinned to his shirtfront. "Does Phee have to go to jail?"

"Not today," the sheriff said.

Scout thought for a moment. "Okay," she said and slid off the bed.

Zane led the twins out of the room. When they were gone, the sheriff retrieved the visitor's chair from beside the other bed and put it at the foot of Phee's. He sat down heavily.

"I understand you had a bit of an adventure," he said.

"You have to call the airport! Jungen is the one who took the Trent boards and he's going to Germany and—"

The sheriff held up his hand. "Whoa, slow down. Let's start at the beginning."

With Aunt Helen holding her hand, Phee began with the day of the field trip.

"So the prototypes are marked with some sort of flower?' Sheriff Allerd said.

"A sunflower."

"And you saw this Jungen give them to a guy from Avalanche?"

"Sort of. I saw him carry the boards to the truck with the A on it and I saw them talk. When he walked back, he didn't have the prototypes anymore."

Sheriff Allerd wrote in a notebook he had taken from his shirt pocket. "Go on."

When she got to the part about what Jurgen said in the lift shack, he stopped her. "I have to make a call." He stepped into the hallway.

". . . need an APB . . ."

Phee didn't hear anything after that, largely because of the roaring in her ears. A blush warmed her cheeks as she thought about how dorky she looked in a hospital gown.

Standing where the sheriff had been moments before was Peter Allerd.

Chapter 70

"Hey," Peter said.

Phee's brain went cuckoo. *Are you here because you like me? Or because you happened to be with your dad when he got sidetracked by the call to go to the hospital? Or because when you found out your dad had to talk to me, you said you wanted to come too so you could tell me the kiss the other day was a total mistake and it wasn't going to happen again?*

"Phee?" Aunt Helen said. She and Peter were staring at her, waiting for her to say something.

Phee clutched the sheet around her. "What are you doing here?"

Peter looked taken aback. "Um, I wanted to see if you were okay."

Because you're curious about a kid in your class? Or because you like me?

Aunt Helen offered her hand. "Hi. I'm Phee's aunt, Helen."

"Nice to meet you."

Phee said nothing. If this was what her brain was going to do when she liked a boy, she wouldn't have to worry about college. Her synapses would burn out before she finished high school.

Sheriff Allerd returned.

"I need to finish up with Phee here," he said to Peter. "I'll come get you when I'm done and you two can talk." To Phee, he said, "When he heard who I was interviewing, he insisted on coming along."

Now it was Peter's turn to blush. "I'll see ya," he mumbled and left.

"Bye," Phee said to the empty doorway. *Peter Allerd wanted to visit me. PETER ALLERD WANTED TO VISIT ME.*

"What happened after Jurgen left the shack?" the sheriff said.

Phee told him. When she was finished, he had her go through the story once more, interrupting only a couple of times to ask a question or clarify a detail. When she was finished, he said, "I'd like to talk to your aunt in the corridor. That okay with you?"

"It's okay."

After the adults left, Phee smoothed her hair with her hand. She wished she could take a shower before Peter came back. Phee wasn't a primper like Veronica, but she drew the line at being able to smell herself.

And wetting the bed. Phee realized she had to pee.

"Hello? Aunt Helen?"

No response. Phee twisted to look at the pole holding the IV bag. Maybe she could unhook the bag and carry it with her. She sat up and swung her legs over the side of the bed. The movement made her slightly nauseated and she waited to let her head clear. She noticed the pole holding the IV was on a stand with wheels. She could just walk into the bathroom and pull it along with her.

Tentatively she touched her feet to the cool linoleum floor and pushed herself to standing. She swayed, willing the dizziness to subside. Her gown was bunched loosely around her, and she pulled at its drooping neck. That made the back of the gown hang open, exposing her underpants. Phee reached behind herself and tried to grab the gown's flapping ends.

"What do you think you're doing?"

Phee swiveled toward the doorway—and lost her balance. She toppled onto the bed. The nurse closed the door behind her and bustled into the room.

"Um, I have to go to the bathroom," Phee said.

"That's why we have bedpans." The nurse bent over and lifted Phee's legs into bed, then tucked the sheet in around her, working her way up from Phee's feet to her shoulders.

"How does a bedpan . . ." Phee's voice died away when the nurse loomed above her. It was Mrs. Risborough.

Rusty's mom pulled the covers tight across Phee's chest, pinning her arms underneath. "Heard you got lost sticking your nose into somebody else's business," she whispered, her face inches from Phee's. Her pupils were so dilated, Phee couldn't tell what color her eyes were. "That should teach you—bad things happen when you meddle in things that don't concern you."

Mrs. Risborough straightened up, dipped a hand into her pocket, and withdrew a hypodermic needle.

Phee tried to pull her arms free, making the IV needle in her hand wiggle. The insertion spot burned. "Help! Aunt Helen, anybody—help!"

Mrs. Risborough smiled, her eyes dark and glassy. "Don't bother. No one can hear you. Your aunt and the sheriff are gone and the door is solid wood."

Phee scooted to the far side of the bed, ignoring the pain from the IV. "Aunt Helen!" she called again.

"Oh, shut up," Mrs. Risborough said. She uncapped the needle. Phee balled her hands into fists, ready to punch and kick when Mrs. Risborough leaned over to give her the shot.

But Mrs. Risborough didn't even try. Instead she stuck the needle into the top of the IV bag. She pushed the plunger home, emptying the needle's contents into the saline solution. Phee opened her mouth to scream as a warmth crept through her. Her fists relaxed, so did her bladder. Wetness puddled underneath her. Phee wanted to move away from the damp spot but her legs and arms were too heavy to move. Her eyelids drooped. She glimpsed Mrs. Risborough's smile, then her eyes closed.

Chapter 71

When Phee woke up, the first thing she realized was that she was in her own bed. She pulled the flannel sheets up to her chin and regarded the white furniture, the striped bedspread, Mr. Scruffy—a stuffed bear she'd had since third grade who'd lost an eye and an arm to Brooklyn—and everything else in the room with an affection she'd never felt for inanimate objects. There were moments during the last twenty-four hours she never thought she'd see them again.

She got up carefully, but the dizziness was gone. She was dressed in her own nightgown. She had no memory of how she'd gotten there. She wasn't sure what day it was.

No one was in the bathroom. With her arm sticking out around the edge of the curtain so her cast wouldn't get wet, she took a long, steamy-hot shower until her skin was as wrinkled as the outside of a walnut.

As she got dressed, a large truck engine ground outside. *Garbage truck.* That would make it Tuesday. So she'd spent all day yesterday in the hospital? Had the poison Mrs. Risborough tried to give her not worked?

That was what Rusty's mom had tried to do, Phee was sure of it. The question was, why? Mrs. Risborough was crazy, no doubt about it, but she didn't seem to be the kind of crazy that went around killing eighth-grade girls.

Phee heard a hiss of air as the truck outside released its brakes. She walked to the window. An orange moving van was backed up to the garage of Mrs. Heckler's house. As she watched, a man wheeled cartons on a dolly up the ramp and into the truck.

Phee started down the stairs. Homicide was stretched out on the landing, his ears swiveling like satellite dishes. She paused to scratch him under the chin, expecting a hiss or claws batting her hand away. Instead, his throat vibrated with a purr and his eyes narrowed to slits. His paws kneaded biscuits on the carpet.

"You really are a cat. Or seriously OD'd on kitty Prozac." Homicide opened one eye and looked at her.

"Don't worry. I won't tell." She stepped over him and continued down to the kitchen.

Aunt Helen sat at the wooden table sipping coffee from a mug. Beside her on the table was the pink hat. It looked freshly washed. Aunt Helen's hair was pulled into a messy bun and gray roots were coming through. Phee had never thought of Aunt Helen as being old enough to have to dye her hair. She wasn't wearing makeup, either, and there were lines on her face Phee hadn't noticed before. *Move in with the Mahoneys and turn into a grandma overnight.*

Aunt Helen looked up and saw Phee. She set down her coffee, came around the table, and enveloped her in a hug.

"How are you feeling, sweetie?" She tucked Phee's hair behind her ears.

"I'm fine. Did you talk to Dad?"

"I decided to wait until he's back to tell him what happened. You're okay, thank goodness, and I didn't want to stress him out more." Seeing Phee's look, she added, "There's no news on your mom."

Phee shrugged, but inside, the weight squashing her heart became heavier. "What about Zane and the twins?"

"Zane's with his friend and Mrs. Barrows took the twins to the hospital to get their casts off. Scout said hers was too itchy and Brooklyn kept hitting the furniture with his."

The Barrowses had triplets, all girls, the same age as Scout and Brooklyn.

Phee's mom and Mrs. Barrows took turns watching each other's children and taking them places.

Phee sat down. "We need to call Sheriff Allerd."

Aunt Helen had been pouring herself another cup of coffee. She set the pot down and faced Phee. "Did you remember something else about the man who—about that man?"

Phee shook her head. "It's Mrs. Risborough. She's leaving!"

Aunt Helen took Phee's hands and led her to the table. "Something happened while you were in the hospital."

"I know! Mrs. Risborough tried to—"

"It's not about Mrs. Risborough. It's about your friend, Mrs. Heckler."

Phee went still. "Is she dead?" she whispered.

Aunt Helen squeezed Phee's hands. "Oh, no. But something went wrong with her heart. Mrs. Risborough said she was taken to the hospital yesterday."

"Nothing is wrong with her heart! Mrs. Risborough tried to murder her, too."

"Sweetie, did you just wake up from a bad dream?"

Phee pulled her hands free. "No! When I was in the hospital and you were somewhere talking to Sheriff Allerd, Mrs. Risborough tried to poison me. I know she did the same to Mrs. Heckler!"

"No one tried to poison you, Phee," Aunt Helen said gently. "You stayed an extra day because you were so tired. I don't think anyone appreciated what an ordeal you went through."

"I wasn't tired! The poison she gave me didn't work!"

Aunt Helen got up from the table. "You must be hungry. Would you like some cereal? I can make eggs if you want." She went to the refrigerator and opened it. "That boy from the hospital has called twice and one of your teachers, a Mrs. Vlachos, brought those by." She gestured to the bouquet of red and white flowers in a vase on the counter.

Phee was gratified to hear about Peter and Ms. Vlachos. But only for a moment.

"We need to go to the hospital so they can test me for poison. And we need to find out where Mrs. Heckler is."

Aunt Helen shut the refrigerator door and placed her palms on the counter. "Phee, you are fine. The doctor said you might be a little confused and have bad dreams for a while. But other than that, you're one-hundred-percent a-okay. And Mrs. Heckler is being taken care of."

"You don't know that! You don't know anything!" She snatched the hat and stalked through the door that led to the garage, slamming it behind her.

Chapter 72

Phee felt a little better after slamming the door. Why were adults so dense? Just because something *likely* didn't happen didn't mean it *didn't* happen. Frustration sizzled through her. She wished she could drive. Right now would be the time to jump into her yellow Jeep—no, red convertible, no, black SUV—and zoom away. She was so engrossed in imagining her perfect getaway car, she didn't notice Austin until he spoke.

"Hey," he said.

Phee jumped as though she'd been hit with an electrical charge. "Hey," she managed to say after making sure her heart hadn't leaped out of her chest. "What are you doing here?"

Austin was standing in front of the workbench, the toy helicopter in front of him, along with some other electronic parts. "Waiting for Zane. He took the truck for a pickup. There's so much stuff, only one person could go." He twiddled a screwdriver, rolling the tool over the tops of his fingers. "I heard about you getting kidnapped. Glad you're okay."

"Me, too."

"Riding a backboard down the mountain? Pretty rad."

Phee didn't want to talk about it. "What are you doing?" she said, indicating the helicopter.

"I fixed the tail rotor. Now I'm mounting my GoPro on it."

"Are you seriously going to spy on Missy Fairheitz?"

"No!" Austin said, looking embarrassed. "I just wanted to see if I could do it." He wound a zip tie around the little camera, tightened it, and snipped off the plastic end. "There."

He set the helicopter on the garage floor. Mounted on top was a tiny camera like the kind Phee had seen on snowboarders' helmets. Austin hit a button on the remote. The helicopter levitated until it was hovering a foot off the ground.

"I had to put counterweights on the tail to compensate for the weight of the camera," he said over the insect drone of the tiny engine.

Phee nodded like she knew what he was talking about. Using the remote, Austin guided the copter back to the ground.

"Watch this," he said when the blades stopped spinning. He flipped a switch on the camera, then swiped the touchpad on his laptop, which was on the workbench. A photo filled the screen. Phee saw the concrete floor, the bottom of the rakes and shovels behind her, and one of her scruffy purple Keds.

"Cool!" she exclaimed, meaning it.

Austin started the copter again. This time he guided it upward until it hovered about four feet off the floor. Using the joystick on the remote, he made the machine rotate in a circle. On the screen appeared a three-hundred-and-sixty-degree pan of the garage. Phee saw the workbench, her plaid shirt, Austin's jacket, and the windows of her mom's car flash by. Austin landed the copter.

"Zane and I are thinking about making kits and selling them on the Internet. You'd have to have the RCC and the camera. What we'd sell is the piece that allows you to attach them together, along with the tail weights."

"It's a great idea," Phee said.

Austin looked glum. "All we need is seed money."

Phee imagined dollar bills growing on bushes. She wasn't sure what that had to do with the helicopter kits. "Seed money?"

"Cash to get us going—you know, money to buy the parts to make the first batch of kits. After we sell them, we'd use the money we made to pay back the seed money plus make more kits. That's how you start a business. "

"Where are you going to get your seed money from?"

"I dunno. Know any millionaires who like backing new products?"

Phee thought about that. But before she came up with an answer, from outside came the rumble of an engine turning over, followed by a grind of gears as the orange truck moved away.

"Your neighbors are moving," Austin said.

"Yeah." At the hospital Mrs. Risborough had tried to kill her or at least make her really sick. Phee was certain of it. She was also sure that unless she could prove it, no one would believe her.

"I have an idea how you could get some seed money," she said.

"How?" Austin didn't keep the disbelief out of his voice.

"What if you used the camera to find out things people wanted to know? You could sell them the information."

"You mean we could be like private spies?" Austin now sounded interested.

"Something like that."

"How would we get customers?"

"I'm not sure, but I want to be your first one."

Chapter 73

"Why are we doing this again?" Austin said. They were crouched by the bushes that grew against the rear of Mrs. Heckler's house, the ones with bright red berries and sharp thorns. One of the thorns was stabbing Phee in the butt of her jeans and squished berries were stuck to her knees.

"I want to see if Mrs. Heckler's in there," Phee said. The movers were gone and the driveway was empty.

"The old lady? I thought they took her away."

"I just want to make sure." If Mrs. Heckler wasn't in the house, Phee planned to track down where she'd been taken, starting with the hospital. But after Mrs. Risborough tried to poison her, Phee didn't trust anything Rusty's mom said or did. She thought it was entirely possible that Mrs. Heckler was tied up in one of the bedrooms, forced to eat bread and water until she signed over her house or did whatever it was Mrs. Risborough wanted.

"Wouldn't it be easier just to go inside and look around?" Austin said. "The lock on the back door looks pretty cheap. I could probably pop it."

Phee didn't want to think about how Austin knew about popping locks. And after her experience climbing out of the bathroom window, she didn't want to go back into Mrs. Heckler's house. With her luck, Mrs. Risborough would come home as soon as Phee was inside.

"Look, does this camera thing work or not?" she said. "'Cause if it doesn't, I'm finding somebody else."

"You're acting like you're a paying customer," Austin said as he adjusted one of the zip ties binding the camera to the copter.

"You have to give stuff away for free when you're starting a business. Besides, I am paying. I told you I'd write a good review on Yelp."

"Okay, okay." He switched the camera on and looked through the viewfinder.

"Can't you hurry?"

"You want the shots in focus or not? Open the laptop."

Phee lifted the computer's lid and balanced it on her thighs. She clicked on an icon and waited impatiently for the webpage to open.

"How's it look?" Austin said.

"Pretty cool," Phee admitted. The image on the screen showed dark glossy leaves and waxy red berries.

"Three, two, one . . . lift off!"

The toy helicopter rose off the ground. Phee and Austin watched as it climbed to the window above them.

"Check that out," Austin said.

Phee studied the image on the laptop. It showed what used to be Mrs. Heckler's bedroom. There were dark rectangles on the wall where pictures had hung and dents in the carpet from furniture legs. The door to the closet was open, showing a few wire hangers dangling inside. Two cardboard cartons, sealed with tape, were in the middle of the room. Otherwise, the space was empty.

"You said this was the old lady's room?" Austin said. "Looks like they moved her out."

Phee chewed on her bottom lip. "We have to check the rest of the house."

With Austin guiding the copter cam and Phee following him with the laptop, they circled the building, checking each window. Austin was even able to maneuver the copter up to the second floor. Every room looked pretty much the same as Mrs. Heckler's bedroom.

They returned to their starting point in the backyard.

"Now what are you going to do?" Austin said.

"Find out where they took her."

"How are you going to do that?"

Phee thought for a moment. On principle, she was against torture, but this was an emergency. Since she was six years old, she had known her neighbor's tickle spots. "I think Rusty will tell me."

"Except for those two boxes, looks like they took everything out of the house. Let's go check out the garage. There might be stuff there that Zane and I can sell."

Phee trailed him across the yard. Beside the garage a tarp covered a stack about five feet long, a foot and a half wide, and a foot high. Austin set the copter on it. Phee realized she'd seen the tarp before. At the time she'd assumed it was wrapped around lumber. She'd been wrong.

"Pick up your toy. Hurry!" she said.

"It's not a toy," Austin said, sounding irritated, but he did as she asked. "What are you doing—oh, wow."

Phee had found one corner of the tarp and pulled it back far enough to expose a stack of snowboard decks with the Trent logo. Austin ran a hand along the top board.

"Check out that rocker. I've never seen anything like it," he said.

"No one has." Phee pointed out the sunflower decal. "It's a prototype. Jungen stole it and the other ones from Trent."

Austin looked skeptical. "And he kept them at your *neighbor's*?"

It didn't make sense to Phee, either. If Mrs. Risborough and Jungen weren't boyfriend-girlfriend, why would she let him keep snowboards—*stolen* snowboards—at Mrs. Heckler's house? It's not like Rusty's mom went around doing favors for people.

"I saw him drop 'em off." Phee flipped the tarp back into place. "Forget about it for now. I want to look in the garage before anybody comes back."

"Roger that." Austin set up the copter and it took off. There were three windows high up, near the eaves, and the machine headed for the closest one. As it hovered before the glass, Phee opened the webpage on the laptop.

"What do you see?" Austin said as he concentrated on keeping the helicopter in position.

"Dust and cobwebs." Phee squinted at the screen. "A lot of, you know, garage junk. And a car."

"What kind?"

"I can't tell. It's covered with a sheet or something."

"Let me see," Austin said. Phee turned the screen toward him.

"Oh, man," he said after studying the laptop image. "That isn't just a car. That's a Citroën."

Chapter 74

"A what?" Phee said.

"A Citroën. C-I-T-R-O-E-N, with those funny dots over the *e*. It's this really cool car from France. The old ones had hydraulic suspension and headlights that could look around the corners like eyes."

"A Citroën," Phee repeated, not caring about the car's features. She was trying to remember what Mrs. Heckler had said. Phee thought the older woman had been talking about her favorite candy. Instead, it was her car.

I can't take the Citroën.

As soon as she gets rid of the Citroën, I'll be next!

This isn't about me—it's about her. Her and the Citroën. She thinks I don't know her secrets, but I do.

Phee now understood some of what Mrs. Heckler had been saying. She wanted to take her car to the nursing home, but Mrs. Risborough wouldn't let her. But what did Mrs. Risborough's secrets have to do with the car?

"I'm going to check it out," Austin said. While Phee had been thinking, he'd brought the copter back to earth. "Hold this and wait here. If someone comes, throw some of that gravel at the window."

"Hold your own helicopter. I'm coming in with you."

There was a door in the rear wall of the garage, not visible from the street. Austin took out his multi-tool, and after a minute of poking at the space between the door and the jamb with one of the blades, the door opened.

"Ta-da," he said, bowing low and gesturing with his hand that she should enter first.

Phee rolled her eyes.

The garage was a typical suburban one. Garden tools hung on one wall over a barbecue. Miscellaneous cartons were stacked on metal shelves. A boy's bike hung from the rafters. Cobwebs were draped like garlands in the corners and dust coated everything.

Almost everything. The sheet covering the car looked relatively clean, as though it had been shaken out recently. Austin lifted a corner.

"It's a 2CV!" he said. "Probably early sixties. Like in that old James Bond movie."

Phee no longer questioned how boys seemed to know the most obscure information about cars, just as she was no longer surprised that girls like Veronica knew the names of all the OPI nail polish shades by year.

Austin pulled the rest of the sheet off. Before them was a small four-door car. Its metal hood was ridged and a canvas top, now mottled with age, covered where the moonroof would be on modern cars. Headlights perched on top of the bulging front fenders like frogs' eyes. The rear fenders covered the tires like sleepy eyelids. The car was yellow, almost the same shade as the candy Phee brought Mrs. Heckler.

Austin opened the driver's door. "Check this out." He indicated the single-spoke steering wheel and shifter protruding from the dash.

"Mmm," Phee said. She peered into the car, looking for . . . what? So far she hadn't come across anything that might be something Mrs. Risborough wanted to keep secret. Maybe Mrs. Risborough just wanted to sell it for the money.

Phee looked over the roof at Austin, who'd walked around to the car's other side. "How much is it worth?"

"I'm presuming it's got a lot of miles on it, so probably around ten thousand dollars. It'd be worth more if it hadn't been in an accident."

Chapter 75

"Accident?" Phee said.

She joined Austin and they both looked at the right front bumper, crumpled like the skin of one of those wrinkly dogs. The headlight on that side dangled like a detached eyeball from a zombie movie.

"It's been hit twice," Austin said. "See?"

Phee didn't. He pointed to the middle of the hood.

"Someone used a dent puller there, and filled in the ones they couldn't get out with Bondo. And you can see where the yellow paint doesn't match exactly. It was done a while ago. The Bondo's started to crack." He nodded at a box on the floor of the garage marked KOLATA AUTO. It held two cans of spray paint, a glass jar with something white in it, and what looked like a metal spatula, along with other stuff.

"Looks like they're trying to fix the damage themselves. They really should take it to a garage." He flipped the sheet back over the car. "Hope your little old lady friend drives her wheelchair better than her car."

"She's not in a wheel—"

A car horn blasted outside, making them jump.

"Zane," Austin said. He took a last look around the garage. "I doubt they'll leave the car. But if they don't take this other stuff, we could sell it." He headed for the door.

Phee didn't move. Something tickled her brain. She couldn't figure out what it was.

"Hey," Austin said. "You coming?"

"In a minute." She could feel the idea teetering on the edge of her brain, almost but not quite falling into her consciousness.

"Lock the door on your way out."

When she was alone, Phee peeled back the sheet covering the front of the car. Her fingers traced the area where the damage had been repaired, a narrow band that ran from the bottom of the bumper to the top of the hood. She squatted to examine the newer injury. Just the fender and the base of the headlight were involved.

The connection clicked. She stood beside the car to be sure. The damage from the first crash was what you'd expect if the car ran into something tall and narrow. Something that both crunched under the fender and landed on the hood after being struck. Something like a cyclist and his bike. The newer impact looked like something low to the ground had been hit. Something like a hand bike.

The Citroën had been the car that hit Johnny—twice. What Phee couldn't get her head around was Mrs. Heckler doing something like that and not stopping to help Johnny or reporting it to the police.

No, her friend wouldn't do that, not if she was driving.

Not if she was driving.

Phee thought about Mrs. Risborough and Rusty moving away right after Johnny's accident, not telling anyone where they were going. Mrs. Heckler thought her daughter was selling her house out from under her. Maybe she was, but that wasn't what Mrs. Risborough cared about. It was the car she wanted to get rid of. Because Mrs. Risborough had been behind the wheel both times when Johnny was hit. No wonder she freaked out when she saw Phee with him in the van. Had she thought Johnny figured it out? Had she tried to run over him again before he could tell? Phee felt a prickle of nervousness. Did Mrs. Risborough think Phee knew, too? That would explain the syringe in the hospital.

Phee hurried toward the garage door. She had to get out of there and talk to the sheriff. The rear door opened. Relief coursed through Phee. Austin had come back, probably to show Zane their potential treasures.

Mrs. Risborough walked into the garage. "Hello, Ophelia."

Chapter 76

Phee stopped. "Hi, Mrs. Risborough." Her voice cracked on *borough*. "I heard Mrs. Heckler was leaving and I came to say good-bye."

"In the garage?" Mrs. Risborough was staring at Phee in an unpleasant, boiled sort of way—lips tight, eyes bulging, red creeping up her neck.

"Um, no one answered the door, so I came out here and—"

Mrs. Risborough reached into her shoulder bag. Phee tensed, ready to run, yell, kick—whatever it took to get away—if she pulled out another hypodermic.

This time it wasn't a needle. It was a gun.

"If you scream or do anything I don't tell you to do, I'll shoot you." Mrs. Risborough's regular voice was gone, replaced by one that sounded like a robot's. "Pull the sheet off the car and get in."

The hinges squealed when Phee opened the passenger side door. She sat on the red cloth seat.

Mrs. Risborough pushed open the two garage doors, keeping the gun in her hand. When her back was turned, Phee cracked the window a few inches. If she had a chance to call for help, she wanted someone to hear her.

Mrs. Risborough returned to the car and got in.

"This is a stick shift. You know what that is?" Mrs. Risborough said.

Phee kept her voice even. "Yes."

"Then you know it takes two hands to drive it. I'm putting the gun in my lap. If you reach for it, I will get to it first and shoot you. If you open the door and try to run, I will shoot you. Or maybe I'll just run you over." Her laugh was high and thin. "I seem to be rather good at it." She dug into her bag, which she'd stuck between the seat and the driver's side door, coming out with an orange bottle of pills. She flipped off the cap and shook several into her mouth, gulping them down dry.

After she put away the pills, Mrs. Risborough started the car. They drove slowly down the driveway. Phee looked for Austin's truck, Aunt Helen in the yard, anybody. The neighborhood was deserted.

Faking nonchalance, she passed a hand over her hair, sweeping the pink hat off and stuffing it through the cracked window. It wasn't much of a *Master Spy Handbook* move, but it was the best she could come up with.

Mrs. Risborough hit the street and shifted. The Citroën picked up speed. The engine didn't feel like much compared with modern cars but the Citroën was moving at a decent clip. The broken headlight bounced up and down like a paddleball.

Phee broke the silence. "What's with the snowboards? I know Jungen stole them, but why'd he give them to you?"

"Jungen . . . I was his nurse when he came to the ER . . . what a *nice* man . . . " Her tone became as sour as an unripe orange. "I heard you're the reason he had to leave. Now I'll have to find someone else to buy from."

Buy what? Snowboards?

At the bottom of the hill, Mrs. Risborough turned right.

"Where are we going?" Phee said.

"Shut up." Mrs. Risborough twirled one of the radio knobs. An announcer's voice speaking rapid Spanish came through a tinny speaker.

"I hate that AM crap." Mrs. Risborough snapped the radio off.

They followed the road where Phee had driven Johnny's van. The Citroën's engine started to labor and Mrs. Risborough downshifted. She began to hum under her breath.

Phee thought of the chapter in the spy handbook on interrogations. *Don't assume your interrogator knows as much as you do. Watch for guesses disguised as assertions of fact.* Phee knew this meant she should pretend she had no idea Mrs. Risborough was responsible for hitting Johnny twice. If she could convince Mrs. Risborough of this, maybe she'd let Phee go.

"Thanks for the ride. I've always wanted to see what one of these cars was like."

"You're not an idiot," Mrs. Risborough said. "I'm not, either." Her humming got louder. It sounded like one of the marches the band played at football games.

So much for her interrogator not knowing as much as Phee did.

She was pretty sure the first hit-and-run had been an accident. Johnny said there'd been no skid marks, so Mrs. Risborough probably hadn't seen him on his bike until it was too late. That still didn't excuse leaving the scene and never coming forward. But *another* accidental hit? Phee didn't believe it was coincidence.

The humming stopped. Mrs. Risborough retrieved the pill bottle from her bag and poured several more into her mouth. "You don't think this car qualifies as heavy machinery, do you?" Another giggle.

"Why'd you hit him the second time?"

"I don't know who you're talking about." Mrs. Risborough airily waved a hand.

"Johnny. Why did you run him off the road again?"

The breeziness vanished. "Because he was going to tell! You and him, cruising by my house, taunting me. Well, I got to him first."

"No, you didn't. He's still alive."

Mrs. Risborough smirked. "But not talking. And he won't be until after I'm long gone." She glanced over at Phee. The smirk became a smile—if that's what you called lips stretched over clenched teeth. "And you won't be, either."

Chapter 77

They passed the turnoff to Thorne.

"Where are we going?" Phee said again.

Mrs. Risborough resumed her humming. Another ten minutes went by. Phee wondered if anyone had noticed she was missing. Not Kimiko—she was probably hanging with Chord. Joshua-Alex was probably playing with his stupid metal detector. Zane and Austin were off getting more stuff to sell on eBay and Aunt Helen was probably stopping Brooklyn from teasing Scout. And her mother and father were thousands of miles away. They were getting a D- in the parenting department lately as far as Phee was concerned.

And Mrs. Risborough was getting an A in Crazy—certifiable around-the-bend loony. Phee considered grabbing the steering wheel, but she didn't see what that would do other than crash the car or send it off the road, rolling a time or two. As it didn't have seatbelts and half the roof was canvas, she didn't think that would be a great idea.

Mrs. Risborough abruptly jerked the wheel to the right. The car headed down a snow-covered dirt road, the narrow tires jouncing in and out of the frozen ruts.

"Too bad the hydraulics are broken," Mrs. Risborough said as their heads barely missed hitting the ceiling on a particularly bad rebound. Phee's bottom flew off the seat with every bounce. She gripped the armrest and gritted her teeth to keep from biting her tongue.

Mrs. Risborough swerved to miss the next pothole. A branch from a tree beside the track sheared off the dangling headlight. Another poked through the car's canvas roof, tearing a slit. Mrs. Risborough didn't seem to notice.

The road ended in a turnaround at the edge of a plateau. A wooden hand-painted sign read CLIMBER'S ROOST. It was an abandoned quarry where local rock climbers came to practice. Phee had been here once, to watch Zane and Austin rappel off the cliff as part of their rescue patrol training.

She quickly discovered why Zane had asked her—it was BYOV: bring your own victim. While Phee pretended to be unconscious, Zane and Austin had run ropes through an anchor point at the top, clipped in their climbing harnesses and Phee's rig, and—feeding the rope hand-over-hand—walked backward down the nearly vertical face to the quarry floor below. Even with her eyes closed, Phee's fear of heights had kicked in. After two trips she'd resigned, and spent the rest of the afternoon watching the free climbers and slack liners.

No one had been here recently. The boulders that had been dusted with chalk handprints were now topped with snow. There were no footprints around the slack line set up between two trees. Phee had tried walking on one that day. The nylon webbing had stretched and bounced like a long and narrow trampoline. Two steps were all she could manage before being catapulted off.

Mrs. Risborough stopped a few feet from the cliff, shifted into neutral, and turned off the car. She swallowed the last of the pills and flipped the empty bottle into the footwell.

"This is where you go down," she said and giggled. The giggle was one of the creepiest sounds Phee had ever heard. It reminded her of the stoner kid's laugh, the one who stole his mom's marijuana and smoked it behind the gym.

The pill bottle had come to rest against Phee's shoe. Phee thought about seeing Mrs. Risborough at the grocery store, the wrong names on the prescription there and the bottle Phee had taken from her bathroom. There could be another reason no skid marks were present the first time Johnny was hit.

"You were high," she said. "When you first hit Johnny."

Mrs. Risborough stared straight ahead. "Not my fault. Not my fault." Her voice picked up speed. "Notmyfaultnotmyfault."

"So it was an accident. If we went to Sheriff Allerd—"

Mrs. Risborough turned to Phee. Scribbles of red filled the whites of her eyes. "I didn't ask to be T-boned by that drunk. Screwed up my back. Do you know how many hours a nurse is on her feet? *Take these, they'll make the pain go away.* That's what the doctor said, the SOB I was married to. Then he leaves me because I've changed." Her lips turned into a snarl on *I've changed.*

"I get it," Phee said. And she did. Mrs. Risborough needed her pills like her mom needed her work. It was an addiction, what Mrs. Moss spent all that time in health class warning them against.

"You don't have a clue," Mrs. Risborough said. "And now no one else will, either." She giggled again.

"Your mom knows." Mrs. Heckler had been trying to tell Phee, but Phee hadn't understood.

Mrs. Risborough's face got ugly. She picked up the gun and rapped Phee's broken wrist with the barrel. Hot pain shot through her wrist and up her arm. Tears blurred her vision.

Mrs. Risborough put on her fake-normal face again. "That doesn't matter. With the car wrecked and you dead, no one will believe a senile old lady."

The word *dead* bounced around in Phee's head.

"Don't move," Mrs. Risborough said. She opened the door and got out. "I heard you like to joy ride. This will be your trip that went wrong." Still holding the gun, she propped a fist on the steering wheel and braced the other against the door. She leaned forward and grunted. The Citroën began to roll forward.

"Hey!" Phee said. She groped for the door handle.

The car kept rolling.

Then the gun went off.

Chapter 78

The *bang* was like fifty firecrackers exploding at once. A mini-sonic boom punched Phee's ears. She clapped her hands over them, but the painful ringing wouldn't stop. Through her tears she saw a bullet hole in the radio, right next to one of the knobs.

Mrs. Risborough was hurting, too. She staggered backward, shaking her head.

Phee opened the door and ran. She couldn't hear anything—not her footsteps on the dirt, not whether Mrs. Risborough was still shooting at her. There was something wrong with her balance, too. Instead of going straight, her feet kept veering left. She reeled across the clearing. She needed cover, but her body was betraying her. It sent her lurching toward the cliff's edge.

She risked a look over her shoulder. Mrs. Risborough stood with her feet apart, both arms extended in front of her, holding the gun. Pointing it at Phee. Her arms swayed slightly, like she was having trouble aiming.

Phee dropped to the ground and scrabbled backward. Her feet hit air and the ground under her was falling away, and then she was falling, like into a tree well. But there was no snow to catch her. Only air.

She tried to grab hold of the shrubs and rocks as she slid by them, but she was moving too fast and the thin covering of frozen snow made the surfaces slick. The front of her jacket shredded. So did the skin on her hands and arms. How far was it to the bottom? She'd be torn apart before she got there. Down, down, down.

Her feet slammed into solid rock, and she collapsed, pain shooting up through an ankle. She'd hit an outcrop, a small ledge of rock. She scooted as close to the cliff as she could and looked up.

Mrs. Risborough's face hovered above her. She aimed the gun at Phee and yelled something, but Phee's hearing hadn't come back all the way yet. All she heard was *wah wah wah* followed by the awful giggle. Mrs. Risborough's hand jerked. *Pop*. The crazy lady was shooting at her!

Phee pressed herself into the rock face. *Pop, pop.* After thirty long seconds, Phee dared to look up again. Mrs. Risborough had disappeared. To get more bullets? To find a boulder to roll down the cliff?

Phee looked down. The bottom of the quarry was still a long ways away. She looked up. She really hadn't fallen that far, maybe twenty feet. It might as well be a hundred and twenty.

Phee scanned the nearly vertical face. To her left, about thirty feet away, a black-and-red rope dangled. It hung from the summit and extended about ten feet below the outcrop. Someone's forgotten rappel or belay line.

If she stayed where she was, she'd be a sitting duck. It was too steep to go down—she'd tumble to her death.

Phee stood, keeping as much weight as she could off her sprained ankle. Already it was swelling inside her shoe. She examined the cliff face between her and the rope. Small pockets and knobs of rock dotted the surface. Were the pockets deep enough for toe and finger holds? Would the knobs break off in her hands or from the weight of her feet? A fall meant serious injury or death. Maybe she should wait for the police to come. Someone had to have heard the gunshots.

Mrs. Risborough's voice floated down from above. Phee's hearing was improving. It sounded like Rusty's mom was saying, "Dig, Kathryn, dig!" A shiver knifed through her. Was she talking to herself about Phee's grave?

Rule #8 in *The Master Spy Handbook: If trapped, don't wait for your enemies to come to you.* Phee wiped her palms as best she could on her jeans. She had to get out of there.

Phee took hold of a shallow pocket in the granite. She thought of the climbing wall in gym class. Her hand went sweaty and her grip slipped slightly. She wished she had some of that chalk climbers used.

Slowly she pulled herself along the vertical slab, her left toe reaching for a foothold. She found it. Transferring her weight to her left side, she crimped her right hand around a shallow ledge and stepped sideways with her right foot. The injured ankle burned. She ignored it.

Several inches at a time, she moved across the front of the cliff. Once, her right foot slipped out of a crack and dangled in space. Phee fought back the panic as she felt for a toehold. When both feet were secure again, she took a moment to catch her breath, then tipped her head to one side, trying to loosen the knots in her left shoulder.

The rope hung less than three feet away. Her back and arms trembled with fatigue. Balancing on her good leg, Phee reached for it. The nylon brushed against her fingertips. She stretched her arm as far as it would go, her tendons, ligaments, and muscles elongated to the max.

She gathered the rope into her fist and pulled it toward her. Hand over hand, she started to climb. The cast made it hard for her to grip, and tightening the muscles in that hand sent shocks of pain through her wrist. But this wasn't gym class. No medical excuses, no teacher to help her. Failure would mean more than an F.

The rope stung her abraded hands. She kept going, putting most of her weight on her good leg as she walked up the nearly vertical surface. She tried to whisper, "You got this," but her teeth were chattering too much from the cold.

Thirty seconds later, the top of the cliff was only inches from the top of her head. What if Mrs. Risborough was waiting there to shoot her? Phee took a deep breath and hoisted herself over the rim. She was about eighteen feet from where she'd gone over the edge. The Citroën was where Mrs. Risborough had parked it. The passenger side door was closed. Mrs. Risborough wasn't in sight.

Phee lay still, panting, letting the muscles in her arms and shoulders relax.

Her cast felt heavy and the wrist sore under it. She crawled toward the trees and boulders, wiggling her toes and fingers to get the circulation going. It was afternoon. If she could stay hidden until dark or Mrs. Risborough gave up looking, Phee would then get herself down the hill.

She elbowed across the rough ground. Something hard was in her jacket pocket, pressing into her side. She fished it out. It was the bottle of pills she'd taken from Mrs. Heckler's medicine cabinet. She put it away and kept going.

"Stop." Phee looked up to see Mrs. Risborough standing on the other side of the Citroën. She rested the gun on the roof. It was pointed at Phee, the muzzle like a black open angry mouth.

Phee stopped crawling.

Chapter 79

"Come here."

Phee didn't move. Mrs. Risborough pulled the trigger. This time the sound wasn't as deafening. A spurt of snow kicked up a yard in front of her. Phee pushed herself to her feet and hobbled reluctantly toward the car.

Mrs. Risborough gestured with the gun. "Open the door and push."

Phee saw what the problem was. The Citroën had gotten stuck. From the look of things, Mrs. Risborough had tried to back it up. The wheels had probably spun, turning the snow to slush and miring the car deeper. There was a thick stick next to the car on the passenger side. It had been used to scrape snow away from the front of the tires.

Phee opened the passenger door and leaned into it. Mrs. Risborough did the same. Nothing happened.

"Push harder!" Mrs. Risborough screamed, grunting with effort. Phee did the best she could, trying not to put weight on her injured ankle. The little car rolled forward until its front bumper hung over the chasm. Mrs. Risborough reached in and pushed down on the foot brake with her left hand. The right one still held the gun.

"Get in," she said.

Phee was going to die. Mrs. Risborough was going to push the Citroën over the cliff. Phee trembled with fear, shaking so badly the pills in her pocket rattled.

Addiction. The word came to her, along with an idea. Phee held up the orange bottle.

"I've got your pills."

Mrs. Risborough's face went funny, like Homicide's did right before Phee set down his dinner plate. "Give them to me."

Phee held the bottle out, shaking it.

Mrs. Risborough let go of the brake pedal and held out her hand. Phee tossed the bottle at her, the throw deliberately short. Mrs. Risborough lunged for it.

With the brake off, the car rolled forward. The side beam knocked Mrs. Risborough onto the front seats. She waved and kicked like a swimmer fighting a riptide, but she couldn't get back on her feet before the Citroën's front wheels dropped over the cliff.

The car hung, balanced for a heartbeat, and then it was gone, like it had been sucked down a drain. Phee stood and listened to the clang and clatter of metal hitting rock. There was a stupendous final crash, and then a high whoop that hurt Phee's ears. She thought her hearing was still playing tricks on her until she caught the blue and red lights strobing through the trees. It was a siren, several of them.

Phee turned and nearly fell as she put weight on her sprained ankle. Police cars streamed out of the woods onto the plateau. Sheriff Allerd got out of the first one. So did someone else. The person ran to her, faster than Phee had ever seen a grown-up run, and scooped her up like she was the twins' age again.

"Phee," her mom said. "Oh, Phee."

Chapter 80

Brooklyn had saved her. He and the winter hiker who heard gunshots at Climber's Roost. Aunt Helen a little, too. In the excitement of Phee's mom and dad's homecoming, no one noticed right away that Phee wasn't there. At some point Brooklyn spied the pink hat in Mrs. Heckler's driveway, retrieved it, and put it on. Aunt Helen asked him where he found it. When he told her, she put it together with Phee's poisoning story and called Sheriff Allerd. The report of gunshots came in soon after, and the sheriff took a leap and made the connection.

Phee went back to the hospital to have her cast replaced and her ankle taped. The doctor wanted to keep her overnight but she insisted on coming home. Before she left, she and Aunt Helen stopped by to see Johnny.

"Phee!" he said happily as she walked into the room. He then whistled the opening to The Beatles' *Drive My Car* tune. Phee shot him a warning look, glancing over at Aunt Helen. He grinned.

"How are you?" she said.

"Doc said I can leave tomorrow and start training in two weeks." He indicated his legs. "When you're already paraplegic, a broken leg doesn't slow you down as much. I'm ready to go home. I'm finally sick of Jell-O and really miss Kirby."

Once home, Phee wanted to stay downstairs where everyone else was, but after she nodded off at the kitchen table, her dad and Zane carried her upstairs to her room.

Phee slept the rest of the night and most of the next day. Brooklyn and Scout kept sneaking into her room to check on her, Brooklyn putting his face close to hers to make sure she was still breathing. Even Homicide seemed concerned. For the first time in his kitty life, he curled up at the end of her bed and hissed at anyone besides the twins who tried to come in. When she finally woke up, Phee declared Brooklyn a hero and gave him one of her swimming medals. He wore it all the time, even to bed. She gave the pink hat to Scout.

Phee's mom had been working on one of the outer islands of Vanuatu when the tsunami hit. She did just what Phee had imagined. She rode out the storm hugging a banyan tree. She had a few cracked ribs and scrapes but was otherwise okay. After the water receded, she was stranded—no boat, no communication.

It took some doing to get home. When Phee's dad finally arrived on the main island of Efate, it was several days before he could charter a boat to where Phee's mom was. After he located her at one of the emergency shelters, there was more delay getting back to Vanuatu, booking a flight from there to Australia and on to L.A. Cell phone lines were down, but Phee's dad managed to call Aunt Helen before they got on the plane in Australia. It was the middle of the night in Colorado, his call went to voice mail, and Aunt Helen missed seeing it when she woke up. The first she heard Phee's mom was okay was when Phee's dad had called from the Denver airport.

Mrs. Risborough was dead, pancaked in the Citroën. The police found a syringe full of tranquilizer in the remains of her handbag.

"We think that's what she put in your IV," Sheriff Allerd said. "Injected a sufficient amount to keep you at the hospital for an extra day or two, long enough for her to get out of town." Phee didn't buy it. He hadn't seen the look in Mrs. Risborough's eyes when she'd told Phee "bad things happen when you don't mind your own business."

Mrs. Risborough apparently had been medicating her mother, too, to make her seem like she was losing it so Mrs. Risborough could get control of Mrs. Heckler's assets. Mrs. Heckler, who quickly returned to her old self after the drugs wore off, decided to sell her house and moved to Colorado Springs with Rusty.

"Fresh start," she'd explained to Phee when she stopped in to say goodbye.

"I'm sorry about your dau—Mrs. Risborough," Phee said.

Mrs. Heckler's shoulders slumped and her eyes filled. "Me, too," was all she'd said.

Patients at the hospital stopped complaining so much about their pain. The head nurse figured out Mrs. Risborough had been stealing the patients' OxyContin and substituting aspirin. She'd also taken a doctor's prescription pad and was writing prescriptions in fake names for herself. And Mel got back the auto supplies Mrs. Risborough had shoplifted to fix the Citroën herself, avoiding a record of repair after she hit Johnny the second time.

Jungen was in Germany; the request to detain him had come too late. But Sheriff Allerd said Germany was going to send him back to the US to face trial for kidnapping Phee, the Trent thefts, and selling pills. He was Mrs. Risborough's dealer, supplying OxyContin when she couldn't get enough through her own methods in exchange for storing the Trent boards he'd stolen. Phee imagined sitting in court in the witness chair like people did on TV, pointing a finger at Jungen and saying, "That's him!" But Sheriff Allerd said there probably wouldn't be a trial because Jungen's lawyer would get him a plea bargain. Phee was disappointed. She'd been looking forward to the finger-pointing.

Mr. Trent came by with a snowboard as a thank-you present. Phee refused to ride it, not even once, hanging it on her wall instead, much to Kimiko's annoyance.

Ms. Vlachos was put on probation but wasn't fired. She was also removed from field trip duty. When Phee confessed she'd stolen her Koosh ball, Mrs. Vlachos said she was glad Phee was safe and could keep it. Phee told Ms. Sobel about climbing the cliff face. The gym teacher suggested Phee try out for lacrosse next season. Phee politely declined.

Being kidnapped and nearly killed made her a little famous at school, but not as famous as Chord. Phee was fine with that. He and Kimiko were now an item, which meant Kimiko and Phee didn't hang out together as much as they used to. Chord was invited to join the USA Snowboard Association's junior team. His parents said he could ride as long as he kept up with the violin.

Zane got his driver's license but not a car. He became extraordinarily helpful—running errands for their mom, taking Phee to school, ferrying the twins to playdates. Under Colorado law, drivers under seventeen could carry only one passenger, so that meant separate trips for Brooklyn and Scout. A good thing, Phee thought. Brooklyn by himself was distracting enough. She still babysat the twins, having asked for and, with Aunt Helen's fervent support, received a raise in her babysitting rate. Aunt Helen flew home to Texas, promising to return for Phee's eighth-grade graduation.

Joshua-Alex passed the *Jeopardy!* online test but hadn't received a call to go to L.A. for a taping. If it didn't come soon, Phee was going to suggest he resubmit his application, this time dropping the *Alex* as well as the explanation for why he wanted to change his name.

Her third day back at school, Phee arrived at lunch late. She was on crutches because of her ankle, and her wrist cast made them hard to maneuver. There were only a couple of empty seats left, the closest at the table occupied by Veronica, Ashley, and the rest of the Donner Partiers. Balancing her tray awkwardly with one hand, she caught Veronica's eye. The other girl flipped her pink-ribboned ponytail and turned away. So, Phee thought, things were back to normal.

Not quite. In front of the whole school—at least the whole lunchroom, which was almost the same thing—Peter Allerd got up, walked down the aisle between the tables, and took her tray. He led her to a spot at his table, telling his friends to move over to make room.

"You need help with that?" He said, indicating the hamburger and salad in front of Phee.

"If you offer to cut my meat for me, I will stick you with a fork."

He raised his hands in surrender. "After my dad told me what you went through, I should ask you to cut mine."

They ate lunch under the Donner Partiers' stare. Ashley's jaw actually dropped, making her look like a mailbox with the door open. But Veronica wore a little smile that for once didn't look fake.

For the rest of the week, Peter ate lunch with her, which was pretty much the eighth-grade equivalent of telling the world you were boyfriend-girlfriend. He hadn't tried to kiss her again. Phee was okay with that. Her brain still went a bit haywire when he was around. Kissing might blow a circuit. But she knew it was coming. And she was okay with that, too.

And if he asked her to the graduation dance? Probability she'd say yes: high. Probability she'd wear pink? As Joshua-Alex would say, I'll take Not A Chance for one hundred.

www.ingramcontent.com/pod-product-compliance
Lightning Source LLC
Chambersburg PA
CBHW060555310726
48982CB00008B/1135/J

* 9 7 8 1 9 5 2 4 2 7 4 0 4 *